Brushstroke!

Alice Goldfarb Marquis

Brushstroke!

A Novel

Penny-A-Page Press
Washington, D.C.

Penny-a-Page Press
Washington, D.C.

This book is a work of fiction and any resemblance to actual events, places, or persons living or dead is entirely coincidental.

Published by Penny-a-Page Press, Washington, D.C.
http://pennyapagepress.blogspot.com

10 9 8 7 6 5 4 3 2 1

Library of Congress Cataloging-in-Publication Data is available.

ISBN: 0615988954
ISBN-13: 9780615988955

Table of Contents

Acknowledgments

T hank you John Blankfort for posthumous publication of this manuscript and his author photo; Deborah Wright, for the front cover painting; Wah Keung Chan for the front cover graphic design; and Sandra Betton for taking the picture.

Chapter 1

Passion

It was only 3:30 in the afternoon, but a thin sun was already fading, swallowed in the trough of winter in the big city. Somewhere, a siren wailed hopelessly against the traffic building minute by minute toward its usual rush hour jam. Gloom seeped into the room, like a dark stain, as he switched on a harsh fluorescent lamp above the desk. Below the windows, the radiators struggled like millions of others in the city to counter the chill creeping in around the glass. On the desk strewn with half-opened books, there was barely room for a blocky Underwood typewriter, a fresh sheet in the roller and its keys expectant.

He was studying the painting again and, as always, an erection tightened his pants. Bettman Levin had long ago given up feeling shame at experiencing such a direct erotic tingle from a work of art. To be sure, the first time it had happened, just a month past his fifteenth birthday, he had turned beet-red and had fled to the museum's men's room. While joylessly jerking off into the toilet, Bettman resented the bizarre, illogical imperatives issued by his body. The

1

trigger for his urgency had been, of all things, Picasso's *Guernica*.

Now, Levin allowed the tension to build, savoring his finesse in controlling his own sensations, drawing out the pleasure, and idly adding this talent to the many satisfactions he found in mid-life. It was possible now, pleasurable even, to focus his attention on some other matter and to stifle the clamor of his body.

Again, he turned to the picture before him, drawn first to the brazen gaze which unfailingly flicked what a novelist of his adolescence would have called the fire in his loins. The face in the painting was vulgar, broad and coarse, the face of a common shopgirl, an upstairs maid, an anonymous gum-chewer slopping coffee into a styrofoam cup at some cheap fast food place. Whose fingers had tied the pert bow of narrow black velvet ribbon around her throat? The tiny locket twined into it seemed weightless. Aroused, he forced his eyes to the periphery of the picture. Through a professional squint, he barely made out the green drapery swagged across the upper left corner, its curves pressing the eye almost painfully back toward the figure.

Her body was compact, squat really, and Levin yearned, as he always did, for less torso and more legs. The disproportion provoked him; as his lust swelled, so did his anger at her flawed presence. Not yet, maybe not at all today, he thought, and thrust his scrutiny deeper into the painting, where scumbled patterns of wallpaper and a doorway lent stability to the tousled bedclothes upon which she reclined. Something was wrong with the drawing of her right elbow;

it rested lightly on the pillow instead of punching the deep cleft of her weight upon it.

He rushed away to the edges again, to the carelessly tucked sheet at the lower left. It formed a swag that echoed the green drape at the top. Sheets like that, ample linen sheets with fine picot and lace edges, could be had today only at Bucellatti, at $1,000 the pair. The embroidered silk shawl on which she reclined, by contrast, looked cheap, like a souvenir from Hong Kong.

He followed the shawl's folds to the foot of the bed, where a black cat glowered, its erect tail arched into a C (for carnality?) Considering its importance in the history of modern art the painting was in rather poor condition, Levin thought. The pigment had crackled in most of the flesh areas, but especially across the upper right arm and breast and the right thigh. For a moment he imagined that this bold hussy's body had expanded in the hundred years since she was created, pressing out against its unyielding coating of dried pigment. He pictured himself thickly smeared with an artist's mash of flesh-toned colors and the slow constriction as it dried. He relished the tightness.

Above her body the paint forming a flower bouquet seemed to have aged more gracefully and the tissue paper around it looked crisp, with no trace of the hairlines of age. The black servant proffering the blooms had been one of the picture's most offensive mysteries when it first was displayed in the Salon of 1863. The woman on the bed looked undeserving of a personal retainer, and the flowers could only have come from an admirer, who was perhaps at that very moment waiting in the anteroom. Levin resentfully pictured him as the Victorian lecher of *My Secret Life*. The man might well have bought and paid for the bed and even spent, in the anonymous roué's locution, copiously upon it, Levin reflected, but he could never possess that self-possessed woman.

Levin contemplated her satin mules, the right one resting on the shawl below her bare foot, the left coyly covering her toes, and then his gaze travelled up the leg, noticing the dark hairy shadow where it crossed the right leg. The artist's best draftsmanship was clearly in the hand, as it splayed out, pressing into her crotch. The hand was not languid, as in Titian's *Venus of Urbino*, a painting art students called "The Itch," and which scholars identified as an ancestor of this work. No, this hand pressed into the buttery flesh; if forced it would give way, but the inner being it shielded would never be accessible, even after a hundred years. Examining the pudginess of the fingers, their baby-like nails and their skillful foreshortening, Levin slowly moved his own hand to his gray tweed crotch. He pressed, in a mocking attempt at mirroring the gesture of the painting before him.

Then he released and purposefully closed the book in which the painting *Olympia* occupied a double-page spread, a volume in a popular Time-Life series, *The World of Manet*. He turned to the keyboard and began to type:

January 27, 1962

Age Arno Peller's new work at the Pestle Gallery demands attention by subverting the evidence of our senses. Larger, more expansive than last year's output, his glossy, almost licked surfaces deny sensuality, while asserting the futility of scientific inquiry into the creative act. Peller has frequently cited his debt to Magritte, Max Ernst, the early Dali, Arcimboldo and, of course, Marcel Duchamp. After his trip to Paris last year, in connection with an exhibition at the prestigious Bernhard laFoco Gallery in the Marais, the artist confessed to renewed interest in the works of Eduard Manet.

"The sensuality of his surfaces demanded an answer," said Peller in a taped interview published last year in Art for Tomorrow. "It's not that I want to argue with him, because, after all, he was a very big artist and was very famous and very successful, but, you know, he seemed to be a victim ... a victim of this narrow, academic education. I looked and looked and looked at Olympia and then, you know, well, I couldn't help myself and really began to feel sorry for him."

In the current exhibition Peller deals with his feelings of compassion for Manet by rigidly denying the component of art. "In today's world, sex is a given," he said. "What else is new?" Indeed, this young artist's search for a meaningful dialogue with the history of art, always in the context of today's fast-moving visual scene, is praiseworthy and it deserves close study.

The exhibition will close on March 17.

Levin smiled as he typed the last sentence. It was always a relief to get started on writing his monthly reviews for *Art for*

Tomorrow. More shows, more artists demanding attention all the time, and now that so many galleries scheduled openings on the same day, it was patently infeasible to see everything. The openings he attended were so overrun with people these days that it was impossible to see the art in the crush. Still, it was rewarding when people asked his opinion and downright fun to answer smoothly that his ethics sealed his lips and they would just have to wait and read it in the magazine.

Levin twirled a plaid scarf around his neck and tucked a small red leather notebook into his breast pocket. He was locking the door of the apartment when the phone inside began to ring, but he knew that what with unlocking and then disarming the security system, he would miss it anyhow. Let the answering machine take it. Besides, he was already late for his evening with Zelda.

Waiting for the elevator, Levin studied his silhouette in the hall's old-fashioned console mirror. Not bad for a fifty-two-year-old, he noted. Belly firm, stance erect, garb stylish yet discreet. He continued his inventory in the elevator mirror: spiky black hair receding a bit and greying at the temples; eyes a bright, clear brown; nose definitely Jewish but that, thank heaven, didn't matter much any more; lips curling in a sophisticated smile; cheeks a bit puffy and too pale; chin, well, resolute was too strong a word and adequate was too weak. He completed the self-appraisal while striding through the old-fashioned mirrored lobby: shoulders relaxed, gait brisk, the scarf flapping rakishly.

To set forth into a New York February evening without an overcoat was definitely daring, but a taxi was blessedly at hand and Bettman Levin ordered the driver to swing through Central Park to the St. Moritz.

There is truly such a thing as being too thin, Bettman thought, as he spotted Zelda in a corner of the unfashionable, nearly deserted lobby bar. Her huge black round glasses overwhelmed her small face, sharpened by too-dark hair too severely strained back under a black velvet bow. She had always dressed exquisitely and tonight was no exception. A Turkish peasant woman must have labored for a year to create the lavishly embroidered bolero Zelda had casually slung over her shoulders. Under it, as she stood up and crossed her arms to keep the jacket from slipping, Levin noticed she was wearing a black wool jersey sheath that subtly followed her girlish torso.

He kissed the air next to her ear, and she pecked somewhere near his cheek, careful not to smudge her lipstick. They met often, but never without suffering an embarrassing awkwardness at first. Each time, he felt a twinge of failure, annoyance that their marriage had come to grief. Twelve years after their divorce, he no longer felt anger or pain; in fact, he considered Zelda his best friend and confidante. He looked forward to seeing her and yet her frail form conveyed reproach, a failure on his part to shelter this tiny waif from the world's blind cruelties.

"Still no overcoat?" she asked, playfully tugging at his scarf. "You're welcome to be Rodolfo, just so long as I don't have to play Mimi."

"Edith Piaf will do," he replied, "unless you insist on playing Colette."

An aged waiter set down a plate of tiny, exquisite *canapés* on a doily-covered plate and they both ordered Perrier and chardonnay spritzers. They had once chuckled over the perversity of consuming a hot weather drink in midwinter. Levin watched Zelda's hand hover speculatively over the plate and knew that she was calculating the caloric content of each exquisite morsel. She chose a tiny cucumber circle topped with a pink worm-like shrimp. He settled for liver paté on rye toast. It was a regular ritual, and sharing the secret of such divine canapés in a city where knowing such secrets means much broke their reserve.

"Well, they decided to do it. Naturally, it'll make a tremendous splash and cost a fortune, but," Zelda paused for effect, "when you can get the Rockefellers competing with the Baritsches, there's bound to be an explosion."

"I gather the insurance problem is solved," said Levin.

"There's no problem so immense that these folks can't solve it before breakfast." She delicately nibbled a caviar and egg miniature. "The State Department has been reminded by assorted Rockefellers of the vital role played by exchanges of art in promoting international good will. So the insurance premium has suddenly materialized. And the good Baron Baritsch suddenly finds that he must remodel his villa during the last six months of 1963. So he's delighted to send the paintings over; in fact he's going to spring for crating and shipping."

"What a prince," Levin said sarcastically. "He's so generous that I've just about forgotten about the atrocities that helped to buy all those gorgeous pictures. I'm still wondering how the old Baron acquired a lot of them in the first place." He jiggled the ice in his empty glass and frowned at its jagged configuration, trying to decide if he should have another before they left for dinner. No, but the smoked salmon tidbit on the tray was irresistible.

Zelda sipped frugally.

"Now, now," she patted his forearm, "art is the great consolation of the world, remember? The trustees are just tickled pink about the whole concept. The ladies are already consulting their designers for some simply smashing frocks to wear to the opening. The men hope the show will bring megabucks into the building fund. And they're all one-hundred percent for the appreciation of art."

"Amen," Levin grumbled. "Let us bring aesthetic appreciation to the masses, while our accountants tot up the appreciation of our collections. Next stop, Sotheby's."

"Have done with cynicism, my dear," said Zelda. "Even Bertram Till is going wild for this show. He's been dreaming about it for years. Next to getting the Russians to part with their Impressionists, fat chance, this would cap his career."

"Oh really? That guy's been capping his career regularly for the past thirty years. There's a raving megalomaniac behind that pinched preacher front. He acts so goddamned sanctimonious about the glories of art, when you know he spends most of his time brown-nosing the big donors, graciously dropping by for a drink to view their collections, and swooning over some minor Utrillo. 'It's typical of the artist's middle period,'" Levin mocked in falsetto, "'we have fifteen others like it in the basement and seven more promised in people's wills, but if your tax lawyers believe it would be advantageous, we'll be delighted to relieve you of it.'"

To his chagrin, Levin was getting furious. He always did when he thought about Till, who was Zelda's boss at the museum. For some unfathomable reason, all the women around Till adored him. The man was a dessicated bean-pole, seemingly devoid of testosterone, a wily manueverer and a hypochondriac who took to his bed at the most inopportune times, dumping the extra work on all those cow-eyed women.

"Dear Betty," said Zelda. "Not a jealous bone in your body. Let's eat."

Though he had suffered it ever since prep school, the nickname still rankled. Levin considered the irony of his parents, immigrants who had grown up on the lower East side, carefully choosing the right name to speed their first-born toward professional success. Professor Erwin Bettman was a teacher of American history in the night school on Grand Street. He spoke so beautifully and he looked so distinguished, like a banker, it was hard to believe that he was Jewish. In fact, his ancestors had come to New York from Germany in the 1840's and they were all bankers except Erwin, the black sheep. Levin's parents sat at the minuscule desks four nights a week, improving their English, learning about Custer and the Gold Rush, and drinking in the splendid presence of Erwin Bettman. A professor's name would give the baby the right start in America. Levin's Jewish name, which he had never confided to anyone, was Belzalel, and occasionally he wondered if disinterring it would be an improvement over his nickname. But the urge passed.

Having shared a pizza and Chianti at John's, in the Village, the couple strolled two blocks to Zelda's floor-through apartment on Gay Street. Strolling is hardly the word, since a fierce and frigid wind chased them as Bettman hunched into his inadequate muffler and Zelda clutching her beaver coat around herself. Warm and cozy behind heavy metal bars at the windows, the apartment was a book-lined haven, every open wall crammed with prints and paintings.

"The usual?" she asked, as Bettman sank into the beige corduroy sectional, rubbing his chilled fingers.

"Not tonight. Just give me a club soda." From the glass and chrome coffee table, he picked up the latest *Art in America* and flipped through the glossy pages. "We just love to decorate with fine art," he was reading in an article about the Goldbaum collection, when Zelda returned, carrying his drink and a snifter of brandy for herself. She had changed into a filmy white Moroccan *djellaba*, shot through with golden threads.

"Are you going to the Drinkhill opening?" she asked. "I hear he's planning to attend wearing white overalls and carrying a big bucket filled with white sequins. Which he intends to toss in the faces of all and sundry. It's supposed to be a statement about the inevitable philistinism of everybody in the art scene ... except the artists, of course."

"Whatever it takes to make the cash register ring," said Levin. "The poor man has got to let people know somehow that he's really an artist."

The magazine was still open on his lap and, as she gathered it up, Zelda pressed her hand on his thigh. It was not at all like the hand in the painting; its thin, elongated fingers were as tiny as a child's and they ended with brightly lacquered nails, but his earlier unfulfilled dialogue with *Olympia* now continued, like a film after the reel-change. He reached around Zelda's bony ribcage and pulled her closer, then lightly lifted her and carried her into the bedroom. She was nipping at his neck and he wondered why they had ever parted, as he always did at moments like this.

Like her hands, her body was amazingly child-like, especially for a woman of almost fifty. That never-ending neck (like the Nefertiti in Berlin), those tiny bud-like breasts, the silky wisps of pubic hair: she resembled a Modigliani, as he had often told her in moments of passion. She was uninhibited, too, efficiently unzipping his pants and then removing the rest of his clothing. They tussled on the raccoon bedspread, an extravagance acquired in Greece during their honeymoon and apportioned to her when they had separated.

"It's not right any more to fuck a Modigliani," he said. "They've gotten too valuable."

"Well, then you'll just have to feed your fantasies a deKooning woman."

Experienced lovers, they cuddled and kissed in the fur. Again and again they joined and separated to extend the pleasure, until Zelda hopped on top and zestfully impaled herself. Her hands pressed into Levin's chest with unexpected force. They reminded him of the hand in the painting that had earlier mobilized his juices so deliciously. Now he was suddenly struck by their claw-like parody. He closed his eyes and tried to conjure back the picture in the book and replicate his intense feelings. But the mood ebbed just as Zelda pounded herself down, ecstatically grimacing, panting.

At least he wouldn't have to coax her to climax, although he knew that she could easily come again and again. In fact, he usually provided her with several appetizers before joining her in the main course. But he was in no mood to indulge her in desserts. In fact, he was in no mood even to hold her and caress her until she fell asleep, in the style she normally demanded. Neither could he tolerate a lengthy, painful post-mortem discussion. What went wrong? He didn't want to hear it. Now he was glad that they were divorced.

"That didn't work out too well for you, did it?" she said. "Want me to do something about it?"

That was exactly what he didn't want, some obliging female massaging his dick. He preferred husbanding his rage, illogical as that was, and she, damn it, knew it.

"Never mind," he said sharply. "The old man just wants to lie down. Let him rest."

He dressed hurriedly, pecked her abstractedly on the cheek, and dashed out into the bitter cold. The first gust of wind, as he rounded the corner to Macdougal Street, stabbed through his light clothing and he gave his muffler a futile extra twist. He couldn't possibly hope for a taxi until he reached Sixth Avenue, another two blocks away, and even there, he knew, the competition would be fierce. He crunched through a filthy remnant of last week's blizzard and waved ineffectually at schools of taxis swimming north on Sixth Avenue. All were replete with contented diners and theater-goers smugly homeward-bound.

He had begun to walk to the subway station in desperation, still waving half-heartedly at the passing cars, when a vacant taxi stopped. At least it was warm, although the interior reeked dangerously of exhaust fumes and the springs poked through the back seat. At the corner of Fourteenth Street, a hunched figure waved ineffectually toward the passing traffic. It was striking how abject people looked as they tried to flag down a cab -- and how quickly the beggar turned into a king when installed inside. Levin, however, did not feel particularly regal, not even like the Jewish prince his adoring mother had envisioned. Had she sweated for forty years over a sewing machine in Boorstein's shirtwaist factory only to raise a son nicknamed Betty? Betty, a big *makher* in the art world? Betty, a connoisseur educated at Harvard? Betty, whose eye was so refined and sensitive that he could spot a fake Picasso print from across the room? Betty, whose aesthetic sensibilities were so tender that he could get a hard-on out of a cheap reproduction in a book?

He shoved a wad of bills at the driver and ran into the warm lobby of his building, chased by one last frigid blast. In the elevator mirror he confronted his own tired face, hating the shadows under the eyes, the deep lines connecting nose and mouth, the sallowness of the middle of the night. Smirking insincerely, he offered himself condolences for teeth swarming with plaque and swollen gums announcing periodontal disease. Bitterly, the old man he would soon be offered condolences too, leaning on a cane, voice quavering.

Bettman noticed a sprinkling of pale dust on the carpet as he unlocked his door and then stepped quickly inside to disarm his security system. Punching in the code, he saw that the light on the control was already green. He must have forgotten to arm the system, yet he seemed to remember distinctly that he had done so. The message light was blinking on his answering machine, but the tape gave only a futile, exasperated-sounding click.

At the living room bar he poured himself a hefty cognac and looked forward to the last meager pleasures he could extract from this lousy day: dive into his eiderdown, read a few pages of Steinbeck's *Travels with Charley* while sipping his drink, and then a good, dreamless sleep.

"Good evening, Mr. Bettman Levin. Aren't you going to offer me a drink, Betty?"

She spoke with a harsh, Central European accent as she stepped out from behind the beige monk's cloth drapes.

"You don't even remember me," she said peevishly, "after all the happy times we shared."

She was large but not sloppy. She wore a serviceable pants suit in navy blue polyester and neat black patent leather pumps, and in her right hand she grasped a tiny, nasty-looking pistol.

Levin stiffened in shocked disbelief. Of course, it all added up. The phone call as he was leaving, the dust on the carpet at his front door, the hang-up on his answering machine. This is why people paid a premium for apartments sheltered behind 24-hour doormen.

"Remember Munich in the spring of 1947?" she pressed on. "Remember a Jewish soldier selling chocolate bars in Marienplatz? Remember a Jewish girl offering a drawing for a chocolate bar? And you asked for two because the drawings were small, you said, while the chocolate bar was big.

Remember walking along the Isar River and sitting on a bench talking about art and putting your jacket around her shoulders when it got cool in the evening?"

Levin recalled the day with difficulty. It came during the week he was shipped home, when his thoughts had been monopolized by his imminent discharge from the Army and the prospect of starting graduate school in art history at Harvard in the fall. The girl's drawings had intrigued him because they were so naive and child-like: flowers stiff as popsicles, alpine cabins with shutters and boxes of geraniums at the windows, country roads curving into a pine forest. They were done in colored pencil on thick, cheap paper, and none of them included any people.

Examining the sketches as he strolled, he had wondered at the innocence that would prompt a nineteen-year old girl to draw so immaturely, crudely really, and the brazenness that would send her into the street to peddle such coarse work. Even then he had considered himself something of an art connoisseur and he would have dismissed her without a second glance had he not spotted the number tattooed on her forearm. In those days, the streets of Munich were teeming with the sad human residue of Hitler's concentration camps, men and women and even children with wizened, pinched faces furtively scurrying about on black market errands. Bargaining with her over the drawings had been a reflex; in fact, he recalled thinking that the whole stack of sketches wasn't worth a chocolate bar. But he now remembered thrusting a second bar of chocolate at her when he said goodbye, hurrying back to the base to check whether his travel orders had finally arrived.

"Yes, so?" he said to her now. "I'm beginning to remember. It really was long ago. So?"

"So I've come to ask you for a favor," she said.

"For a favor you don't have to break into my apartment in the middle of the night," he said. "For a favor you don't have to point that thing at me. It must be some big favor."

"No, it's really a small favor, but I want to be as persuasive as possible. I need some information about an art collection, about a museum."

"What about calling me in the morning," he suggested hopelessly. "I'm really bushed after a long, rough day. We could have a nice long lunch somewhere tomorrow and I'll be more than glad to tell you anything you might want to know."

She gravely shook her head. She had filled out a lot since Munich, had bleached her hair platinum, had learned how to apply makeup. Her face was attractive but hard, her hazel eyes flinty and two determined lines bracketing her mouth. He would not have recognized her, had not thought of the incident in Munich for years. He had given away her drawings to a chambermaid in Hamburg on the way home, ashamed to possess such patently amateurish, meaningless work.

"Sit down," she said, pointing with the pistol to a white leather and chrome Barcelona chair. "First of all, you are well-known in the art world as a man of great discretion. Your reputation as a critic depends on it, I hear. Now, your life depends on it as well. The least slip of the lip, as I've heard they used to say during the war, means you're a dead man. Even after what will happen happens, whether it succeeds or fails, you will not breathe a word. Clear?"

"It sounds nefarious," said Levin, "like some sort of crime. Is it a crime?"

"That depends on your point of view. Some would call it justice."

"Only some? That sounds like a complicated crime."

"Never mind the intellectual nit-picking. We don't need your moral input; just your information will do. And by the way, you may have to do some on-the-spot research. I hope you're prepared to travel."

"Where to? I can't stand the food in Spain. The Caribbean bores me. Mexico always gives me the trots. India is out ... all those depressing beggars." He was no longer tired and, since the pistol was not imminently going to be used, he was savoring his own wit. Cool in the face of mortal threat -- that's not the way the preppies would have described their Betty. Perhaps he could amuse her into giving up.

"It's not funny," she said, in a voice from which the laughter had been bleached long ago. "I'm not going to kill you with this gun," she said evenly. "Not yet. Maybe never. But I could hurt you a little bit, or maybe a lot. I just want your assistance. You might call it a professional consultation." She used the gun to wave off his next witty riposte.

"You've heard of the Baritsch collection?" It was not a question. "Quote: 'The world's grandest array of art treasures still in private hands,' unquote. I believe that was how you described it in your article last year in *Art for Tomorrow*. 'Exquisitely selected, without regard for cost, and exquisitely displayed in the Baron's villa in Bellagio, on the shores of Italy's Lake Como,' you wrote. And further, you described the Baron's refined 'instinct for beauty,' his 'aristocratic eye,' and his 'generous sharing of the great patrimony of European culture in opening his private collection to the public.'"

"You read my article." Levin was pleased. "Don't you agree with it?"

"You know it is bullshit," she said roughly. "The man's grandfather was a war criminal. He got a fortune from making poison gas for the Kaiser in the first war. In the second, he expanded production for the Nazis. Oh yes, he was a true art connoisseur. Looking at the great masterpieces of western civilization helped him to get the stink of the trenches and the gas ovens out of his nose. And such a philathropist, too, the way he helped the Jews trying to escape from Germany by buying their Old Masters. About that time, he also got interested in German Expressionists. He picked up a very nice collection, yes, very tastefully selected, from the thousands that the Nazis stole from collectors and museums and even the artists. What compassion! He saved them from being burned. After all, they represented the heritage of European culture; not like the millions of people who were burned."

"Oh, degenerate art," Levin interjected wearily. "That's an old story. Lots of others bought those pictures too, including, I might emphasize, the genuine anti-Nazis at the Museum of the New. They hired a dealer to bid for them in that auction in Zürich. The Rockefellers provided the money. And after the War, they never returned the pictures, even when the German museums pleaded for them. They never dared to send them to Germany in any exhibition because someone might have tried to impound them as stolen goods. So? So morality gets shaky in the rarified realm of art. It's a world of accommodation. Live and let live. Gather ye Rousseaus while ye may. Ha! I should use that some time. So why, my dear lady, are we engaged in this deep philosophical discussion at three in the morning? Especially when tomorrow, I promise, we could dice it all out in a civilized manner, over *truite bleu* at Le Pavillon?"

"I'm not the one dicing out anything," she said sharply. "This is not a theoretical discussion, may I remind you. For me, theory went up the smokestacks in the camps. Nothing bores me more. When I hear the word intellectual, to mimic what Goering said about culture, I reach for my revolver. I piss on your precious thoughts. Who are you to tell me that art is good and what kind of art is best?"

With her free hand she reached into her pocket and extracted a tiny red Swiss Army knife. It was already opened to the fruit blade. Then she stepped to the huge canvas covering an entire wall with its nervously twirling squiggles and splashes, a dizzying dance of pigments that seemed to reach out and suck the viewer into its nervous embrace. She was still pointing the gun at Levin as she delicately used the blade to prick a tiny sliver of paint off the surface.

Levin glared in horrified fascination. The painting was his best loved possession, a Jackson Pollock from 1950, a seminal work from the best period. The artist had impulsively thrust it at Levin during a night-long drip-session at The Springs, even scribbling a cryptic dedication on the back: "To the best fucking critic, if any." Pollock had been drinking steadily while Levin was trying to interview him and maybe he gave away the picture because he had said absolutely nothing usable. It was still wet, not just with paint, but also blood from where Pollock had cut his hand on the edge of a paint can, and Levin had had the very devil of a time schlepping it home. Under the dedication Pollock had scrawled the title: *# 79/1950*, but the next day, his wife, Lee Krasner, had telephoned. Numbers weren't good for sales, she said, and the painting's real title was *Rosy Dawn*. Levin had let Zelda keep the raccoon bedspread in order to keep the painting. And when he moved uptown after after the split, he had settled for a building without doormen in order to afford an apartment with enough wall space for this picture. It was a landmark in the artist's career and valuable, too. At Parke-Bernet only a month ago a similar work (but without the artist's blood) had fetched nearly $100,000.

"Look, Levin. I'm correcting the picture," this mad woman was saying, "I think he made a mistake right here." And she dug her piercing little blade into a delicate whirl of black, flicking the chip in his direction. Then she turned severe. "This painting is in deplorable condition. You really don't deserve to own a great masterpiece if you're not willing to take care of it. It's deteriorating fast. Let's just take a little swatch here..." she pointed with the knife, "... and we'll send it to the lab for spectrographic analysis."

Levin sat horrified as she nattered on and on in a gruesome catalogue of restorers' technical jargon: varnish, underpainting, X-rays, lasergrams, pigment half-life, essential resins, solvent; the woman knew what she was talking about. Furthermore, he was finding her vandalism on his picture perversely erotic. He hunched forward to relieve the pressure on his crotch.

"Now these blue streaks," she went on, forcing the blade-point in again, "they're dangerously degraded from the artist's intentions. It was only house paint to begin with and you've obviously allowed too much daylight to get at it. I'm afraid this entire section will have to be retouched. And here, where the silver enamel overlaps the automobile lacquer, hairline cracks." She was using the blade like a pointer, leaving a distinct scratch over the offending spot.

Seated tensely on his white velour sofa, Levin realized that for the first time he was reacting viscerally to the painting, all too viscerally, to his acute embarrassment, for his body convulsed with a rush and he felt a sticky moistness spread over his lower belly. She viewed the mortifying stain on his pants with clinical detachment, like a nurse contemplating a specimen.

"That's much better I'm sure," she said. "Just think of all the orgasms I could give you by ripping this valuable picture to shreds. But I'm not going to do it now. Now we're going to get serious."

Levin was miserable. He had not been so humiliated since a drizzly November afternoon at Phillips Andover. Gathered in the locker room, the boys had been told that field hockey was cancelled and most of the class shambled off to study for midterms. At the door five of his regular tormentors had jumped him and hustled him into a linen closet. They dragged off his clothes and then held him down while Baxter Worthington III diddled his dick. "Why, I thought they cut off Jew-boys' pricks right after they were born," Baxter had sneered malevolently. "Why, lookee here. This Jew-boy still has one ... well, a part of it anyway." The boys holding him down grunted and giggled in embarrassment. And then the milky semen had spurted out and Baxter had dipped a long, patrician finger into it and smeared it around Levin's mouth. "You can ask the rabbi if it's kosher," Baxter had jeered, as the gang ran off, snickering.

Levin sometimes ran into Baxter these days, usually at the Cosmopolitan Museum, where, it was rumored, his father had purchased a position for him as chief curator of Renaissance art. A husky, athletic boy at prep school, he had gone to flab, and Levin was pleased to hear the gossip about his prodigious homosexual liaisons. Half the artists in New York had succumbed to him, so the talk went, in hopes of an "in" at the museum, especially now that it was beginning to show contemporary work. Baxter, in fact, favored a lithe black graffitist, with whom he shared not only sexual ecstasies but also the heroin needle. When they saw each other at some museum event, Levin usually responded gravely to Baxter's effusive recollections of Phillips Andover, while privately exulting over the man's flaccid belly and slack, razor-burned double chin.

"You're not getting sleepy, are you?" the woman barked harshly. "Because now, at long last, we are really going to get down to the main event. To be brief, what we want from you is a complete floor plan of the Baritsch Museum. By complete, I mean the location of every single painting and sculpture marked, every door and window marked, every skylight and chimney marked. We also would like a full schedule for all the curators, where they work, when they work, as well as where they live and their *curriculum vitas*.

Vitas or *vitae*? I never get that straight; I missed that part of my education."

Levin listened dejectedly to the way she kept digressing. First she was all business and then suddenly she would switch into all this personal stuff, like she was dictating an autobiography into a tape recorder. If she hadn't still been brandishing the knife over the painting (idiotically, it was the knife picking at the painting that bothered him more than the gun), he would have sarcastically pointed this weakness out to her. He would also have explained to her that the Baritsch Collection was about as susceptible to theft as the Crédit Suisse vaults in Lausanne. And besides, there was no point in stealing such a well-known constellation of masterpieces; no one would buy them for a hundred years.

"We also need a full schedule for the guards," she went on briskly, "but we'll find that elsewhere. Likewise for the dogs. So I guess all that's left for you to do right now is to sign the contract."

"What if I refuse?" Levin blurted.

"When you see it, I'm confident you'll sign. And I'm also confident that we won't have to take extraordinary measures to enforce it."

She reached behind the drapes for a large artist's portfolio. From it she fished a tissue-wrapped parcel, less than twelve-inches square, placed it carefully on the floor, and gently nudged it toward Levin with her foot. Pulling away the tissue, Levin found a dark fruitwood panel, the patina of its great age marred by dry splinters. It was slightly bowed and it bore a roughly chalked message, like a bistro menu, which said simply: "I promise," followed by a blank line for a signature. He turned over the panel and caught his breath in astonishment, almost dropping it.

He was face to face with the world's most enigmatic portrait except for the *Mona Lisa*, and many would say even more so. Framed by tight, glossy curls above an ivory-smooth forehead, she haughtily regarded Levin from under heavy waxen lids, with the same grave equanimity with which she might have viewed a beheading. Smudges of darker pigment brought her high cheekbones into relief and delineated a generous Italianate nose. It was the mouth that gave him a chill, as it had to virtually all those who had confronted it for almost five hundred years; as it probably had in life. Firm and slightly pouting, ominous in its gravity, pitiless in its total willfulness, this Renaissance woman projected her self-contained mystery across the centuries.

Behind her, spiky trees ushered the eye into a deep landscape where, on the far horizon, a city raised its towers and steeples. But Levin's gaze was inevitably drawn back into the face, which seemed to regard not only him, but all the rest of humanity with flinty, judgmental disdain.

"It's *Ginevra di Benci*," he gasped.

Chapter 2

Connoisseurs

The Baron woke up annoyed. Time and time again, the fishermen from the west side of the lake had been begged not to start their putt-putting near the villa before nine a.m. He would actually have preferred eleven a.m., but didn't want to give the appearance of a slugabed. Some years ago he had searched out the men who seined this entire section of the lake and simply paid them to go elsewhere. The racket had stopped, but not for long. What with increased demand for the lake's toothsome white fish, the men had returned to their traditional fishing grounds in even greater numbers, and now the sputter of their unmuffled outboards was worse than ever.

He tugged languidly at the tapestry bell-pull and Franz appeared almost immediately bearing a chrome bed-tray on which a steaming Meissen coffee cup, a folded copy of the *Neue Zürcher Zeitung* and a perfect white orchid were artfully arranged on embroidered pink linen.

"There seems to be no way to get a decent night's sleep around here any more," grumbled the Baron, reaching for a second pillow and heaving himself into position to receive the tray. "Maybe it's time for another excursion over there to see how much they want this time to stop the racket."

Franz shook his head sympathetically. "Don't you remember, Herr Baron, we tried that again last year, but the authorities refused to permit any foreigners to negotiate with the fishermen."

"Of course I remember," he said irritably. "Just bring me a half grapefruit, two soft-boiled eggs, and a croissant. No, better make that one egg and a slice of toast, lightly buttered; that should satisfy Dr. Kohler."

Franz backed deftly toward the door and managed to bow slightly while reaching backward for the handle to let himself out. He had virtually the same conversation with the Baron every morning. It was worth leaving Switzerland to work for a man like Karl Baritsch, thought Franz. A man of strict habits, this Herr Baron, so regular in his hours and his routine, his wishes and consumptions, his gestures even, that he could almost be taken for a Swiss. But then, one could only be a real Swiss if one's parents had been Swiss, and their parents and back to at least the days of Wilhelm Tell. But for a foreigner, the Baron came damned close.

The offending boat was chugging away into the mist as the Baron sipped his coffee and unfurled the newspaper. The pilot of the U-2 spy plane shot down by the Russians had now returned to his home town, welcomed by a brass band, following several days of debriefing in Washington. A clinic in Lausanne would begin to supply the Lippes Loop, a new intrauterine birth control device. Both the Arlberg-Orient Express and the Simplon-Orient Express would cease operating, after seventy-nine years, on May 27. Friedrich Dürrenmatt's new drama, *The Physicists*, was about to open in the Zürich *Schauspielhaus*. A fifteen-man delegation of Evangelical seminarians had left Munich for Tel Aviv. They would spend the next six months working on a *kibbutz*, as a gesture of reconciliation, following the conviction of Adolf Eichmann.

The *Zürcher Zeitung's* dignified gray columns imposed a fictitious logic upon the news. In its pages, the heroes and villains of the world's mad parade faded into gray rationality, passing into the calm shoals of history before the full highlights and shadows of their deeds emerged, like a murky film that had not been fully developed. The Baron could imagine the outbreak of nuclear war announced on the front page in type of a decent size and in measured, grammatical prose. On the editorial page, there would be a call for all parties to meet (in Geneva, of course) for a negotiated settlement. The price of gold had spiked sharply upward, the financial section would reveal, while the banks experienced a a massive influx of foreign currency. He had consumed the rest of his breakfast, delivered silently by Franz, and, after lighting the single cigar he allowed himself in the morning, the Baron contemplated the day.

The early morning mist had turned into a thin drizzle (So that's why the noisy boat had gone!), but a bright line at the southern horizon promised the Mediterrannean breezes that often coaxed the mimosas into bloom even in February in Bellagio. It was the climate that had lured the Baron to settle in this delicious corner of northern Italy; that and the perfect site, a long, narrow strip squeezed between the green precipices of the alpine foothills and the pebbled shore of the lake. The original villa was a tumbledown pile, its cracking stucco smeared over stone walls more than a foot thick. Onto it, the Fascist functionary who had last lived there had added a grandiose pavilion. Leaks riddled its roof and by the time Baron Karl bought the place in 1952, rainwater also seeped in around its French doors and the mansard dormers on the second floor. The whole place required massive renovation, but at least there was plenty of space for expansion and for exquisite and fragrant gardens as well. Cliffs formed a formidable boundary all around the perimeter, except for a single entrance at the west end. It was a natural fortress, a perfect location for the magnificent collection of art he had just inherited.

Acquiring pictures had been the only distraction from work and duty Karl's grandfather had allowed himself. A quixotic patriarch whose somber furies had shadowed not only his family but the pages of European history as well, he never missed a Sunday mass and proudly rode the streetcar to his office among his workmen. Trained as a chemist, Gerhardt Baritsch tinkered with coal tar derivatives in his laboratory to produce the earliest aniline dyes and then translated his discoveries into a vast industrial empire, one of the engines of Germany's economic surge during the last two decades of the nineteenth century. The title the Kaiser had bestowed upon him was a source of great satisfaction to this son of a provincial postmaster. But, as he all too often reminded his grandson, he was even more gratified by the creative avenues his discoveries had opened up for artists.

"Renoir, Degas, Monet -- none of them could have painted such brilliant colors," he would declaim, dragging the youngster from one brilliant Impressionist canvas to the next. "None of this would have been possible without my dyes." Eight-year-old Karl would shift impatiently from one foot to the other as his grandfather paused interminably to examine this passage of viridian green and that one of ultramarine violet. They were in Paris, and little Karl considered it a total waste of time to dawdle in front of paintings of haystacks and water lilies when they could be riding on the open platform at the back of a bus or having a parfait in the Café de l'Opera. One time they had even encountered a street riot and watched from a doorway as the police lunged into the demonstrators, swinging their weighted capes.

"Lousy Jews," his grandfather had muttered. "Now the French are paying for electing one of that scum to lead them. At least such a disgrace will never happen now in Germany." Karl was fascinated by one of the *flics* jumping energetically onto a cardboard sign dropped by one of the marchers. "*A bas Blum*," it said and the boy wondered why anyone was opposed to flowers -- *blumen*, in German. He knew better than to ask his grandfather, however, because anything connected with the Jews, or anything connected with the French (except for the paintings that showed off his dyes) would provoke the old man into a sputtering red-faced rage. And then he might forget completely about riding on the bus or having a parfait.

While recalling this mid-Thirties excursion to Paris, Karl Baritsch washed and shaved, regarding, in the magnifying mirror, the distinctly aquiline nose above his mustache. His grandfather had always been at pains to point out that it was a Roman nose, distinguished by its refined, narrow bridge, he said, from the typically thick, fleshy Jewish kind. From the armoire, the Baron selected gray slacks, an ivory Viyella shirt and a navy-blue cashmere cardigan, which he donned while studying the garden and the lake beyond it, from the window. The forsythia were already in bud and even the lilacs were turning green. An elderly gardener in a green cotton apron was weeding the bulb beds, where hyacinths, daffodils and tulips would soon erupt, perhaps just after he returned from his annual ski trip to Zermatt.

Franz knocked softly and entered, extending a silver salver on which rested a discreet ivory business card.

"I know," said the Baron, sighing, "that must be Rosenfeld. He wants to show me a new Picasso that he's managed to pry out of the old man. That shrewd Spaniard, you know, he's always teasing the dealers into coming to see him and then he chases them out empty-handed and ships his pictures to the Paris vault. Rosenfeld must have been especially charming. I hope he's also brought the Matisse and the Braque. I'll meet him in the gallery annex, the little office there, where the light is decent. Please see that an easel is set up in there, and maybe you'd better bring in a floodlamp, as well. I want to be sure I can see all the values of the chrome orange. Matisse was about the only one who could handle that particular shade."

The irony was lost on Franz, who nodded and stepped off to obey.

"And Franz," the Baron called after him, "please see also that I can meet with the restorer this afternoon. We'll have to decide how to treat the Van Gogh."

There was never an end to the problems posed by the collection, he thought, especially now that Rosalinda was gone. She was really the one who knew about art, who never tired of acquiring this or that, who loved spending long afternoons in the gallery, hanging and re-hanging the pictures. "When they're arranged just right," she would say, "they can speak to each other; they have a dialogue, just like actors in the theater, and all we have to do is sit in the audience and try to understand and enjoy it."

After the carpenter and the picture-handler were gone, they would often sit together on the divan in the center of the gallery. They would hold hands and she would tell him tall tales about the painters: how Gauguin had spent the proceeds from sale of a year's pictures on a shipment of *marrons glacées* from Paris; that Degas chose to paint ballerinas because he found their deformed feet especially erotic; that Toulouse-Lautrec smoked hashish to dull the pain in his crippled legs. Then she would giggle conspiratorially and recline luxuriantly into his lap. Sometimes they would have sex right there on the carpet in the gallery. Once, their thrashings had even brought a guard rushing in and she had snickered about the man's discomfiture and imagined him dashing home to his pudgy wife for a vigorous session.

But Rosalinda also knew a great many truths about art. She had studied art history at the Munich Pinakothek and then stayed on as a library assistant. That's where Karl had first seen her, unpacking books sent by an American museum to replenish the library ruined by a wartime bomb. His grandfather had been offered a Dürer drawing at a bargain price and had sent Karl to get information about its provenance.

"My dear friend," Rosalinda had said mockingly, "of course the price is low. I'm just surprised that the seller is willing to take money at all. Last week I heard about a Monet, yes, genuine, although damaged from being stored all through the war, rolled up, in a cow barn. The owner traded it for a pound of butter."

She was wearing rough gray pants, cut down from an army officer's uniform, a burgundy hand-knitted turtleneck and gloves, for the building, in that hard January of 1948, remained unheated. Her hard work in the chill had raised a glow in her face, a broad and generous face, with lively gray eyes and a playful mouth. A dark plaid wool scarf was wound around her head and throat, and from it emerged a long, thick, blond braid tied with a tiny pink bow. With a sweeping gesture, she cleared a space among the piles of books on one of the tables and pulled up two venerable oak arm chairs.

"Thank heaven for these zealous cleaning ladies we have here, she said. "Every month, they pulled all the chairs and tables out of this library so they could really give the floor a good scouring with a brush. And they'd leave them out in the corridor until the floor dried. By golly, that was the night the bombers visited us. So we ended up with all our tables and chairs ... but the books were burned to cinders. However, with Dürer, I think you're in luck. Seems to me just last week I unpacked huge crate that arrived from Detroit. Can you imagine? A huge crate ... and it was crammed with duplicates from their library. The director there used to be a curator in our museum. He had to leave when Hitler came, naturally, being half-Jewish. I thought it was damned nice of him to give us all those books."

Karl sat back contentedly as she jabbered on. He had never been talkative and when he encountered someone who was, he was relieved. Besides, he found what she had to say interesting and he was taken by her brisk, offhand manner. The fat yellow braid with its tiny pink bow intrigued him.

"What about a cup of real coffee?" she now asked. "It so happens that this very cultivated American lieutenant, yes really, was in here last week, looking for -- you won't believe it -- a book about Bavarian glass painting. I sent him to Dr. Brenner at the university, the only remaining specialist in that field. And the very next day, that lieutenant came back with a jar of Nescafé. So, I'll just be a minute and meanwhile you can look over the Dürer book."

While recalling this scene, the Baron was striding dutifully toward the gallery, glancing with a pang of sadness at the Dürer *Annunciation*. She had insisted that it should hang right next to Grünewald's version of the same subject. "So they can talk to each other and won't get lonely when we're not here," she had said.

Helmut Rosenfeld rose to greet the Baron. "The breezes from the south must agree with you, Herr Baron," he intoned. "I've never seen you look so hale and fit." The dealer wore a dark double-breasted blue suit with a subtle pinstripe, tailored in Milan to emphasize his lean build. He

looked liked an aging pixie, his pinkish face framed by ring-
lets of prematurely white hair and his hazel eyes crinkled
under bushy brows.

On the easel, bathed in a blinding light, was a recent
Picasso, a jagged figure of a woman holding an elongated
infant on her lap. Above her head, doves were wheeling in
flight and at her feet lay a jumble of what appeared to be ribbons twined in tormented strands. The colors overall were
somber, relieved by alizarin crimson brushstrokes around
the woman's breasts and by touches of Prussian blue shading the infant's body. The ribbons, Karl now noticed, were
in fact snakes and they glistened in a black tangled mass.

"You have no idea how difficult it is to get anything out
of Picasso these days," the dealer began. "It was always difficult, as you know, but now," he threw up his hands, "it's
an ordeal. First he keeps you waiting for days in some hotel
near his villa. You can't go anywhere because at any moment
The Call might come. Then when he finally deigns to see
you, he spends the whole day clowning around in funny
hats and refuses to get down to business. There's no place
to sit because every level surface is covered with stuff. They
have to eat every meal out because there's no place to sit.
He drags paintings and drawings out from the bottom of all
the debris, or out from under his bed and often they're not
even finished. He waves them under your nose -- and then
he pulls them all back. Finally, he might give you one piece
and you're so glad to get it, you don't even examine it. Then
you can spend half a day humoring him into signing it.

"How I wish I had been in Kahnweiler's shoes," the
dealer went on. "Back then, that wily Spaniard was still

hungry, he was still grateful for a few francs. But now he demands a fortune -- and in cash -- for any scribble he makes on a paper napkin. He keeps the dealers competing with each other, makes appointments with several of us all at the same time and when we leave, I swear, I can hear his laughter down the street. But then, what can we do? He's the genius of the twentieth century and I guess he's entitled to eccentricity. And besides, the Americans will pay the moon for anything his hand has touched, yes, even the paper napkin with the doodle on it."

Karl patiently listened to this diatribe, even though he had heard it in all its variations quite a few times -- and not just from Rosenfeld. He admired the dealer's way with words, the ease and humor of his description and the way he was able to imply that there were plenty of customers for this rather unattractive picture if the Baron did not buy. Karl felt deeply, but a false sense of decorum kept him from making easy conversation. Maybe it was his strict schooling, or else the way his grandfather had so forcefully expressed his strong opinions ... and been proven so wrong.

"It's not the prettiest Picasso," he now ventured.

"No, not pretty," the dealer quickly agreed. "But then, one tires of pretty pictures. I'll always remember being in Wesley Till's office at the Museum of the New and hearing him carry on about how suspicious we should be of pretty pictures. 'They're not profound,' he would say. 'You'll tire of pretty pictures.' Nelson Rockefeller was in the room on that occasion, along with the museum president, Alex Clarendon, whom, as you know, Till also advised on his collection."

Even politeness could not keep Karl from breaking in; Rosenfeld could easily go on in this vein for the rest of the morning. Then he would have to be invited to stay for lunch.

"What kind of a price are we talking about?"

That sent Rosenfeld into a long disquisition on recent sales:

"At the Sarlie sale of Picassos in 1960, just to give you an idea, Herr Baron, a 1938 *Man with a Red Glove* went for more than $64,000 and a 1944 *Still Life with Candle* fetched almost $41,000. Last year, Somerset Maugham's *La Greque*, one of those overblown women Picasso was doing in 1924, brought $72,000. Of course, the works from the Blue and Rose Period have been bringing considerably more, but the Cubist works are beginning to find eager buyers as well. This picture is a late work and is therefore of somewhat lesser value. On the other hand, we must remember that the artist is now eighty-one years old, and one day soon there will be no more new Picassos."

"Not counting the hundreds, maybe thousands of things he's got stashed in his Paris vault," Karl interrupted. "The French government will get its share and may dump everything on the market. Then there'll be the family to contend with -- wives, former wives, mistresses, children legitimate and illegitimate, who knows how many and what they intend to do. This won't be a nice, clean situation like Pollock -- the man slams his car into a tree and the long-suffering wife gathers everything into her well-manicured little iron fist. She doles out only a few pictures every year. The prices take off into the stratosphere and she ends up with a magnificent reward for putting up with that madman all those years."

"Concerning Pollock, I will agree with you, Herr Baron," the dealer said. "Without Lee, nothing. But you must understand that Picasso is in a different category. He's the artistic genius of our time. Anything touched by his hand is likely to appreciate substantially, even more so because of these inflationary times. Those who have the foresight to buy early always will benefit. Your grandfather, if I may be so bold as to mention it, had that kind of perception combined with financial prudence when he bought into the Impressionists and the Post-Impressionists at such an early stage."

Karl rose to peer more closely at the picture on the easel. He felt like telling Rosenfeld the truth about his grandfather. Perception? Prudence? The old man had bought those pictures because they demonstrated the elegance of the dyes he had invented. The beauty of a chemical formula is what he appreciated. Those pictures never meant more to him than the triumph of a successful laboratory experiment. He had considered the artists who painted them decadent, just like French civilization, and deemed their subject matter frivolous. The Old Masters now, that was something else. They represented the greatness, the enduring values of European culture, German culture.

"We Germans are the only ones who are still really serious about European culture," the old man had told him on the last of their trips to Paris together. "Everywhere else they're playing insane games, trying to turn three thousand years of history into a silly joke."

They had just been to the Surrealist Exhibition, the sensation of Paris in that summer of 1938. Eleven-year-old Karl had no idea of what to make of the taxi rusting under a perpetual synthetic waterfall in the entrance hall. Inexplicably, the mannequin of a woman was sprawled inside. He had found the live snakes writhing around her rather intriguing. Then there were the department store dummies dressed as mocking self-portraits by various artists. A bit pornographic that. Totally baffling was the ceiling draped with 1,200 empty coal sacks by the enigmatic joker Marcel Duchamp. It all struck Karl as lots more fun than the usual boring gallery, but his grandfather emerged red-faced and shaking.

"These vermin," he fumed. "They won't rest until they've stripped the last rags off European civilization. Truth, beauty, honor? They just snicker and dump another garbage can on our heads. At home at least we put an end to all those sorts of pranks. It was unpleasant, but somebody had to say, 'Stop!' And here we are, Karl, at the Café de l'Opera. How about a parfait?"

Thoughfully, Karl ran his forefinger over the Picasso, tracing the outline of that poor, distorted woman.

"She's so damned crude and ugly," he repeated.

"All a matter of taste," replied Rosenfeld smoothly. "Shall we look at the others?"

He removed the Picasso from the easel and carefully positioned the Matisse, a brilliantly colored street scene painted during the artist's stay in Morocco.

"Please, spare me the sales talk," said Karl, surprised at his own gruffness.

Rosenfeld's father had been a dealer in Berlin, one of the first in Germany to specialize in modern art. When the Nazis seized power in 1933, the Berlin brownshirts had made a point of looting his gallery. They had taken particular delight in spreading out some of his most daring Expressionist paintings on the sidewalk and forcing the distinguished dealer to trample over them. A small crowd had gathered to watch the spectacle, but no one intervened. A few of the bullies gathered up the ruined canvases, tittering nervously, and tossed them into a van. That night they were all burned in the courtyard of the central Berlin fire station, along with hundreds of other paintings and sculptures that the Nazis deemed decadent.

Fortunately, Jakob Rosenberg had earlier shipped a few of his most precious paintings to London. That very evening, as the torch was being applied to the paintings, he hustled his family aboard the train to Calais. They carried a few personal belongings in small suitcases and precious forged papers in their pockets. The elegant apartment near the Tiergarten they abandoned, not without tears over the Walter Gropius and Mies van der Rohe furniture. The small Renoir sustained the family in London; the Seurat sketch took them to New York, where Jakob opened a salesroom in their West End Avenue apartment; the Blue Period Picasso paid for Helmut's graduate degree in art history at New York University. The story had been published in *Art for Tomorrow* soon after the war.

Karl had always wanted to discuss this history with the dealer, who now sat across from him, his elegantly pinstriped legs crossed, relaxed in a splendidly restored Louis Seize armchair. Karl wanted to offer some kind of explanation or even an apology, although, God knows, he had been much too young to influence those long-ago events.

He himself had paid dearly for Hitler's madness: his own father frozen in an unmarked grave at Stalingrad. And even his grandfather, one of the men who had financed Hitler in the early days, had become disillusioned, had refused to employ slave laborers in his factories, had emerged from a concentration camp at the end of the war, a teary-eyed and trembling wreck, babbling nonsense.

"I need a little time to study these pictures," Karl said instead. "Leave the Braque here too. I'll examine them all at leisure, maybe hang them in my bedroom for a few days. That's the best way to learn whether they're congenial, don't you think? Then we can settle this business on the phone. Frankly, the Picasso really puts me off right now. It's so ugly. But who knows? It might just bewitch me overnight."

"Of course, Herr Baron," the dealer said evenly, rising to shake Karl' hand. "It's always a pleasure to share some beautiful things with you. Don't bother to see me out. I can find the way very easily. And we'll talk in a few days."

Karl stepped back into the room and again sat facing the easel. He stared hard at the Matisse. He wondered, as he often did, about why this particular scrap of linen should cost as much as a two-story stucco house with a view of the lake on a good street in Bellagio. Stretched on flimsy wooden strips, daubed with these particularly garish colors, the thing challenged him to even find a reason for its existence, not to mention its outlandish value. He even wondered why an object like this could move Hitler to frenzies of rage and his followers to gruesome deeds.

Rosalinda would know, he thought, frowning. She might have pointed to the saturation of pure orange, astonishingly laid down next to a shimmering purple band. Perhaps she would have remarked on the daring jangle of clashing, brilliant colors; on the glaring light of the North African street, conveyed through blinding highlights; on the hubbub of human activity, expressed in dashing, unarticulated figures. For Rosalinda, he would unquestionably have bought this picture today.

"Say something," she had screamed at him during that last, ghastly evening. "Say something, for once, that's real. Say something outrageous, something rude and unreasonable, just so I know that you have some feelings. But you can't. And I can't stand that." And she had left.

Chapter 3

Deals

Helmut Rosenfeld walked carefully and slowly through the Baron's gallery. He stopped before a Cranach portrait -- a canny-looking German Renaissance merchant with pinched lips, draped in wine-red brocade and grasping a silken purse. Beside the elaborate frame, a tiny red light was blinking. He scribbled a few marks in a small notebook and quickly strode on through the long hallway crowded with lesser works and a few of the old Baron's "mistakes," excellent examples of the great German pictorial past, but unfortunately faked.

At the door he passed Franz, who bowed reflexively. The Baron's servants were all Swiss, recruited in little alpine towns where the old values -- discretion, deference, thrift -- had survived Europe's upheavals. Rosenfeld murmured *"Auf Wiedersehen,"* and ducked into the back seat of his waiting beige Mercedes limousine. He knew that Franz would notify the gatekeeper and indeed, by the time the car had negotiated the narrow, curving path which wound through the gardens along the lakeshore, the wrought iron portal was already swinging open. The driver turned sharply to the right and arrived just as the ferryman reached to close the gate. He waved the car aboard.

In less than ten minutes, the boat was bumping into the pier at Menaggio. From there, the car climbed eagerly up the narrow road toward the frontier post at Ona. After barely a glance at his passport the Italian border guard raised the red and white striped barrier, and so did the Swiss fifty feet further on. Helmut savored the scene ahead, the red tile roofs of Lugano blending into the mist rising from the lake, a ghost village fading up into the craggy hills behind.

At a damp intersection, the driver turned sharply right and aimed the car precisely up the steep, winding street toward the summit of the sheer ramparts overlooking the lake. It passed the cemetery, with its opulent graves, and Helmut smiled as he imagined the numbers of their occupants' secret Swiss bank accounts discreetly chiselled under their names. With all the ups and downs the lira had taken, it was only prudent for the well-off Italians who frequented the lake resorts to entrust their savings to the gray gnomes of Geneva. The street snaked dizzily upward. The drizzle had stopped, but the moist haze drifting from the lake's surface created a Chinese-looking landscape in which grayish peaks layered off into the distance, their vegetation virtually drained of all color.

The Hotel Belvedere occupied the choicest spot on the peak, far above the last house even the clever Swiss and Italian architects had dared to embed in the mountain's rocky flanks. It was noticeably colder as Helmut dismissed the driver. Inside, the small lobby opened into a deserted bar and dining room where a tropical forest of ferns and vines trailed luxuriantly from hanging planters. On the terrace beyond, however, the window boxes were empty; in summer, they spilled a profusion of red geraniums. Rosenfeld collected his key from the board and called out to the hotel-keeper, a brisk and stout lady who was wiping nonexistent dust off the bar: "I'll be checking out in ten minutes."

Exactly ten minutes later he signed the credit card chit. "As always, it was delightful, Signora Bellizi," he said. "The new wing is particularly comfortable; I appreciate the feather-beds. Especially," he shivered, "in this kind of weather."

"Have a pleasant journey, Herr Rosenfeld. At least you're dressed for the weather," she replied, accompanying him to the door and shaking his hand.

From the helmet hugging his head to the boxy tip of his boots, Rosenfeld was garbed in smooth black leather. Stout zippers snugged his jacket around his torso and the sleeves around his forearms, and gleamed down the sides of his legs, where they overlapped the tops of his boots. The globe of a black plastic helmet rested in the crook of his left arm, while the hand grasped a pair of bulky gauntlet gloves. In his right hand, he carried a pair of black leather saddlebags. In the hotel garage, he checked the tabs and fastenings of his clothing, donned helmet and gloves, slung the saddlebags over the machine and roared away. To Signora Bellizi, watching discreetly from behind a lace curtain, the flaming red Kawasaki Grand Prix and its black rider conjured up a medieval knight charging off to a crusade.

Rosenfeld guided the powerful machine carefully down the twisting road, leaning gently into the curves and alert for uphill drivers who often crossed the center line as they took the hairpin turns. He again passed the cemetery. The sun had chased away the clouds and the remaining moisture on the lush vegetation glistened like jewels. He swung left just before reaching the foot of the mountain and quickly passed through the somnolent town. A substantial meal with wine and pasta and the obligatory siesta kept the population indoors until mid-afternoon. Helmut slowly negotiated the twisting streets until the houses petered out among stone-walled farmsteads. Then he picked up speed, relishing the cool wind that crept under his dark plastic face shield.

In the summer, he would have taken the high route through Introbio and Ballabio, with its challenging four-teen per cent grades snaking through forbidding peaks. But in mid-February, heavy snow could arrive suddenly and dangerously; the alpine passes were frequently closed and even if the roads were open, long lines of cars heading for a cluster of ski areas set a sluggish pace. Today he would follow the main road hugging Lake Como, dropping south to Lecco, then skirting Bergamo on the way to Brescia. From there, he would head northeast, reaching the spectacularly winding road north along Lake Garda at about dusk. It would be easier to negotiate the endless series of tunnels on this road while there was still a bit of daylight, but he could handle it in the dark, if need be, though the cold would bite.

He slowed down briefly as he passed through the tiny village of Lierna, whose fisherfolk disturbed the Baron's sleep, and then Mandello del Lago, where the mountains squeezed the lake into a narrow defile. Then he leaned forward on his roaring steed and gained speed, revelling in the steady vibrations beneath him and the anticipation of the evening's encounter.

What fun it would be to barge in on the Baron right now, Helmut thought, dressed just as he was and riding his red charger. That might awaken the poor man's feelings. There might even be an honest conversation, man to man, instead of the polite minuet that passed for communication between them. Never had Helmut seen delight, enthusiasm, sadness, or rage in Karl Baritsch's eyes; only correctness, totally predictable and bland as porridge. The man was so maddeningly reasonable. And so trapped in that magnificent house, eternally chained to that magnificent collection: conserving it, insuring it, judiciously augmenting it. Rather than being energized by the joy of possessing beautiful things, the Baron appeared to be weighed down by the sober duties of a caretaker, For him, the gold of art had been transmuted into leaden anxieties over insurance, temperature and humidity, lighting, insect infestation, decay of canvas or wood, the tendency of old pigments to fade or darken, or develop nasty flakings and cracks.

Helmut had detested old Gerhardt Baritsch, and not only because his (and his kind's) early and generous support for Hitler had made the whole rise of the Nazis possible. The old man also expressed nothing but contempt for modern art. Yet, except for a few mistakes, the old man had a fine eye for old masters. True, his cockamamie racial theories drove him to favor northern Europeans, but who could complain about a collection featuring Dürer, Van der Goes, Grünewald, and the Van Eycks? For these, the old Baron displayed a passion that was almost sexual in its purity.

For Helmut, thinking about art was most enchanting at moments like this, when the road rushed toward him in a blue-grey blur and he anonymous, helmeted and black, a hell's angel. Not that he belonged to that rough gang. Rather, the garb and the quivering motor between his legs stimulated his senses, allowing him to recall the unbridled colors of the Matisse with a sensuous rush. Here, on the road, he could rip through the dead veil of intellectualism and experience directly the voluptuous delight in a work of art.

This was the kind of passion which had driven Helmut's father to his career as an art dealer. The only son of a banker, he was expected to carry on the business. Then, during a student visit to Paris in 1905, he had fallen in love with the brilliantly colored canvases whose makers the critics denounced as Wild Beasts, *Fauves*. Through a banking connection, Jakob Rosenfeld had been invited for an evening at the home of two Americans, brother and sister, who had recently taken up residence in Paris. They were feverishly cultivating the city's avant-garde artists, buying some of their most outrageous productions and inviting them to bohemian soirées. The brother, Leo Stein, bustled about pompously, showing off his arcane assortment of aesthetic jargon. The sister, Gertrude, sat on a carved wooden armchair, like a massive sphynx on a throne, and droned cryptic, oracular pronouncements.

"Berlin will be ready one day for the work of M. Matisse," she said, "but not yet; Germans are too orderly for it; they are bound to fear his strident palette. The Americans? The colors could bewitch them, but their art education is sadly lacking. True understanding may never come. No matter.

They have no cultivated taste. In the end they'll worship whatever an expert places on the altar, especially if it's expensive."

Jakob had never heard anyone speak so portentously, as though her words were being dictated into a book. He was intimidated by it, and quietly spent the evening examining the pictures on the walls, while a hubbub of talk in French and English buzzed around him. This Matisse, who happened to be in the room, hardly resembled a wild beast, nor did his appearance match the screaming colors he favored in his palette. Seated primly on a bentwood chair, he looked like a provincial schoolmaster. The youthful Spaniard, by contrast, restlessly paced, his black eyes burning with a fiery passion, and volubly disputed everything, mercilessly rolling the R's in his poor French. Jakob found it strange that this vibrant man produced paintings of sad, destitute people in melancholy blue tones. On the wall above Gertrude, however, Jakob noticed a new work by this Pablo Picasso, lonely-looking clowns and mountebanks tinged with pink.

That evening, Jakob quite simply fell in love with the new art and its brave artists. Their imaginative fervor left Jakob exhilarated; it seemed to embody the rosy promise of this new twentieth century in which anything seemed possible. Two years later, after dutifully completing his education as a banker, he was back in Paris. This time, he was selecting stock for the new Berlin gallery his father had reluctantly agreed to finance. He cheerfully trudged up reeking staircases to the cramped studios, single rooms where the new artists slept and cooked and made love -- and feverishly created. Often, they were too poor even to buy firewood. Once,

Jakob had arrived at Picasso's place just in time to snatch away a bundle of drawings that the artist was about to feed into stove. Cold they might be, but the artists never seemed too poor to gather at the *Lapin Agile* for cheap wine, a bowl of onion soup and boisterous talk late into the night.

"Before the war," Jakob would start one of his inexhaustible stories, and Helmut knew that this meant before August 1914. To his father, that was clearly the crucial 20th century date, with all the horrors that followed merely a grisly postscript. "I shut the gallery immediately," Helmut would hear him tell a client. "At that time in Germany there was such a hate campaign against the French. I was afraid that a mob would destroy my pictures. Some people sent their families to the country," he would add, "but I sent my pictures."

Hearing this, Helmut would seethe. He knew exactly why his father re-told these tales: he was trying to convey to his customers a properly reverent attitude toward art, an attitude that he hoped would transfer to whatever picture was on the easel in the saleroom. Still, Helmut resented the notion that pictures were more precious than one's flesh and blood.

Helmut was only two years old when the pictures were sent away. He didn't remember that event; rather, one of his earliest memories was of his father in a gray uniform, bending to pat his head before leaving for the Western front in 1914. Jakob returned only when the war ended in 1918, but it was 1920 before the gallery re-opened. There was a party, with uniformed waiters passing champagne and canapés, and Helmut squirmed among the guests in his navy-blue sailor suit. The crowd, the heated room, the vinegary champagne he had swilled, and the handfuls of canapés he had gobbled made him dizzy. The pictures on the walls blended into a whirling kaleidoscope and his mother had snatched him up just as he was about vomit all over a Renoir drawing.

That, too, had become one of his father's interminable stories, a way of pouring soothing and amusing talk over clients while they were viewing a prospective purchase. "People don't know what to say about art," Jakob explained to his son. "They feel uncomfortable because most of them really know nothing about it. They don't know the vocabulary and if they do, they misuse it. The erotic feelings one gets from great art frighten a lot of people. Some of them feel guilty about spending a great deal of money on a small colored rectangle. Others are wondering if it will clash with the upholstery on the sofa, but they don't dare say that."

When Helmut had entered the business in 1949, he was unable to summon his father's kind of effortless, meaningless talk. A trained art historian, he wanted to tell clients about influences and affinities, about brushstrokes and composition, about hues and scumblings. Pedantically, he would start to lecture purchasers on the symbolism in the Max Beckmann on the easel before them, only to notice their polite resignation, followed by discreet yawns. By the time his father retired, ten years later, Helmut realized not only that his clients were bored, but rightfully so; no lectures were needed: to the occasional sensitive viewer, the picture itself was the text, and to the rest, it was only useful to talk about money.

Leaning into the tight hairpin curves hugging the shore of Lake Como, Helmut spotted the toy-like ferry leaving

Belllagio on its ten-minute voyage to Menaggio on the western shore. Otherwise, the lake was deserted on this wintry day, except for one brave, swaddled soul guiding a sailboat southward into the narrow dogleg of water toward Como. In an hour, Helmut would see the medieval city of Bergamo on his right, a fortress town of red tile roofs draped atop an impregnable crag.

From there, it was all first-class road to his destination and he would be able to make excellent time. Despite the many winding tunnels along the western shore of Lake Garda, he should be arriving just as the last light faded. Finding the driveway into the inn could be tricky. It branched off unexpectedly from the middle of one of those tunnels; Helmut hoped he would remember which one it was. He had been there only once before and someone else, the Count, had been driving. Helmut recalled just one sign for it on the highway, a roughly lettered "Hotel Bellavista" daubed in white where the tunnel wall opened into the parking lot.

Near Brescia, he stopped for gas and a bowl of minestrone, pale, over-boiled vegetables and pasty lumps of macaroni, but warming nevertheless. Because of the constant small movements required to balance the motorcycle, his body was not cold; only his hands were freezing. Before re-mounting the machine, he dug a pair of wool liners out of a saddlebag and slipped them on under his leather gauntlets. Then he roared northward toward Gardone Riviera and his first view of Lake Garda since the previous summer.

Despite his vigilance, it was too late to turn right when the sign for the hotel flashed by; he had to veer sharply off the road and make a U-turn into the packed dirt parking lot. He was elated to see that the one car in it was Filippo's ice-blue Maserati coupe. Helmut was quite certain that no other guests would turn up at this season of the year. Later, he would lash a protective tarpaulin around the Kawasaki, but now he leaped nimbly down three flights of cracked concrete steps to the forlorn terrace, with its hopelesssly shredded palm frond umbrellas.

The reception area doubled as a bar and, during this slow season, apparently also as a storage area. It was cluttered with sacks of dirty laundry, piles of clean sheets, and discarded kitchen equipment. A huge German shepherd bounded toward him, dragging its chain, followed by a sloppy blonde in a stained smock and felt slippers.

"About time you arrived," she said rudely. "We can't keep the kitchen help waiting around to serve dinner at this time of the year; not with just two guests. Dinner is at seven. Your friend is in number 5, over there, across the terrace. Leave your passport here."

She reached for the dog's chain and snapped the end onto an even stouter chain around her thick waist, from which a great bunch of keys dangled. Without another word she padded away, dragging the dog behind her.

Count Filippo Bolza Pietruccino Vergazzi Cardini was stretched full-length on one of the two narrow cots that nearly filled the room. His dark, curly hair emphasized the pallor of his complexion and his liquid brown eyes. At forty, he was losing the freshness of youth and even in the thrifty light from a single bulb, the beginnings of pudgy jowls were visible. On a thin gold chain around his neck, he wore an immense diamond, ringed with smaller emeralds. The rest of his body, soft, white, languorous, virtually hairless, was naked.

Without knocking, Helmut swiftly stepped into the room and shut the door behind him. Not a word passed between the two men. Then the art dealer threw his leather clad length over the pale figure on the bed. They embraced wordlessly and remained entwined, barely moving, breathing deeply of each other's scents. Against the Count's pallid body, Helmut's black leather squeaked moistly. Then he rose and stood by the window.

"Not quite yet," he said. "That dragon of a hotelier up there insists that we eat right now. The Excelsior this is not. And besides, I don't want your come all over my leather pants."

The Count rose lazily onto one elbow. "My dear Helmut, no dragon can spoil my delight at seeing you. The digs are a bit grubby, I grant you, but after we've dined I suspect you'll forget all about the cool drafts. I have a special treat for us both."

He jumped off the bed and retrieved a pair of Rose Madder paisley shorts from the floor.

"Should I wear them or not," he said. "That was my big decision before you got here. or should I bring out the pink tights with the white polka dots?"

Helmut had zipped off his leather jacket.

"Don't be vulgar," he said soberly and walked out to use the bathroom across the hall.

The Count meanwhile stepped into his beige wool jersey slacks, pulled a creamy Aran fisherman knit over his head. He tossed the diamond pendant carelessly onto the dresser. Not to worry: it was paste. While looping a navy foulard ascot around his neck, he stepped onto the narrow balcony and surveyed the deep, black expanse of the lake, the water lapping frigidly at the foundations below. In the summer, he thought, it would be possible to dive right off here into the water. He heard the toilet flush and saw the effluent spray out of a broken sewage pipe. No, swimming here at any season was definitely not recommended.

They had their pick among all twenty tables in the chilly, deserted dining room. A cowed youth in a wrinkled white jacket unfurled suspiciously ample menus and then announced that the evening's special was lake trout with garlic. Nothing else on the menu was available, except an omelette. The fish was surprisingly fresh, however, although the garlic tended to overwhelm the flavor of it.

"Nothing like chilled Mumm's to make the meal," said Helmut.

"Indeed," agreed the Count. "I picked it up in Milano."

Helmut wished that this soft and handsome man across the table were less frivolous, more substantial. When he had first met him, more than half a decade ago, Helmut had been enchanted by the Count's soft black curls, his velvety eyes, his vermilion lips curling into a smile at once innocent and mocking. Caravaggio was the artist that came to mind, the Baroque painter of dramatically lit tableaus and of bewitching boys.

The Count had wandered into his gallery and lounged lazily in a chair as Helmut brought out picture after picture for his perusal. The man's indolent posture vividly reminded

Helmut of the *Bacchus* in the Uffizzi, reclining on white draperies while daintily raising a glass beaker in a toast to the viewer. The face was androgynous, full and Orientally inscrutable, the luxuriant dark hair twined with vine leaves. One could almost smell the ripe scent of the fruit before him. Below the strong, muscled right shoulder, the hand fondled a dark ribbon bow. It was a painting that had all the ingredients of a masterpiece: impeccable craftsmanship, of course, but also an air of mystery that drew Helmut back to it and back again to wonder who and what and why.

Helmut had found himself irresistibly attracted to Filippo. But soon his fantasy of the young man as a stunning embodiment of one of Caravaggio's deliciously effete boys began to pall. He wanted the Count also to be a Bronzino prince at the Florentine court of Cosimo I: pale and ascetic in black fustian, a ruler of men, grasping an open book. All this Filippo was not.

Helmut threw the negative image into the balance, fighting against shame at his own peculiar passion, not just for another man, but mostly because the object was such a frail, unfocussed individual. Helplessly enthralled by a painting come to life, he had become a hostage to the whims of this pretty boy.

"I hear that the Baritsch collection is going on an American tour," the Italian said.

"Yes, on September fifteenth, for four months in New York," said Helmut. "Such a long visit should accommodate the crowds the museum expects. They love to ogle valuable goods. Then three weeks in Chicago, three weeks in Los Angeles and a final month at the National Gallery in Washington. I understand the Kennedys will formally attend the show there. But I hear that Jackie can't wait and will sneak in for a preview the night before it opens in New York."

"So our plans suddenly have a timetable," said the Count. "So far, it's been all ifs and maybes. Now, it looks like it's time to get serious."

Helmut smiled. "This is the first time I've ever heard that word from you. You've always been so playful. Are you sure you want to get serious? Why not forget it, carry on with *la dolce vita*?"

"But to me, this project is part of *la dolce vita*. Something new and different. Something thrilling, maybe dangerous. The thought of it makes my blood run faster, like a delectable new drug. Which reminds me, I brought along a surprise for you."

The waiter poured the last of the champagne and shambled away to draw their espressos. They came in tiny glass cups, a rich jolt of pure caffeine.

Filippo had too much enthusiasm for the complex operation, Helmut thought, he was altogether too frivolous. Though on the verge of middle age, the Italian always struck Helmut as a youth, too callow for mature responsibilities. He should never have gotten Filippo involved. Had it been a woman sharing an idyllic weekend last March at the Plaza in New York, Helmut was sure that he would have kept silent. But as two men, they were already conspirators in their desires. Helmut had managed to get through the Saturday with just affectionate chit-chat. It was Sunday morning brunch in bed that had loosened his tongue, lazy talk over the *New York Times*, nothing to do for the rest of the day except to make love. Easy and secure, a taste of being like a happily married couple.

"Did you ever hear of Rachel Haberman?" Helmut asked.

Filippo lowered the travel section. "The art restorer? Some tough bitch. Sure, she's the one who insisted nothing could be done to save my Barquettis. Said the man used inferior pigments and it served me right for buying so many of his pictures without consulting her."

"Well, she's had a tough life," Helmut had said. "God knows what she had to do to survive Auschwitz. Afterwards, she wanted to be an artist, but with a childhood like that, her imagination was too frightening. That's how she got into restoring paintings. In which, of course, she has become the best in the world."

"So why are we discussing this bitch's life history?" the Count demanded.

"I'm not sure myself, replied Helmut. "Except that she has some kind of crazy plot in mind. She wants to abstract, to put it delicately, a very large, very valuable collection."

"If it's very large and very valuable," Filippo immediately broke in, "it can't possibly be sold. So what's the point? You'd have to keep the stuff in a vault for a hundred years and who knows what prices will be like then? The police might stop looking for it after a while. But the insurance companies? Never. She's a crazy woman."

"Just hear me out," said Helmut, sorry already that he had begun this conversation. "She's not doing it for the money."

Filippo fell back into the pillows in a mock swoon. "Don't tell me there's a principle involved. You're a dealer. You see these collectors and these museum people every day. What do they talk about? Art appreciation? Sure, the kind of appreciation you get in a business deal. Money, money, money. That's all."

"Just forget I mentioned anything," said Helmut, "We're here for a pleasant weekend. Besides, it's just a notion. Nothing's likely to come of it." He grasped Filippo's soft shoulders and hugged them close. He kissed the Caravaggio boy's lips and pushed a pile of crumpled newspapers onto the floor, to caress the white buttocks, the milky legs, almost devoid of hair. Danger, just the thought of it, always inflamed his desire. Maybe that's why he had taken up with this boyish man in the first place, to create a sharp contrast to his sober, careful nature by taking risks, courting destruction to bring on almost unbearable ecstasy.

The waves on the lake outside the dining room phosphoresced in the moonlight. Grasping the Count's hand, Helmut pulled him up and away from the table. He scooped a bunch of grapes out of the fruit bowl and propelled his lover toward the door, across the windswept terrace and into their room. From his alligator attaché case, Filippo fished a square white envelope, along with a small mirror.

"I promised you a surprise and here it is," he said, chuckling while extracting a crisp ten-thousand lira bill from his wallet and rolling it into a tight cylinder. From the envelope, he poured a tiny hill of white powder onto the mirror. He arranged it into a neat, elongated pile, using the rolled bill and then stuck the other end into his nose. After inhaling with a sigh of pleasure, he handed the bill to Helmut.

"Try it," he said. "It's a new treat the people in Rome have been enjoying. Just don't sneeze; don't even breathe out."

"It looks like baking soda," said Helmut. "And you look totally ridiculous."

Nevertheless, he sniffed his portion, puzzled. He felt nothing at all. It certainly wasn't like pot, which seared the throat on the way down and then expanded inside the body with a soft and languid ease. He sniffed up a little more, and then Filippo poured out another neat dose.

"What's it supposed to do?" Helmut asked.

"You'll see," said Filippo, inhaling luxuriantly. "No, you won't see anything, you'll just love it."

Helmut never did directly feel any effect all that long night. He just felt more alert, more in control, elated, cheerful, and, above all, more brilliant. His wit was sharper, sending Filippo into gales of laughter. He danced around the room like a satyr, picturing the rude drawings on some of the erotic Greek vases and then he performed what was pictured, finding his senses extraordinarily sharp and his performance everlasting. He arranged Filippo in provocative poses and shamelessly pummelled and pinched him, while the Italian giggled tantalizingly. He crushed grapes on Filippo's chest and between his testicles, and lasciviously licked off the juice. Finally, he entered him from behind and felt a monumental, unheard-of surge of release.

There was no guilt, no ambivalence, no pain, and time was abolished. Early in the morning, they fell asleep in exhaustion, clutching each other's weary bodies like two innocent children.

When Helmut awoke, large white puffs of snow were drifting slowly down into the lake, like a blessing. Helmut felt his body drifting too, in lassitude and total satiety. He shivered. He could barely remember the wild saturnalia of the night, but he marvelled at the intellectual fireworks that the white powder had evoked. And then he was afraid. There had to be a price for such plenitude. He studied Filippo's sleeping features and spotted the seed of a grape tucked into a fold of his neck, just where a slight pulse regularly swelled the pasty skin.

It was after eleven, he noticed with surprise. A part of him wished that time would stop forever. But another part knew that it was impossible. The Caravaggio boy was just a magical image torn from the imagination of a rash and reckless painter. The day-to-day reality of Filippo was quite different: impulsive, self-indulgent, possibly even dangerous. That was why Helmut so angrily blamed himself for even mentioning Rachel Haberman's name to him, let alone her peculiar obsession.

Quietly, he rose and dressed. The highway north along the lake was wet, but none of the snow had stuck and there was virtually no traffic. In an hour he would be in Trento, where he could catch the train north over the Alps.

Chapter 4

Exhibition

As the bus plodded down Fifth Avenue, Wesley Calvin Till gazed abstractedly at the jagged, leafless trees of Central Park. He felt slightly queasy. It had been a particularly bad night; catnaps that might add up to a couple of hours' sleep, but mostly restless tossing and wakeful anxiety. None of his usual sleep strategies had worked. The good music station was celebrating Brahms' birthday with cavalcades of romantic noise. The talk shows were hopeless. He had read a good portion of a new book arguing that the Abominable Snowman was really a descendant of the woolly mammoth. Interesting, but he would much have preferred sound sleep. After a miserable night like this, he would normally have called in sick. The staff at the museum knew that he often worked at home following this kind of night.

That was out of the question on the first Wednesday of the month. That was when the trustees of the New Museum had their meetings. Without Till to guide them, there was no telling what sort of foolishness they might get into. There was that time when he had been out with stomach flu and they had impulsively voted to sell half of the works in storage. Afterward, Till had the very devil of a time pleading with each trustee individually to reverse the decision. Not that any of them understood how important it was to acquire examples of every ripple and trend illustrating the complex development of modern art. To be useful, the collection had to be complete, if only for study by scholars. No, the argument that had carried the day was purely financial: Selling off so many works would dangerously depress the market.

A few well-bundled nannies were already pushing elegant baby carriages into the wintry park, as the bus ponderously moved toward midtown. At 57th Street, Till looked longingly at the names of galleries lettered in gold on the windows of upstairs offices. Years ago, he had spent every Saturday roaming through those buildings; there was not a show of modern art in the city that he did not view. Now he was working harder than ever, but seldom got to an exhibition. His time leaked away in meetings about fund-raising or insurance, in legal consultations to provide maximum tax benefits to donors, in haggling with other museums to borrow or lend works.

Officially, the trustees were endlessly lauded as the museum's benefactors, but to the staff they were more like wild beasts to be lassoed and eventually domesticated. Few of them these days took the large view. Instead, there were the penny-pinchers, like Henrietta de Vries, who questioned every roll of toilet paper in the budget, or successful executives, like Henry Eckridge, a snowy-haired despot who refused to see any reason why a museum should not be run like an airline. Then there were the social butterflies, like Anita Deckman, whose sole passion seemed to be planning and attending parties.

All of the trustees, without exception, were immensely wealthy, but there was a sharp line between the "old" money and the "new." The old money tended to side with the penny-pinchers, while the new money preferred lavish parties. The love of art was supposed to be at the core of their activities but they had little patience with such a vague and old-fashioned concept.

In the early days of the museum, the concept had been much clearer. The trustees then had been vanguard collectors of modern art, crusaders for the wildly imaginative new forms pioneered by European artists early in the twentieth century. For them, the purchase of a Cubist Picasso or a Surrealist Miro had been a bold adventure, slightly wicked, an endearing eccentricity, perhaps a foolish extravagance. Connoisseurs of modern art, they also often favored progressive ideas in other areas, such as divorce or birth control or the various radical political movements of the 1930s.

But soon after the Second World War, many members of this motley band of enthusiasts were surprised -- and, in some instances, shocked -- to discover that the works they had bought for love were achieving considerable monetary value. Then, as prices rose steeply, a new kind of trustee appeared on the museum's board. Gradually, almost all the connoisseur-collectors were replaced by investors in art. They professed their love of art more ardently than ever before, but underneath the highflown generalities lurked obscenely naked greed.

These changes had come about so gradually that Till was horrified to discover, one day, that most of the trustees were actually using his long-range exhibition calendar as a kind of tip-sheet. They would load up on works by artists scheduled for one-person shows in confident expectation of a massive price rise after the exhibition opened. Their confidence had not been misplaced.

Over the years, Till's staff had developed a long glossary of locutions to convey the financial subtext under a decent cloak of scholarship. Acquisition of an "important" work meant that its value was likely to rise quickly. A "significant" contemporary artist was one who could command high prices now. A "promising" artist was one to bet on for the future.

Until the past few years, most of the trustees had quietly purchased works in accordance with these obvious tips, personally visiting galleries to express their love for this or that artist or school. But many of the museum's newer breed of trustees had discovered a time-saving short-cut: following the lead of the board's new president, Alex Clarendon, they simply asked the museum's director to purchase works directly for them. The man was constantly buying pictures anyway; it was far more efficient to have this acclaimed expert picking their purchases. Best of all, Till often obtained bargains by dickering with dealers for two or three examples of an artist's work, rather than just one.

"What do you think, Wes, about our acquiring a really first-rate Rauschenberg," Clarendon would begin, in his fruity baritone.

And the museum director would understand exactly what the board president meant: find two first-rate Rauschenbergs, one for the museum and one for me. Till was no longer shocked by such crass ploys. He had choked back his original revulsion with rationalizations about the ultimate benefit to his one and only love -- the museum.

After more than thirty years on the job, Wesley C. Till had come to recognize just about every nuance of human greed. As an idealistic young man, fresh from his academic journey through the long history of human creative genius, he had been revolted by the crassness of some collectors and trustees. But gradually, he had accepted the reality that the desire to possess a rare object powerfully motivated collectors, not only in modern times, but as far back in history as scholars had explored. What was different now, however, was that collectors also seemed to be obsessed with possibilities for profit.

In the early days, Till had seen himself as a kind of missionary for modernism. Tall and thin in his decent navy-blue suit and steel-rimmed glasses, he would earnestly lecture the trustees on the inventiveness, the sheer risks that so many great modern artists took. Patiently, he dragged them to galleries and sent educational articles to their homes. They gave him no money at all to buy pictures, but they all promised that some day, in their wills, they would leave what they owned to the museum.

That was when he began to advise them on their private collections. He was quite frank about it: "I wish you would buy this artist's work," he would write to one or another trustee. "It will help to complete our collection, should you see fit to give it to us, one day."

For some years now, the bequests had been arriving by bonded messengers, at first just a few long-awaited landmark works, and then tumbling in, a torrent of tax-deductible goods. In a few instances, the recipients of Till's advice had dared to change their minds, leaving him furious. In almost every respect, however, the imaginary museum he had once constructed on paper was now complete. More than complete.

Till stepped off the bus and walked mechanically toward the colorful banners which proclaimed the museum's current Braque exhibition. Despite his poor night's sleep, he was eager for the trustees' meeting. A Methodist minister's son from St. Louis, he was working his will--well, mostly--upon a group of New York's wealthiest people. A scholar, stooped from his labors in dusty archives, he was now almost guaranteeing success to this or that artist by his friendly, "Hmmm, interesting" ... and banishing another to the hinterlands with a dismissive "Derivative work."

Early on the day of the meeting, Till would rehearse the agenda and remind his curators to remain in the building and on call, just in case any question in their area of expertise came up. While the trustees relied on Till's personal advice in forming their own collections, they also insisted on full access to every specialist whose salary they paid, and some outsiders as well, summoned as expert consultants.

In practice, the specialists were seldom called, but Till sensed that the trustees were flattered by the dislocations their meeting caused to the staff. Shut inside their rosewood-panelled meeting room, they savored the bustle of anxious anticipation in the offices outside; they relished their power. But for many years now, the most important matters had been handled by a small executive committee, while the full board devoted itself to trivia: the design of uniforms for the guards; the profits from the gift shop and restaurant; the location, theme, menu, and program for the next party.

Years before, the board had actually been elected by the museum membership. There had been artists and architects among them, even a dealer, although many had looked askance at such a vulgar mingling of art and commerce. But as the museum had grown and prospered, the board had slipped more and more into ritualized triviality. First it had been enlarged, to the point where any serious questions by one member could be harmlessly diverted into a staff study, or simply left to drown in the disinterest of the rest. Then the museum by-laws were changed so that trustees were no longer elected by museum members, but by the board itself. At last, the board consisted solely of individuals who had already donated generously to the museum and whose wills promised even more.

These arrangements guaranteed that no fresh ideas emanating from the trustees would ever jar the routines established by the staff. The object of all the staff activity to prepare for the upcoming trustees' meeting was to create the illusion that momentous decisions were at hand. Thus, on the day before the meeting, a uniformed messenger would deliver several pounds of illustrated reports to each trustee's home. It was obvious that no one could digest any of this material before the meeting. Experienced trustees hardly bothered to open the package; they knew that the director would cover whatever they needed to know during the meeting. In any event, Till would have telephoned if anything important needed deciding.

Only one tradition dating back to the museum's founding was still observed: the trustees gathered for coffee and croissants in a different gallery each time, prior to trooping up to the board room for their deliberations. In the old days, they had assembled promptly at nine, so that the gallery could be cleared before the museum opened an hour later. But a battle with the city over funding some years ago had forced the museum to close every Wednesday, and, even though the funds had been more than restored, the closing remained. So it was after 10:30 a.m. when Till was finally able to shepherd his flock upstairs to its duties.

He made a special point of humoring Agnes Devaney, a sharp-eyed, white-haired lady in a sedate black and white printed silk frock, who was the last survivor of the original board. At the previous meeting, she had demanded to know why more than eighty per cent of the museum's collection was in storage. Till had patiently explained that it was needed for "depth," to be lent out to other institutions, and for scholars to consult in their research. Miss Devaney, the walls of whose Park Avenue apartment were virtually papered with first-rate Van Goghs, Gauguins, early Picassos, and the city's largest collection of Georgia O'Keeffes, was unconvinced. She wanted the trustees to review the storage collection and perhaps the whole policy of what she called "hoarding the art."

Till hated that word; it was so vulgar. But he had smoothly suggested that perhaps the trustees would care to have a special meeting to "review storage policy." He knew that these people would have great difficulty fitting an extra meeting into their busy social and travel calendars, so he scheduled the review two weeks hence. And he was right. Only eleven trustees, most of whom never said a word at the meetings, showed up in the eight-story windowless brick warehouse which occupied an entire block on West 58th Street, near the Hudson River.

First, they had toured the drawing collection, a full floor holding more than 15,000 works, all carefully collated in racks and drawers. The curator was near retirement, having devoted his entire career to amassing this collection. He now officiously opened and closed several drawers and called the trustees' attention to several easels on which his most recent acquisitions were displayed. "We are moving toward a comprehensive selection from all periods and styles of modernism," he had said, "but we still have many gaps." He looked sad, and even sadder when Till abruptly rose to shepherd his flock onward. Till reserved for himself all discussion of gaps in the collection.

Next, they were greeted by the curator of prints and artists' books, who whisked them around two floors of the museum's holdings in this department. The prints were in steel drawers, while the books were stored on shelves, each one swathed in acid-free tissue paper. Here, also, the curator had a small display of his latest acquisitions, an array of Paul Klee etchings. "The Maurice Bowen bequest," he explained. "Mr. Bowen was a lifelong friend of the museum. He bought these etchings from the artist himself. Although he is no longer with us, I'm sure Mr. Bowen would be overjoyed to know that the addition of these forty-six works gives our museum an example of every etching ever created by the immortal Paul Klee. Would that our holdings in other artists were equally rich," he added morosely.

By the time the little band of explorers reached the sculpture floor, they were staggered to see aisle upon aisle, shelf upon shelf, all laden with magnificent-looking bronzes, woodcarvings, and marbles. Several aisles were devoted to untraditional materials: plastic, welded metal, cloth, rubber tires, paper, crumpled automobile parts, and unidentifiable debris. Fortunately, the curator there did not insist on showing them anything in detail. Instead, they perched on folding chairs and viewed slides of representative works. The curator had flaming red hair and her ample form was draped in what looked like a batik tablecloth. "Of course, we have the world's greatest assemblage of sculptures, illustrating almost every facet of the astonishing creativeness of modern sculptors," she said. "And yet, we are not as strong as we should be in a number of areas." Miss Devaney ventured to ask what these areas might be, but Till suggested that the curator prepare a private memo for her on that subject and swept the group onward.

They rode to the top floor in a cavernous padded freight elevator, and when the doors opened, found themselves in a re-creation of a *fin de siècle* Paris *bistro*. "We've worked hard all morning," said Till in a lame attempt at playfulness, "and we have a long afternoon ahead of us. Now, we need to relax for a bit." Screens hung with paintings by Toulouse-Lautrec, Degas, and Pissarro set off the space from the rest of the warehouse floor. In the center were several tables covered with red-checked tablecloths. A formal waiter served *salade Niçoise* and poured a respectable Chablis.

Till tried his best to enter into the spirit of the setting, but without success. Distracted by his work on large and complicated exhibitions, not to mention building fund campaigns, he had not visited the warehouse for several years. All he knew about its contents came from inventories and from periodic memos from the various curators pleading for more money to fill "gaps." Traipsing through the "study collection" was a revelation, the more so since he had not encountered a single scholar all morning who was studying anything.

After the *meringue glaceé* and espresso, Till ushered the committee to one of the three floors where the museum's surplus paintings were stored, rack upon rack. Gratefully the trustees sank into easy chairs. Henrietta De Vries, who all morning had been badgering Till about the cost of all those metal drawers and the exorbitant price of acid-free tissue, leaned back and almost immediately began to snore peacefully. The rest of the group tried hard to concentrate as white-gloved handlers eased one precious canvas after another onto the viewing easels before them. The curator of painting, a cadaverous bearded young man in bronze corduroy stood by, but it was Till himself who gave the commentary.

He towered over the group, pale but animated, not handsome but sincere, with an air of academic fussiness. His crinkled graying hair was slightly too long, in the opinion of some of the more conservative trustees, but it was neatly trimmed. His gray flannel slacks and Harris Tweed sportcoat gave him a false air of casualness; in reality, he was shy and studious, and totally bereft of the small change of breezy conversation. To his father's disappointment, Wesley Calvin Till had not heard a call to the ministry. Yet, as he addressed his flock, his voice resonated richly, persuasively of the pulpit.

"We can all be proud of the magnificent collection our museum has built up over the past thirty years," he began. "Thanks to the generosity of our friends, we now own more works by more modern artists than any other museum in the world. We have, for example, the best works from every period in the careers of such great masters as Picasso, Matisse, Braque, Mondrian, and Miró. Alas, our success has imposed upon us the heavy burden of guarding this treasure for coming generations of art lovers, and of constantly adding to it the best work of contemporary artists...."

Miss Devaney shifted impatiently and sat on the edge of her armchair. She had heard this speech, with little variation, for at least ten years. Literally thousands of works -- paintings, sculptures, drawings, prints, posters, books, sketches, models --had showered into the museum's collections during that time, mostly as gifts from collectors needing tax deductions. And here most of these treasures sat, piled up in an ugly brick warehouse, unloved, seldom viewed, inaccessible to the public, monuments to little more than acquisitiveness.

"But why do we need to keep adding to all this?" she now asked mildly. "If we don't have space in the museum, why don't we just lend out these things to less fortunate museums? Or give them away. Maybe we should even sell some of them."

"I'm surprised to hear such sentiments from one of the museum's oldest friends," Till chided gently. "We've gone over this so many times. We really can't take the valuable time of our trustees today to discuss all this again. But of course, I'll be happy to go over it with you in person, perhaps next week."

Why did she have to keep making such a nuisance of herself, Till thought irritably. There's not a shred of support on the board for her unfashionable notions. He should really ease her out, with profuse thanks for a job well done, perhaps an intimate banquet, and an engraved certificate of appreciation. However, the disposition of her collection remained unsettled. For years, Miss Devaney had been assuring Till that she would leave it all to the museum. Yet every time he had suggested including her treasures in one of the museum's periodic exhibitions of "works promised," she had coyly put him off. Nor had she allowed the museum's attorney to help with the precise wording of the bequest in her will.

The matter had come up again when Till met with her the following week. Saving on current income taxes did not impress her in the least. Neither did saving on estate taxes. Nor did she care to impress anyone with the magnitude of her gift to the museum. "Don't rush me, Wes," she had said. "I'm planning to enjoy my treasures within my own four walls for many, many years. An old lady like me needs the consolation of beautiful things a lot more than your young curators. Who knows?" She laughed slyly. "They might condemn Van Gogh's *Flowering Chestnut Trees* to that prison of a warehouse. Don't worry, Wes, the public will get its chance to enjoy my things some day. But not yet."

Till was still irritated with her coyness as the trustees were settling into the fawn-colored plush armchairs around a thirty-foot oval table veneered in perfectly matched rosewood. In front of each place there was a precise geometric arrangement of notepad, two freshly sharpened pencils, a glass of ice water, and a small crystal vase containing one perfect pink rosebud. The lighting was even and the walls bare, the better to focus attention on a vast painting that reached from the floor to within an inch of the ceiling at one end. A mass of minute liver-brown spots danced over the electric blue background, except for the upper right corner, where an orange crescent moon hung precariously.

"Ladies and Gentlemen, I wish to present to you our latest acquisition," said Till. "Burt Itlin, as you know, is the leading painter in the Visualist School and this painting is a truly important work, the purest expression of his abiding concerns. It's called *Excrescence I*, a subtle title, don't you think?"

"But can we afford it?" asked Henrietta de Vries.

"Of course we can afford it," snapped Henry Eckridge. "It's a gift from his dealer, Harry Zick. The Itlin market looks like it's about to take off ... a big article in *Art for Tomorrow*, shows scheduled in Frankfurt, Zürich, and Milan, plus, of course, the big promotion Zick is planning for Itlin's spring show in New York. So now is the time, I thought, to invest in a couple of his works. And, surprise!, Zick offers to donate this one to the museum."

"That calls for at least a cocktail party to celebrate its accession," added Anita Deckman. "Or maybe it should be a dinner dance. We could adapt the color scheme…"

"I'm sure the hospitality committee will welcome that suggestion," Till broke in, "especially to benefit our annual fund drive. Now, to move to the next item on the agenda, I have truly electrifying news to share with you. The insurance problems are solved, and so are the travel arrangements, so it's official. The Baritsch collection, every bit of it, will open to the public on September 15."

An excited hubbub broke out around the table.

"It's very short notice," Till continued, "but the Baron insisted on that. He believes that the collection will travel more securely if the timing is tight. Naturally, our plans will be top secret. We'll have to forego our usual advance publicity and make the announcement less than a month before the opening. The catalog, an extremely lavish production, I might add, will be prepared in Munich and printed in Budapest, where the security, I am told, can be guaranteed. Likewise the reproductions to be sold in our gift shop. Everything will arrive ready to hang, but no more than two days before we open. That means we will have to find storage for our entire permanent collection. As an alternative, we are now considering the possibility of sending our own collection on tour to several other museums."

"Isn't the Baritsch Collection mostly old masters?" asked Miss Devaney.

"Glad you brought that up, Agnes," said Till. "I had thought so too. It turns out, however, that during the past two years the Baron has been buying heavily into contemporary art. He has hinted that we might be allowed to show the modern works in the near future. Fewer than one-third of the 459 items in the collection could be called old masters. As you know, the history of modernism can be traced back deep into the past, so I don't really see a conflict. Besides, the tremendous attendance this exhibition will generate will put a rosy glow on our balance sheet. It will bring a vast audience into our museum, many of them for the first time. It's a wonderful way to pursue our educational mission and wipe out or budget deficit too."

As the excited discussion ranged around the room, Till recalled the first time he had encountered the Baritsch collection. It was June 1945 and he was still euphoric at having survived almost a year of tough, dirty, wet, cold, tiresome, and intensely frightening combat. The campaign had followed with amazing fidelity, a tour of the grand artistic monuments of northern Europe which he had made as a student: Bayeux, where the charming tapestry depicting William's conquest of Britain had spent the war hidden in the basement of the local church; Caen, where his unit's artillery spotter holed up in the stark Gothic tower of the *Abbaye aux Hommes*; the old marketplace in Rouen, where Joan of Arc was burned on May 30, 1431, and which now was a welter of rubble. On a sudden two-day leave in November, he had hitched rides on ambulances and a farmer's apple wagon to Mont St. Michel and stood in rapt solitude before the soaring Gothic pile called, without exaggeration, *La Merveille*.

Returning to his unit, he thought the rest would be easy -- until the Battle of the Bulge in December and January left him hollow-eyed and trembling, with frostbite on his nose and toes. But by early spring, everyone could see the end, except Hitler, who threw pitifully untrained young boys and old men against the Allies' tanks. Then in May it was suddenly over.

Almost immediately, Till was ordered to join the art detail, a motley unit of art specialists whose mission was to track down the thousands of art works which had been stolen by the Nazis. He was cataloging a cache of Rembrandts, which had been hidden deep in a salt mine in Bavaria, when the old Baron Baritsch telephoned him. Could he get a few days' leave for a professional consultation in Liechtenstein?

A week later, a venerable Daimler touring car deposited him in the courtyard of the castle, high above the shuttered windows and huddled red tile roofs of Vaduz, capital of the ancient principality. A stooped retainer led him through chilly stone corridors to the library, where the old Baron sat morosely in a brocaded wing chair next to the fire. He looked pale and ill, his sparse white hair in disarray, and his hand, as Till shook it, cold and dry. On a footstool at his side sat a gangling youth. "My grandson," said the Baron, as though describing a piece of furniture. Opposite him sat the Prince of Liechtenstein, a slender middle-aged patrician with a sharp acquiline nose and piercing blue eyes.

"So we meet at last," the Baron said. "I've followed your illustrious career for a long time. Too bad that tragic circumstances have prevented me from meeting you sooner." He snuffled into a white linen handkerchief. "I wish that we now had a happier reason for getting together. The truth is, the Prince and I ... no, I should say the heirs of all Western civilization face an inconceivable loss. On top of all the other catastrophes of recent years, it's almost more than I can bear."

Till was stunned to watch his face crumple and tears run down the deep lines in his cheeks.

"Perhaps we should show Herr Professor the problem," said the Prince, rising. He led the way through a cavernous banqueting hall and through a low stone archway to a heavy, splintered wooden door. His six-inch long key rasped in the lock and then they were descending a dimly lit circular stairway, its stone steps chipped and worn.

"Here's where, I'm afraid, the electricity ends," the Prince said at last. "For the rest of the way, we should each carry a candle and extra matches, just in case we get separated."

He pressed a thick candle into Till's hand and lit it, before leading them farther down. They descended steadily for five minutes more. The stairs were of uneven height and several times Till almost lost his footing, bumping heavily into the clammy stone wall. Their steps echoed eerily; they must be deep inside the mountain, Till surmised. Finally, the stairs ended. In the flickering candlelight, he made out a huge space, perhaps a man-made cavern hacked out of the living rock. The Baron was leaning against one of the wooden racks which lined the walls, sobbing inconsolably and feebly pounding his fist into the upright.

"We had no idea such a thing could happen," said the Prince. "Our only thought was to protect these treasures. Since the religious wars of the sixteenth century, whenever there was strife, my family has stored its valuables in this ancient dungeon. So, this time, as soon as I saw what was coming, I offered this refuge for the Baron's collection. Now our question to you is whether anything can be done and if so, what."

Till gingerly pulled one of the objects out of the rack. It was a rectangle about three feet tall and a foot wide, ornately framed in what had once been gilt, but was now a mass of green mold. The wooden panel inside it was swathed in woolly, gray tatters of mingled fungus and cobwebs. Till carefully brushed away a bit of the debris, but, much to his chagrin, could make out nothing but a few grayish patches.

"Dürer's *St. John the Baptist*," said the Baron tonelessly, "a panel from the triptych in the Bremen Museum. The rest all look about the same. No need to pull them all out. I can't bear it. You will see from the catalog that 183 items were deposited here, among them ninety-six old masters. The modern works, in some ways, are in considerably better condition; at least the pigments, being largely composed of synthetic aniline dyes, have held up. With them, however, the canvas backing has seriously decayed."

"That's not all," said the Prince quietly. "I happen to have stored here also my own collection, which a similar fate has befallen. It also contains many masterpieces accumulated over centuries in my family -- Rubens, Franz Hals, Van Dyke, Brueghel, no need to enumerate. Perhaps you would be good enough to examine only the most precious item..." He led Till deeper into the cavern and removed a dusty sheet from a small picture hanging from a nail. Till hardly dared to bring his candle closer for fear that its flame would ignite the thick film of dust and mold that covered everything.

"The other pictures I left as they were," said the Prince, "but this one," he sighed, "this one I had to know whether it survived. Just a camel's hair brush, very softly applied, is what I used. So you can see most clearly the condition."

"*Ginevra di Benci.*" Till said the words like a prayer. Then he bent close to the panel, torn between the strong desire to examine the ruin and fear that his moist breath would nourish the fetid mildew that pocked the entire surface. He could have joined the Baron in shedding bitter tears, but instead he patted the Prince consolingly on the arm.

"I suggest the most difficult course for you both -- patience," said Till at last. "No rash moves. Sudden changes of temperature or humidity will surely aggravate the damage. The paintings should stay here until a conservator arrives, the best one you can find, of course. Frankly, I'm pessimistic because the damage appears to be so deep and so widespread. But perhaps, now that the world has exhausted itself in war, mankind will appply its ingenuity to the restoration of beautiful things."

Till was amused at recollecting his youthful pomposity. He looked around the board room at the self-important men and women who were still examining, in trivial detail, the implications of the Baritsch exhibition.

"We'll have to check with the State Department's protocol people," Anita Deckman was saying. "How many guns' salute is there for a Baron? I'm assuming that we can persuade him to attend the opening gala. A serious problem is that it's so early in the season; lots of people will just have gotten back from their summer places. They'll hardly have time to shop for gowns. One blessing is we'll certainly have our choice of caterers, what with no competing events."

"I'm sure our inventive hospitality committee will be able to surmount all these hurdles," said Till soothingly. "Now, if we can please move forward in our agenda, we still have to deal with the revision of our guidelines for docents, not to mention a review of our insurance values. You may recall that we last had a re-appraisal of our holdings almost two years ago. And we all know how wildly art prices have escalated since then."

As he sat through the insurance agent's droning report, Till reflected sourly on how these housekeeping details had gradually stolen most of his time. He seldom had a chance to visit art galleries these days, and often spent evenings and weekends with months-old issues of scholarly magazines, in a losing struggle to keep up with his profession.

There was a time when any artist who appeared at his door was guaranteed a critique of his work and perhaps some suggestions about galleries. Now, the guard downstairs had instructions to turn away anyone without an appointment and most artists had long despaired of ever seeing him.

Years ago, he relished the creative challenge of hanging exhibitions; it was immensely exciting, like a theater opening. Till realized with a pang that he had not hung an exhibition for four years; on a few occasions he had even welcomed the imperious summons to the apartment of the museum's president and gleefully wielded a hammer to help hang a new acquisition.

Even the delicate and complicated negotiations for the Baritsch exhibition had left him detached and somehow unfulfilled. The young Baron was not exactly lighthearted company, nor did he seem to take pleasure in the ownership of so many masterpieces. On a gloomy February morning, with the wind whipping the lake outside into frothy white-caps, they had paced through the deserted galleries in the Villa Tazzi, accompanied by a fussy conservator. Whenever Till had expressed enthusiasm for a particular work, the Baron talked about insurance values, while the conservator pointed out fragile passages of paint.

The tour with Agnes Devaney's group through the museum's warehouse had also troubled him. Even as he had diverted the old lady's sharp questions, he felt uneasy in that yawning space crammed as it was, floor upon floor, with such a massive quantity of the world's most beautiful art treasures. Separated from those who had created them, as well as from most of those who could appreciate them, the works appeared lifeless, mere bundles of goods.

In the early days, before there was any collection at all, he had spent many exhilarated hours and days in a fever of creating his fantasy museum on paper. He had sketched out the contents of each gallery, imaginatively grouped for contrast or harmony -- or surprise. For years, he had kept a notebook in which he listed every work he viewed and rated it, like a schoolmaster: A- for this Cézanne, C+ for that small Seurat, straight B for a charming, too pretty Degas.

And now? The museum had grown beyond his wildest dreams. The public flocked to it in throngs so dense that admission often had to be limited and the lines of visitors stretched on the street outside in merry anticipation of a stimulating tour of the masterpieces inside. The works on display had become icons, objects of worship unquestioningly adored by viewers, but no longer interrogated. The staff that he had built with such discrimination now smoothly dealt with donors and galleries, prepared learned articles and catalogs, tracked down attributions, saw to it that every item was minutely described. A full-time photographer recorded every acquisition and every event and the white-coated specialists in an elaborate laboratory inspected, cleaned, and repaired each work on a precise rotation.

Professionalism. That's what he had sought to provide to a corner of art then dominated by amateurs. But after all the scholars had presented their reports, after all the lengthy catalog essays were written and the lavish illustrations selected, the works appeared to be less, rather than more, significant. The welter of well-chosen explanatory words often obscured the artists' true intentions. It was a general problem with artists that they were unusually clumsy with words. Perhaps that's why they had turned to art, trying to convey visually what they found verbally unsayable.

Till had been inordinately successful in bridging the gap he perceived between the artist and his audience. He was considered the most innovative museum man in the world. He was invited to so many international congresses, seminars, conventions, dinners, luncheons, openings, lecture series, and convocations that his secretary had prepared several stock letters of regret and kept a log so that the same wording would not be sent a second time to the

same organization. He had won awards from every professional organization, not to mention the French Legion of
Honor, the German Order of Merit, and even the Russian
Lenin Trophy. He had been to the White House to receive
the Medal of Freedom. On that occasion, there had been an
editorial lauding him in *The New York Times*.

But today, Wesley C. Till felt uncommonly weary. He
realized, with a pang of nostalgia, that he was damned
bored.

Chapter 5

Restoration

No matter how many times she had made it, the flight from New York was always a miserable experience: the take-off invariably delayed; the meal late and unappetizing; the sleep, if any, restless and brief; then the jolt of a sudden dawn over the Atlantic, followed by a hurried breakfast and the landing in Paris.

By now, Rachel Haberman had learned all the tricks of making herself comfortable for the flight. She wore a deep purple velour running suit, loose around the waist, and tennis shoes as soft as slippers. In her flight bag she carried a black eyeshade and a small down pillow. Frequent tooth brushing helped, but as she pulled her battered leather bag off the baggage belt at Orly, her mouth tasted stale and slightly metallic.

Fortunately, Luc was at the curb with the Citroen, and the traffic was light as they headed south and then west onto the A10 autoroute. Rachel leaned back into the coffee-colored leather seat and closed her eyes. "So what's the latest crisis?" she asked.

"Crisis?" said Luc, mockingly. "Never heard the word. Everything's been smooth as butter. You're back just in time to look over the Rubens. We put the last little touch of pink on the last little Cupid's fat little bottom yesterday. Then Marie sprayed the acetate and that's that."

"What a relief," said Rachel. "That means it'll be dry by the end of the week and we can ship that monster back to the Prado. The Garden of Love, indeed. Four months of piddling around in those miles of satin drapery and I'm ready to call it the yard goods store."

"The bad news is that we're not through yet with the yard goods," replied Luc. "The National Gallery called from London yesterday. A keeper was dusting Gainsborough's The Morning Walk and somehow left a twelve-inch scratch right through the lady's bodice and skirt. They think it's confined to the surface, but I sent Ilana over there to take a look, just to be sure. We may have to bring it in."

"What about the Mantegna St. Sebastian from Vienna?"

"The courier arrived with it yesterday. We checked the little holes in the panel. Definitely woodlice. We dusted it with DDT and now it's ready for you to figure out the repairs. What's exciting in New York?"

"You know those Americans," Rachel replied wearily. "They're always in a frenzy of excitement. Hirschhorn is on a wholesale buying spree. Thinks he can corner the market on Pop and Op, like he did on uranium. Not likely. Those artists are churning out pictures by the thousands. And in a few years, if we can keep our sanity, we'll be operating on hundreds of those pictures, they're so carelessly painted."

There was no speed limit on the straight divided highway and Luc pushed the speedometer to 85. On either side, the perfectly flat fields of the Ile de France rushed by, the brown stubble of last summer's wheat poking through a thin crust of frost. Rachel scanned the vista to the south. She didn't want to miss her first glimpse of Chartres Cathedral, and not only because it marked the spot she now called home.

The view of that bulk and those spires, rising like a ghostly ship on the horizon, had made her heart ache the very first time she had come upon it as a tourist, in high summer of 1948. The town huddled under the towering embrace of those paradoxically mismatched towers. Finally, she had reached the cramped little square with its benches under ancient linden trees and had sat for days absorbing the benign, healing warmth exuded by those old stones. Life was possible, she had decided then, but only within the shadow of that towering monument to eternal life.

The road to Chartres then had been a narrow high-crowned cobblestone street, lined with poplars, probably not too different from the road trod by pilgrims to that sacred shrine for more than five hundred years. In the fourteen years since her first trip there, she had covered that street -- and later the autoroute -- hundreds of times, especially since 1952, when she had opened her atelier for the restoration of paintings in the very shadow of Chartres Cathedral.

"What did the famous New York art critic have to say?" Luc now asked her.

"I think he's agreed. He took one look at the little souvenir I brought him. The rest was easy. He's taking a photographer to Bellagio next month. The Baron's already agreed to a major article in *Art for Tomorrow*. He's delighted to get some good publicity about the collection."

"And the famous New York art dealer?"

"Funny you should ask. He happened to be on his way to Bellagio with a couple of pictures for the Baron's perusal. I told him to make a few preliminary observations about security, nothing obtrusive, and he was more than cooperative. Especially when we discussed the prospect of unpleasant publicity concerning his close relationship with that slug of an Italian Count."

"That one's a weak fish," observed Luc. "Too desperate for money."

"What he's desperate about right now is that all the junk pictures he's piled up in that spooky palazzo of his are practically worthless. He needs to exhibit them in a major museum and fast. Otherwise he can't unload them and then ... no more white powder. He'll have to find honest work, poor devil."

"And the famous New York museum director?"

"My dear Luc, I didn't survive Auschwitz in order to be cross-examined, even by you. Don't worry. The museum director will play his appointed role. I don't think he would mind giving up his life; it seems to bore him. But he'll never endanger his precious collection."

Luc was threading the car up a narrow cobbled lane and stopped at a massive wooden gate, which opened at their approach. A thin winter sun illuminated a courtyard beyond which a second gate was now opening. "What a find this place was," Rachel said. "The perfect location, just a few steps from the cathedral, and also perfect security."

When she had first settled on this spot, back in 1952, Rachel already knew more about security -- and how to elude it -- than the most seasoned prison director would have learned in a lifetime. For four years, one month, and seventeen days, her survival had depended on stealth and cunning -- plus an iron constitution, her parents' sole legacy.

She had been a chubby, apple-cheeked girl of fourteen when the horror began. Her apple cheeks were gone after the interminable nightmare train ride from Munich, but her sturdy body and quick smile had enabled her to survive the first grisly selection on the platform. Life meant a sixteen-hour day in the evil-smelling chemical plant conveniently located right next door to the camp. Life meant a chipped enamel bowl of watery soup and a slab of gray bread in the evening. Life meant achieving sound sleep on a plank. Above all, life meant avoiding illness, which was an immediate death sentence.

And then one day, the horror was over. Rachel found herself back in Munich, this time living in a camp for survivors, a settlement of living ghosts. Like most of the others, she simply could not stop eating. After wolfing down huge portions of rich stew and potatoes in the canteen, she would stuff her pockets with bread and cake to be consumed later, during the night, when the memories were the worst. After a few months, she was free to go, but where? She could not bring herself even to visit the neighborhood where she had grown up, although it was just a streetcar ride away.

A Red Cross worker had set up a small art studio in the camp, and there Rachel spent her first peaceful hours. She loved the feel of pastels on rough paper and the subtle tints of a watercolor wash. She took delight in drawing accurately and quickly. Then she found a small set of oils and discovered the joy -- and challenge -- of painting textures: the velvet of flowers, the gleam of glass, the folds satin of drapery. But whenever she tried to depart from bland subject matter and loosen her imagination, horrible scenes rushed in and she would end up screaming and weeping. She knew that she could never be an artist, not a creative artist drawing on an inner vision. Because the only inner visions she had left were phantasmagoric nightmares.

Entering the main studio, Rachel marched straight to the window and contemplated the view of Chartres cathedral. She had picked this location precisely for this panorama of the west portal, with its careful rows and arches of carved stone figures representing a divinely ordered universe, the gates of paradise. Kings and queens, prophets and saints, their bodies frozen in draperies of columnar gravity; and then the exquisite contrast of their faces, smiling so wisely, so sweetly, so serenely. Dominating the ensemble was a loving god whose blessing implied eternal justice and truth. To this god, the last judgement was not a fiery *Götterdämmerung* but the imposition of divine order on the chaos made by men.

The first time she saw it, the force of the ensemble had struck Rachel with such power that she cringed and felt tears rolling down her cheeks. Over a cup of tea at a cafe nearby, she felt an extraordinary exaltation. Calm and peaceful, this place was the perfect antithesis to the horror and chaos that so far had shaped her life. To survive and experience this, she had stolen a crust of bread from a dying old man; had pulled a stinking blanket off a corpse; had bartered her body for an extra portion of gray soup. Mauled by the perfection of evil, she exulted here, in the perfection of art. Life was not dirt alone, but also glory. There was an antidote to human bestiality and it was this: noble, serene, harmonious.

She watched a group of tourists gaping upward at the mismatched spires, saw their guide's lips moving and knew that his pedantic droning about dates and stylistic variations could hardly add to the emotional power of their experience, would probably dilute it. She thought about the long lines of pilgrims who had trudged in ignorance to this structure and had found exaltation. Perhaps there was even something magical about the spot; archaeologists had already found a pagan shrine beneath the cathedral's crypt, and they were still digging. The vast majority of the people who had gathered here for millennia to worship ... something ... or someone ... came for spiritual nourishment. Until recent decades, few cared that the columnar figures on the west facade represented the turn from the crude and sometimes demoniacal Romanesque style to the refined classical Gothic style of sculpture. Neither did they know or care that the figures flanking the central portal were carved by the progressive "Headmaster," while those on the flanking portals were the work of a more conservative sculptor. The crowds came, until very recently, not to learn, but to feel.

"Enough of window-gazing," said Ilana from the doorway. "The vacation's over, my dear. The patients are crying for a visit from their doctor."

She was a petite woman in her early forties, her dark hair falling long and straight over a starched white lab coat. Briskly, she embraced Rachel and led her into an adjoining room, where the Viennese St. Sebastian lay prone on a stainless steel table. Lights of operating room intensity glared down onto the saint's face, smiling beatifically despite the multitude of arrows which cruelly pierced his body. Rachel now peered through a microscope focussed on one corner of the panel.

"Those Viennese never learn, do they," she said. "Last year, we had to re-paint a whole corner of their Brueghel where the rats nibbled. And now worms. They keep promising to crack down on the guards sneaking pastries while on duty. That's what attracts all this vermin."

"Why lecture me?" said Ilana. "I spent only a week there last year. I must say that Herr Direktor Flieder sounded pretty embarrassed on the phone. He thought the Ministry of Culture might question another big bill for vermin damage so soon so I told him we'd mark the invoice 'Wear and tear due to natural aging.'"

"Sounds suitably vague," said Rachel. "He's lucky he doesn't have to extract funds from trustees, like the Americans. Those people fork over millions for new purchases, but upkeep? No glamor there, so no money."

"Which brings me to the purpose of your New York trip. What's happening?"

"Right now, I'm exhausted," replied Rachel. "Let me get a good night's sleep. Tomorrow morning at nine sharp I want to meet with our whole crew in the board room. We have lots to discuss."

Rachel wearily climbed up two narrow, steep flights to the top floor of the building. There, under the Mansard roof, in what had been the servants' quarters, she had her private apartment. It was small, only a couple of rooms and minimal kitchen and bath, but each window framed stunning views of her beloved cathedral. She soaked long in the deep old-fashioned tub and then snuggled under her French provincial quilt, hoping only that there would be no dreams.

Sleep itself, however, wasn't all that easy. How lucky she had been to run into Ilana in that camp for "displaced persons" in Munich. They had first met in the little art studio there, and for weeks they had worked quietly with pastels and charcoal, talking only about the food, about art, about the prospects of getting out and at last starting a new life. There was a certain etiquette among the wounded waifs in the camp that precluded asking troubling questions. The past was too disturbing. It poked easily through the thin film of composure achieved by the luckiest of survivors.

One day, a bluff and hearty young man from the Jewish underground army, the Haganah, appeared in the studio. He was gathering young people for the illegal voyage to Israel. Some camp inmates had already left on this dangerous journey: by train to a port in Italy or southern France, then on leaky, overcrowded boats across the Mediterrannean to a clandestine midnight landing on a strange and barren shore. Word had filtered back that some boats sank along the way, suffocation in the water ironically overtaking those who had cheated it in the gas chamber. Others were intercepted by British gunboats and forced to return to Europe. Having voluntarily left the DP camps, they were not allowed to return and languished in hopeless misery in the ports from which they had embarked.

It was at a meeting for prospective passengers on the underground journey to Israel that Rachel and Ilana had met the two other members of "the crew," Maria and Luc. They were the only four among twenty in that room who decided to stay behind. No one asked their reasons, nor did they explain to each other why the prospect of any risk at all was totally unacceptable just then. On the other hand, each of them knew that soon he or she would be forced to move on; every day, it seemed, they were seeing another group depart, the lucky ones going back to the homelands from which they had been ripped, and a very few even re-united with parents or siblings; even finding a remote cousin appeared miraculous.

Among the four, however, there was the certain knowledge that everyone was gone; they had seen them die. Not that they talked about it for many months. Friendship was something they approached like a threatening stranger. But gradually, they began to share useful information: a shipment of donated winter clothing had just arrived; the cook was doling out double desserts to people who helped to peel potatoes; there was extra soap in the storeroom and the lock was flimsy.

On a spring evening in 1947, Rachel drew two American chocolate bars out of her pocket and ceremoniously broke them into four precisely equal portions. Luc admitted sheepishly that he could not recall ever tasting chocolate. His parents were Communists, he had been told. They had fled Germany in 1933 for France, when he was just four. Three years later, his parents left him with a trusted party colleague in Tours, and went off to Spain, where civil war had broken out. They did not return. In 1940, Luc's foster parents had hastily deposited the boy in a monastery, "just for a brief vacation," they had told him. Two years later, he was picked up by the Vichy police, identified as the offspring of "public enemies," and became part of the pitiful human cargo packed into the trains travelling east.

"Never tasted chocolate," hooted Maria. She was all of fifteen, a curvaceous bleached blonde tottering on impossibly high heels. The others did not approve of her garish makeup and the tight sweaters and short skirts she habitually wore. One evening, Rachel had encountered her lounging provocatively against a lamppost on Marienplatz, Munich's central square. Her greeting died as she saw Maria walk away arm in arm with a squat, sandy-haired American soldier. They disappeared into a cheap hotel.

After all that had happened, these survivors shrank from judgments. One did what one had to do. Maria willingly shared chocolate, coffee, cigarettes, chewing gum, toilet soap and -- the ultimate sacrifice -- she even allowed Rachel and Ilana to use her red Revlon lipstick.

While standing at her post one afternoon, Maria spotted a gruesomely familiar figure, a beefy woman named Bella, who had taken particular delight in tormenting the inmates at Ravensbrück concentration camp. Often, Maria had watched her swagger among the starved prisoners as the day's soup was being ladled out, casually shoving their half-filled bowls out of their hands.

Maria followed the woman in hypnotic fascination, without really knowing why. Bella was carrying a shopping net filled with bundles. She was thinner than in her camp days, her splayed shoes shuffling slightly, but she walked fast and Maria had trouble keeping her in view. Finally, she boarded a streetcar and Maria followed, after swaddling her head in a kerchief to hide her face. It was doubtful that Bella would recognize her, but the camp had taught Maria to take no chances.

The streetcar was leaving the city and speeded up, its iron wheels singing on the rails alongside a deserted highway. Bella got off, at last, when they reached an area of allotment gardens, and Maria unobtrusively followed. She loitered behind, watching the other woman's broad back as she trudged down a narrow country lane. About a half mile from the road, she turned into one of the gardens. By the time Maria arrived to peer over the rude scrub-covered fence, the woman was pulling weeds from the black, loamy soil in a vegetable bed, where onions and radishes were beginning to sprout.

Exactly two weeks later, Maria, Ilana, Rachel, and Luc were aboard the same streetcar. They got off at separate stops and made their way to Bella's garden by separate routes. Seeing the woman already at work, delicately setting out tomato shoots, Maria walked boldly in.

"I seem to have gotten lost," she said. "Do you know where the Mayers' garden might be?"

"You've gone too far, my dear," said the woman, gently taking Maria's shoulder and leading her to the fence. "It's back about one-hundred meters. Right there, where you see the sweetpea vines."

"Could I bother you for a drink of water?" Maria asked. The woman walked heavily toward a gazebo, her wooden clogs leaving deep imprints in the moist earth. She emerged with a gray enamel cup and turned to a garden faucet to fill it.

"I'll let it run a bit so it's nice and cool," she said, awkwardly bending over and fastidiously straddling the water gushing from the hose bib.

By the time she turned back an instant later, the three others were crowded around her, silent, staring expressionlessly. Maria roughly knocked the cup out of her hand, and then all four wrestled her efficiently to the ground. Maria shoved a wadded handkerchief into her mouth, while the others rapidly looped clothesline around her hands and thick legs. Then Ilana brought a garden spade from the gazebo and wordlessly handed it to Maria. The woman's eyes turned dark and liquid; her tangled gray hair mingled with the garden loam. Then the spade descended swiftly.

Afterward, still not speaking, they dug a shallow pit next to a bed of nasturtiums and dropped the body in, followed by the severed head. They sprinkled fresh earth over the dark spots where the blood had spurted.

And that was the point, in Rachel's recurrent dream about this event, when she always awoke. Unlike her nightmares, from which she awakened in a sweat and panting, this dream left her feeling refreshed, somehow renewed.

In fact, the deed in the garden was a turning point in her life, as well as the lives of her companions. It was only a week afterward that she began systematically visiting the museums in Munich, which were gradually re-opening their galleries. In the Alte Pinakothek, she fell in love with the works of Albrecht Dürer, the artist who almost single-handedly had brought the sunny Italian Renaissance to the dour, thrifty burghers of Germany.

Soon, she had moved an easel into the gallery and contentedly spent her days copying several magnificently detailed portraits of velvet and sable-clad merchants and then a tender Virgin proffering a red carnation to her pudgy child.

Chapter 6

Sketch

The cathedral's bell woke Rachel on the dot of seven. That was a small side benefit of living in the shadow of its divine bulk: one needed no clocks or watches. Her body still said two a.m., New York time, but her mind moved restlessly forward to the day ahead.

Dressing, she contemplated the view from her window, so familiar and yet ever changing. The carved figures on the cathedral front smiled as appealingly as ever, but the thin winter light emphasized their cold stone reality. A young priest, his nose pinched and his cheeks reddened by the cold, was hurrying up the steps. His black gown flapped in the wind, revealing black, laced boots, and he grabbed for his wide, flat Breton hat as he reached the portal. He was swinging a worn black leather briefcase. Otherwise, the square was totally bare, allowing Rachel to embroider it with an imaginative medieval pageant. The place had then been the bustling heart of the community, serving as a law court, or a theater, a place to see and be seen as well as a church. Now, the priests were still saying mass inside this immense space, whose stained glass windows spelled out a complete explanation of the world. But the many multilingual signs inside reminding visitors to dress decently, to maintain decorum during mass, and to speak softly, were only one signal that this place was now just a museum.

Instead of the intricate fabric of medieval life, with the cathedral as its focal point, modern people had only a monument, a souvenir. In the days when the cathedral was fully functional, people walked hundreds of miles on pilgrimages to commune with the relics of saints and martyrs. And now, people were travelling thousands of miles to visit this entire building as a relic. Poor, noble stones, Rachel thought, prodded and poked by scholars, photographed by tourists, but, alas, just a museum, another trophy for travelers.

She pulled on her blue mechanic's coveralls, clean but paint-stained, thick white cotton socks, and tennis shoes. It was wonderful not to have to put on "city clothes." How could people get any work done, she wondered, when their bodies were squeezed here and tightly belted there and draped in altogether too much fabric. The smell of strong, over-roasted coffee drifted into the chilly room as Rachel hurried downstairs.

In the dining room, Lisette greeted her with a great hug and enthusiastic kisses on both cheeks.

"It's wonderful to have Madame back among us," she cried. "I was desolated while you were gone. What about a nice soft-boiled egg this morning? Straight from François' chicken coop."

"You'd think instead of a week in New York, I'd been on a year's crusade to the Holy Land," said Rachel, pouring herself *café au lait.* "I've missed you too, Lisette. No eggs today, thank you, but I've been dreaming of fresh croissants and maybe a bit of François' butter and just a drop of your wild strawberry jam."

The cook bustled back into the kitchen. She had lost her father in the First World War and her husband in the Second. Left childless and alone, she had adopted the four younger people with a maternal passion so intense that they sometimes cringed. Most of the time, however, they basked in her fussy ministrations, especially the endless parade of succulent meals she produced. After almost ten years, new miracles were still emerging from her kitchen and she had yet to suffer a fallen soufflé.

Rachel was glad to have the breakfast table to herself. Her colleagues seldom came down for that meal, preferring the luxury of breakfast in bed. She glanced at *Le Monde.* The Congo, newly liberated from Belgian colonial exploiters, continued in bloody turmoil despite the arrival of United Nations forces. A shopping bag containing a bomb had exploded in a popular Algiers cafe leaving twelve dead and forty-six wounded. A young woman was being sought. The mutinous officers of the French "secret army" were adamantly opposed to DeGaulle's plan for peaceful French withdrawal from Algeria; they promised reprisals. A new center-left cabinet under Premier Amintore Fanfani had been formed in Italy. Wasn't that the twenty-third government there since the end of the Second World War? What a gift the Italians had for detouring their lives around the modern political *circus maximus.*

Ruminatively, she munched her croissant. As she ate, Rachel wiped up the buttery crumbs that accumulated on her plate with her forefinger and ate them all, an old habit brought from the camp. Her colleagues did the same, she had noticed. In that dining room in the shadow of Chartres Cathedral, there were never leftovers. Rising, she chugalugged the last of her coffee, called out cheerfully to Lisette, and skipped briskly down three flights of stairs to a small, windowless chamber furnished with several comfortable easy chairs.

"Welcome home," said Maria, pecking her cheek. "Ilana and Luc are on the way and I'm dying to hear your news."

"Not all that much to tell," replied Rachel coyly. "New York is dirtier than ever, in every way. The Cosmopolitan wants us to refurbish all its Rembrandts, beginning with the 1660 *Self-Portrait*. The unusually greasy grime in the New York air seeps right into the building and before you know it, there's a layer on the picture surface. They say it's especially hard on the Rembrandts because of the very subtle details he painted within his large, dark areas. These get degraded first and then it all turns to mud. I told them we couldn't begin until next winter and they understood. Me? I couldn't wait to leave."

Ilana and Luc arrived and nestled into two deep chairs.

"So let's get started," said Ilana, briskly rubbing her hands together. "I gather there's a lot to cover."

"Not really all that much," said Rachel tantalizingly. "Just that we're definitely on, and sooner than expected. You remember the rumors about the Baron wanting to sell a few things? Turns out it's not just a few. It's everything we worked on."

Rachel described her meeting with Helmut Rosenfeld at his New York gallery. In the midst of art world gossip, the dealer lightly mentioned that the Baritsch Old Masters were for sale. The market had quieted considerably in the last few years, now that most of the best old pictures were safely tucked into public institutions. So the Baron considered it the perfect time to sell. He would keep the modern works, which were appreciating at a far greater rate than Old Masters. To her billowing rage, he had described the arrangement the Baron had made with the New Museum.

"How could he do all that?" Maria broke in. "His grandfather agreed that none of the pieces we worked on would ever be sold."

"Didn't I tell you that New York is dirtier than ever? This is part of it. The New Museum is desperate for money, if you can believe that. The trustees are furious over continuing budget deficits. So they're going to use the Baritsch exhibition to wipe out the deficit and also raise a tidy sum for their endowment."

"Sure, they'll make quite a bit in admissions," said Ilana. "Plus fancy rental fees from the other participating museums. But there has to be more to it."

"Well, there is. The museum president has discovered a new wrinkle. It's really an old wrinkle with an extra crease. Remember the great Futurist exhibition they had in the late Forties? And then a lot of the trustees' collections blossomed out with these same Futurists? And it turned out that all the pictures in the exhibition had been for sale. After the insiders picked what they wanted, the price list circulated all over New York. The museum put its prestige behind the exhibition and also got a regular dealer's commission on every sale. And we all know what's happened to Futurist prices since then ... up, up, and away..."

"So what you're saying," said Luc, "is that they're going to do the same thing with the Baritsch collection."

"Precisely. The sixty pieces they're showing are just the bait. They'll get so much publicity that even the Las Vegas high rollers and the Texas oil hillbillies will be bidding for a little piece of colored canvas."

"Bidding? Won't they have an announced price?" asked Ilana.

"No, that's really a new wrinkle. They've decided to have a silent auction. That way, if the bids should be too low, they don't have to sell anything to anybody. But don't worry. The way prices have been going in the last few years, everything will go at a premium. Afterwards, the Baron will sell directly all the items not in the exhibition. The museum will get its cut on that, too."

"But what about Till?" asked Maria. "I can't believe that straight-laced preacher would go along with a scheme like that."

"Neither could I," said Rachel. "He's not comfortable about it." She told them about her lunch with Zelda Bettman, Till's assistant. They had met in the quiet back dining room of a discreet hotel in the West Fifties. To Rachel's inquiries about the Baritsch sale, Zelda had replied guardedly. Till was not altogether comfortable about it. However, he was tiring of the museum's constant struggle to raise money and his own increasing diversion from scholarly work to crass appeals for donations.

"He's on some kind of treadmill," Zelda confided to Rachel. "First he spent years persuading people to give the museum masterpieces. Now the gifts are cascading in and so there's big crunch for space. That means more building, more costs for upkeep and guards, more insurance and storage expenses." Zelda shrugged disconsolately. "It's not exactly what I thought we'd be dealing with when I first arrived at the museum. Art and artists? This money beast has gobbled them up."

"And the Baron? Surely he doesn't need the money. What's his motive?" Maria looked hopeful, as though she had discovered a fatal flaw in the whole story.

"The Baron is simply tired of all the fuss in owning a collection. At least that's what he told Helmut Rosenfeld. He doesn't want to fool around any more with the insurance and the security and the conservation and the cataloguing. He says he hates what the art world has become. He plans to store the modern works in a vault in Zürich and then unload them when the market is right. He says he wants to concentrate on developing a huge new ski resort in the mountains of Colorado," said Rachel. "I think it's a lot simpler than that."

"Rosalinda," said Luc.

"Exactly. The collection reminds him of her. She's gone. He can't deal with that."

"But surely he knows about his grandfather's agreement with us," said Ilana.

"Yes, indeed. Rosenfeld discreetly brought it up just last week. The Baron said he didn't think the agreement was valid. He showed Rosenberg a letter from a fancy Liechtenstein lawyer saying that an agreement signed there was null and void elsewhere. Besides, how could we enforce it? The Baron also doubted that we would really care to spend the money and effort to litigate it now that we were so successful. Maybe he's right," added Rachel. "Maybe we ought to reconsider. So far, we haven't done anything overt. We could peacefully go on with our lives and just forget anything happened."

Rachel was still seething with the rage she had felt in New York. Those pictures were her own work. She had brought them back to life. They belonged to her more than they did to the artists who had originally painted them. Certainly she had more claim to them than Karl Baritsch. They were her own masterworks. How dare the Baron consign them to the overstuffed rooms of the rich? Rachel knew that she, for one was committed. But what about the others?

"We can't just sit by and watch this happen," said Maria heatedly. "There's no reason for our existence if we don't stand up for what's right. We might as well have died in the camps."

"I feel the same way," said Ilana. "What the man is doing is totally wrong. I don't think we should allow it."

"And Luc?" said Rachel. "What's the male point of view?"

"What disgusts me most is the museum," he said. "Such greed when they're supposed to be serving the public. It's infuriating. They've got enough stuff in the warehouse to fill a half-dozen more museums and they just sit on it, like a miser with his gold. I say let's go."

They adjourned to the living room for midmorning coffee and discussed their plans.

Chapter 7

Speculations

T he day's last wave of double-trailer truck traffic was inching along in a cloud of exhaust fumes when Count Filippo Cardini thrust the Maserati onto National Route 11, heading eastward toward Vicenza. He was annoyed that Helmut had abandoned him so abruptly -- stealthily, too -- at that ghastly inn on the lake. He tried to push the car forward along the unpaved shoulder of the road, but a long line of trucks had discovered that space long before him and it, too, was jammed.

In the dusk, the belching mass gave a fair representation of what Dante had described in the Inferno. Not that Filippo had read that classic. While the professor lectured on it in his course in Italian literature at University of Padua, he was involved in that torrid affair with Angelina, he recalled sourly. Luckily, his friend, Antonio, was able to provide a quick briefing in five minutes of frantic whispering, just before the examination.

Filippo was cheered to see a good many of the trucks lumbering off the highway at Verona. He was not even pushing that hard on the pedal, but the car eagerly leaped forward. The needle pressed toward ninety, when a sodden white cloud came down like a curtain. Dammit. Fog. Who knows how the history of northern Italy would have veered without the persistent, dense fogs that swept across the valley of the Po River? That damned fog had saved many an undeserving duchy from various condottieri and their marauding mercenaries. And the ill-starred lovers of Verona?

Was it not under the moist cover of a fog bank that Romeo had absconded with Juliet?

Again, Filippo was uncertain, as the professor had covered Shakespeare during his profound involvement with Isabella, the 32-year-old red-headed daughter of the Milanese industrialist, Angelo Percotti. The only fact that remained crystal-clear in the white and woolly world that enveloped him was that he would reach Vicenza too late for a decent dinner; that old Carmina would grumble and shuffle around the kitchen and finally produce, if he was lucky, an overcooked omelet.

He should have insisted that Helmut come along with him to Vicenza. He could have lured him into spending a few days and not just by presenting his willing, suggestive body. The collection might have interested Helmut even more, especially if Filippo could convince the dealer that he really had some important funds to spend on additions to it. But then he would have had to endure Helmut's polite recriminations for lying. In the end, he would be alone again anyway and facing, to put it mildly, financial embarrassment, without a single ally.

He crept miserably on, the fog billowing over the hood of the car as though it wished to swallow him entirely. He was sensing, rather than seeing, other vehicles around him, the growl of their motors muffled and subdued. Occasionally, white or yellow halos of headlamps materialized, and once he had to swerve sharply onto the gravel shoulder to avoid a pair bearing down upon him. Ghostly red tail lights appeared ahead of him and then were lost in swirling mist. At this rate, Carmina might give him up entirely, and trudge off to her sagging bed. Filippo hated fiddling around in the kitchen. He had hoped years ago to find a forgiving woman willing to take care of all that junk on a permanent basis, but when it came down to it, they had all made impossible demands. Those willing to put up with his compulsive philandering wanted at least to have children and to be supported in comfort.

Those who had money to bring into the marriage also insisted on fidelity. Everything was so damned complicated; nothing worked out to Filippo's satisfaction.

The gray and dripping outlines of his abode at last emerged from the mist. With a last angry spray of gravel he pulled the car up in the driveway. Everything was dark. Filippo tentatively honked the horn; perhaps Carmina or her husband Boldo were still awake; perhaps a compassionate impulse would draw them out to welcome him, carry in his bag, fix him something warm to eat. But nothing stirred. Filippo had long ago worn out their last twinge of compassion. Old family retainers, they stayed only because they had nowhere else to go.

Icy drops fell from the palazzo's stained and lichen-covered eaves as Filippo resentfully shoved open the heavy carved front door and tossed his bag carelessly into a corner. He glanced at a pile of mail on an antique console table and moved directly into the kitchen. My God, he was hungry and that bitch Carmina, he knew, was lying in her bed next door, crowing at his discomfort.

In the ancient wheezing refrigerator he found a bowl of *pasta e fagioli*, a yellowish circle of fat congealed around the rim. Amazing how much those two could eat, he thought; you wouldn't think two old people who did hardly any work could eat so much. He carried the cold pasta and a pitcher of white wine from the keg into the dining room, and set them noisily down on the scarred oak table. Let them know he was displeased. He ate.

The room was cavernous, large enough to seat fifty at a formal banquet. Its high ceiling was ornately coffered and carved, but the intricate paintwork was faded, peeling, and water-stained. There was a hole in the center, where an elaborate Venetian chandelier had once hung. Carvings of two monumental women representing Night and Day in a faintly Michelangesque style reclined on the mantle of a huge marble fireplace at the center of one long wall. The damask wallpaper had once been striped burgundy and gray, but had faded into yellowish pastels. Aside from the cheap oak table and the splintery chair on which Filippo sat, despondently spooning up chilled pasta, the room was empty.

Last to go had been the richly colored Anatolian carpet, woven in a pattern called Holbein, because its intricately interlaced ribbons were depicted so frequently in that artist's paintings. The importation of these carpets into Venice had formed the underpinning of the Cardini family fortune early in the sixteenth century. The palazzo had been built in 1567, after a design by the great architect Andrea Palladio, as a summer retreat from the humid miasmas and fevers of Venice.

Filippo drained the last of the wine and clattered upstairs, his footsteps echoing through the long stone corridors. Sad, it was all so sad the way this place had fallen into neglect and ruin. It was all his father's fault. The man should have known better than to get so close to that bombastic pretender, Mussolini. Still, things had gone quite well for a while. The Fascisti had made regular payments on the land they had bought, adjoining the villa, where they had hoped to establish a model farm, a brave harbinger of Italia Nuovo.

Then war came. Soon, the starving settlers were beating on the palazzo's gate, demanding food. They plundered the kitchen garden, forcing Boldo to spend the long summer nights sleeping on a mat in the midst of the ripening beans and tomatoes, a shotgun by his side. The Count installed an electrified fence to keep out the rabble, but soon the electricity in the entire district became unreliable: when the lights failed, it was the signal for the marauders to climb over.

Filippo had witnessed a good many of these confrontations after his return from the army. At first, his father's influence with the Party had kept him out and he had started university at Padua. For a few months he had even attended classes in uniform; his billowing, fawn-gray, whipcord jodphurs and gleaming boots certainly had attracted the girls' attention, while intimidating the professors into giving him passing grades.

In the winter of 1941, however, he was suddenly ordered to report to Brindisi and was shipped, aboard an inhumanly crowded transport, across the Mediterranean to Benghazi. In the camp, where they were herded and left to graze like cattle, Filippo had never witnessed such confusion. No one seemed to care that he had no extra boots or blankets, that the sand blew mercilessly in under the tent flaps and into the food and water, or even that his father had important friends in Rome. Every day, the rumor swept around the disheveled encampment that the British were coming, until Filippo, in a fever of discomfort and boredom, prayed for this, or anything else, to happen. He awoke early on Christmas morning to the drone of an observation plane and then there was shouting: "Attenzione! Ecco! Inglesi!"

The tanks seemed to sprout out of the faint line between sand and sky on the eastern horizon. The camp was seething with the panic of ten thousand frightened men, and soon the trails through the desert heading west was a mass of struggling humanity, slipping and falling among the dunes. Filippo had just dropped his bedroll and carbine when he spotted another line of tanks advancing toward him from the west. A staff car with a swastika flag raced across the sand toward him and then an officer leaped out, waving a pistol.

"Halt," he shouted. "Fall in, you godforsaken Italian turds."

A machine gun crew had rushed up behind the German and was now pointing its weapon in Filippo's direction.

Under its gaze, the Italians abruptly stopped and then formed into ragged ranks. Meanwhile, the advancing German tanks arrived and behind them were large open trucks into which Filippo and his companions were unceremoniously herded. The trucks followed the tanks toward the battle. Behind the Italians were more trucks jammed with fresh-faced German infantry.

The field erupted with the crash and fire of battle, while a squadron of low-flying Spitfires strafed the trucks. Filippo and his companions scrambled underneath their truck and attempted to dig shelter with their hands. A shell landed nearby, spraying up a great geyser of sand and bodies. Another German officer appeared, waving his pistol toward another truck loaded with rifles and ammmunition.

"Fight," he was shouting. "Fight, you lousy Dago pigs."

Filippo had grabbed a rifle and was loading a bullet into it, when a blinding impact lifted him. He woke up to the thunder of distant guns. He felt refreshed, light-headed and peaceful. His left foot felt unbearably itchy and he tried to reach down to scratch it. A wave of pain barrelled over him. He looked down over the thin tent of a blanket and saw that it was flat where his foot should have been. In panic, he lifted the blanket and peered underneath. Nothing. His foot was gone.

"You were lucky," the nurse said later. "They thought it would have to come off just below the knee. But after they cleaned it up, the surgeon decided that the fractures could heal and he took just the foot. You won't have to worry about trimming the toenails any more. And you'll go home. An easy ticket out of all this shit."

But home was not exactly a paradise of pasta and vino. Bands of partisans were forming in the hills. One night, a pack of them attacked the rag-tag fascist farmers next door, using grenades and machine guns. They sent word that Filippo's father would also have to pay for his support of Mussolini. From then on, a cart arrived weekly at the palazzo and was loaded with food before lumbering off into the misty hills. The old Count had never really recovered from the dishonor heaped upon him by this rabble. After the war ended in 1945, he seldom left his room, although he could sometimes be seen by the gardener, standing at the window and gravely surveying his domains.

The old man had died in the very bedroom into which Filippo now stepped. He sat down heavily on the puffy quilt and began to undress, letting the clothes drop to the scratched parquet floor. Finally he unlaced the prosthesis from his left leg, leaving the false foot inside its shoe standing at attention next to his bed, like the last soldier in a war. Life would have been a lot different if he didn't have to wear that thing. A lot of women just fled when they saw it. And even besotted Helmut Rosenfeld had recoiled the first time he saw it. Filippo was proud that he walked without a limp, but inside he remained deeply scarred. How could he consider a serious career with a handicap like that?

Then there was the pain. It just never stopped. Even now, he sometimes woke up in the night feeling this awful throbbing in his left foot. Only his foot wasn't there. Uncanny that. The pills had started because of the pain. Even now, it was beginning to bother him. He reached into the nightstand and pulled out a small brown bottle, hugging it to himself like a talisman. He shook four vermilion capsules into his palm and briefly contemplated them. Then he popped them into his mouth and turned off the lamp.

By morning, the fog had lifted only slightly. Beyond the French doors, a mildewed stone balustrade detached itself faintly from the swirling dirty gray smear beyond. The Palladian fanlights above the doors segmented a lint-gray sky. Filippo swam haltingly toward consciousness, the dust-blossoms in his head complementing the wooziness outside. Like the dining room, this bedchamber had been stripped of its former grandeur, and now was furnished with a cheap, garishly veneered bedroom suite.

Filippo laced on his prosthesis, shrugged into a rumpled brown silk bathrobe and padded, with a single floppy leather mule on his good foot, down to the dining room.

Carmina sullenly took his order for soft boiled eggs and coffee. It seemed to him that she was studiously avoiding any questions about his journey or about the time of his return.

"The man from the electricity board was here again yesterday," she announced tonelessly. "They want their money. He said they'd have to shut everything off by next Wednesday if they didn't get paid before then."

"But surely you told him I was travelling on important business."

"Oh yes. He said his business was important too. He said they tried to be especially patient because of your family name and all that. But then he said Wednesday is it."

Filippo retrieved the mail stacked on the hall table and desultorily tore open envelopes. A brief note informed him that, regrettably, Signor Fellini had no role for him in his upcoming movie, *La dolce vita*. Everything else was bills, mostly small ones from local tradesmen who could be put off. But there was also one for insurance, a demand for a whopping $3,000 premium, due immediately, to cover his art collection.

That's a laugh, he thought, picking at his eggs. Ten years ago, when he had inherited the palazzo, the cost of insuring its furnishings had been maybe $200. All those years, he had gradually sold its old paintings, sculptures, and antiques for enough money to support his aristocratic lifestyle, plus buying well over one hundred contemporary works by young, trendy artists. He had hoped that their prices would rise steeply, as so many other contemporary works had, bringing him a profit to invest in still newer works.

At the time, it had seemed foolproof. That fast-moving dealer in Milan had rolled his eyes and sworn on his mother's head that it was foolproof. "Look what's happening with the Impressionists," he had burbled. "In their own lifetimes, nothing. But once they were dead, prices went straight up and they haven't stopped yet. Quite the contrary."

He thrust before Filippo's face a magazine account of the sale of the Gabriel Cognaq estate in Paris. "Look, a few apples and a couple of cookies on a table by Cezanne -- over $80,000. Only ten years ago, that kind of thing was selling for less than $10,000. And just watch, it'll go even faster with contemporary work."

Filippo's head swam as he recalled the dealer's complicated explanation of why that was so: more rich people in the world, lots more interest in modern art, slick selling methods by auction houses, fears of inflation. The words had flowed smoothly, while Filippo's mind drifted to his dinner engagement with Teresina Vesci, wondering how much vino rosso it would take to get her into bed.

"The smart money is getting into Americans," the dealer went on. "That's where the money is, but more important, they know something about merchandising. You buy an American artist and they don't just leave you hanging. They advertise, they get museum exhibitions, they get articles in magazines, and, poof, up goes the price."

He led Filippo out into his gallery and pointed forcefully to a huge canvas. It was even bigger than *The Rape of the Sabine Women*, the painting that stretched across one entire wall of the salon at home. School of Rubens, Filippo's mother had always told him, but the roiling bodies and rampant horseflesh had left him more bored than awed. By contrast, this painting in the gallery was certainly restful. It was almost entirely pea-green, its soup-like consistency broken only by a dusky sphere floating, like a crouton, in the upper right quadrant.

"This is one of Gelfand's most important pieces," the dealer was saying. "He used to do busy things with lots of color. Now, suddenly, stillness; peacefulness; the essence of meadows and forests without all that distracting, really irrelevant detail. He calls it *Foliar Fall*. Get it? He's a comer; I guarantee it."

Filippo looked thoughtfully at the picture. He was not about to admit that he had never heard of this artist Gelfand and, furthermore, that the picture made him think of a large pool of vomit on an asphalt pavement. Instead, he bought it.

"You're lucky," the dealer had said. "In New York, pictures like this are already going for twice the price. He's about to have a show at the Whitney and that's guaranteed to double the price again. You're getting a bargain because the artist doesn't want to pay for shipping this big work back over there."

The painting arrived at the palazzo two days later and Filippo wondered how it would look in the spot where the *Rape of the Sabine Women* had been. The blank spot in the salon had bothered him ever since he had sold the picture, more than a year earlier, to raise money for roof repairs. Well, yes, there had been a little something left over, but a person had to have some fun after months of dealing with roofers.

New York. That was clearly the place to be. Sure, the prices, as the Milan dealer had explained, were probably higher, but that's where the artists were, hundreds of them, ready to be discovered by somebody with his wits about him. The new painting in the salon made all that Rococo furniture look washed out, downright shabby. It may have been all right for the sedate gatherings his parents had organized in years gone by. To Filippo, those evenings had seemed endless -- Professor Enzi from the local conservatory, his limp gray hair streaming romantically, coaxing Respighi out of the piano, followed by Miss Clemenza Cappodimonte, who was actually in the chorus at La Scala, rocking the chandelier with *O patria mia* from Aida.

After his parents died, Filippo promptly cancelled the musicales. The gatherings he favored did not require a salon at all, but they certainly benefitted from the palazzo's profusion of bedrooms. Young people in fast cars arrived at late hours, danced to raucous beats, cracked antique bedsteads with their fornications, and languidly departed after the sun was high, observed from behind drawn draperies by Carmina, clucking and grumbling.

There was a devil of haggle with the antiquarian over the salon chairs. The tables, the man reluctantly conceded, were definitely Venetian, good ones from the late seventeenth century. However, the paint was severely scuffed, the marble surfaces stained, and, in a few places, even burned; they would require considerable restoration. But the chairs, he insisted, were clearly nineteenth century copies, and not from the better, earlier part of the century. "The tapestry seats and backs are machine woven," the horrid man kept saying, pointing to a spot where the fabric was ripped and the underside clearly visible.

"It's obviously woven, rather than embroidered," the man said pedantically. "That alone wouldn't be all that bad. But, the weave also is much too even. That's fatal. The evenness is typical of machine jacquard looms, the kind that came in during the middle nineteenth century."

"Spare me a dissertation on the history of weaving," snapped Filippo. "What's your best offer?"

The whole scene had reminded Filippo of his father's artful and long drawn-out negotiating sessions. For the old Count, the purchase of so much as a bicycle was an occasion for a day's sociable bargaining. Hands would fly and voices rise, one or the other negotiator would stride purposefully to the door, then turn dramatically to shout one final offer over his shoulder. Just at the point when agreement seemed inconceivable, late in the day, when the give and take seemed impossibly poised in equilibrium, the deal would emerge. Then Carmina would appear, solemnly bearing the decanter of grappa and two glasses.

Filippo had no patience for this kind of delicate minuet.

"Cash today," he said sullenly. His leg was killing him. Cheated of an enjoyable afternoon, the antiquary counted out the bills.

The flight from Rome to New York was advertised as non-stop, a matter of eleven hours, punctuated by sumptuous meals and free-flowing drinks. In fact, the DC-6 had to come down for re-fuelling at Gander. Then a fog rolled in and the passengers lolled disconsolately on uncomfortable chrome chairs in the shabby lounge, waiting for an announcement. Some went for greasy fried fish and chips in the cafe; others napped. Everyone perked up when the public address system hummed to life, only to hear that there would be more delay. Filippo stepped outside and peered resentfully upward into impenetrable, wet, cotton wool. For this, he didn't have to leave the Po Valley.

By the time they landed in New York, the cabin looked like a hospital ward. Rumpled and blinking, the passengers descended the stairway and stumbled toward customs. Filippo was still hearing the roar of the plane's four engines and tasting the sour mint flavor of the candy passed around by the stewardesses to ease the ear-popping agony of the unpressurized plane's final descent.

He felt stripped by the immigration inspector's dubious gaze. The man looked positively threatening as he scrutinized Filippo's passport and then began to leaf leisurely through a bulky volume of mimeographed pages. Ever so slowly, the inspector's cracked fingernail crept down the sheet.

"You're not a communist are you?" he asked with a thin smile, then lowered his rubber stamp deliberately on a clean page of Filippo's passport. "Next."

The cab driver spoke pretty good Italian, though his accent was clearly Sicilian. At the hotel, another Italian speaker, with a Calabrian twang, showed him his room. Amazing. His window looked out on a blank brick wall painted in faded black and white: "Bernstein's Delicatessen -- You Ring, We Bring." By leaning on the sill and twisting his neck, Filippo could glimpse in the very top left corner of the window, the spire of the Empire State Building. The last of the sun was gilding the aluminum roof. He felt as though he had left Rome a month ago, but in fact it was still the same day. Amazing. His leg hurt. On the street fourteen floors below, Filippo saw the last straggling commuters hurrying in skittish flocks toward Pennsylvania station.

Chapter 8

Underpainting

In a burst of blossoms, spring arrives in the little town of Bellagio in mid-March. Occasionally, frosts sweep southward from the Alps nipping the forsythia buds and churning the lake into an unfriendly froth. But by May, the harbingers of summer's tourist horde are already picking their way along quaint cobbled streets, sniffing for the rare bargain among ranks of hand-thrown coffee mugs and bins of silk scarfs. Most of them finally settle on an overpriced trinket or T-shirt, the embossed or printed "Bellagio" across the chest condemning it to instant kitsch. They buy because after one has strolled appreciatively through the gardens of the Villa Serbelloni and viewed the Villa Giulia, once owned by King Leopold I of Belgium, there is little else to do. The lake is still too chilly for swimming or boat excursions. The shopping streets are steep -- many are stairways -- so the elderly visitors tire quickly. And the Villa Tazzi, with its legendary array of paintings -- the Baritsch Collection -- is closed.

Therefore, Signora Tancredi was delighted that a group of younger people had taken a lease on her villa for the month of May. The place was difficult to rent even in high summer because it was more than a stroll from the center of town. Worse, access to the leakefront was totally blocked by the massive grounds of the Villa Tazzi, whose electrified fence confronted the pale yellow facade of the signora's rental house. Until recently, it had been her home, but the upkeep of the garden and two-story dwelling were becoming too troublesome for the elderly widow. She had moved into a flat next door, where she could keep a sharp eye on her tenants.

They seemed a decent enough lot, reserved and old enough to eschew blaring rock radio. Still, they were a strange assortment and, despite considerable discreet observation from behind her lace curtain, Signora Tancredi could not figure out which of the three women -- if any -- belonged with which of the three men. As arranged, they had arrived on the first of May: first a harassed-looking man whose ice-blue Maserati was licensed in Venetia; next, three women and a man in a coffee-colored Citröen with French plates; finally, a fellow encased in black leather clattered up to the door aboard a flashy red Kawasaki.

They certainly kept to themselves, Signora Tancredi noticed. Every other day or so, two or three would stroll out in the late afternoon and soon return with a few bags of groceries. As far as she could tell, the motorcyle never moved from its parking spot next to the back door, while the Citröen stayed locked in the garage. The Maserati, however, departed at strange hours. Several times she had been awakened during the night by the noisy grinding of its motor starting up and then streaking away, headed north.

Consumed by curiosity, Signora Tancredi knocked at the back door one afternoon, bearing a fresh bouquet of mimosa. After an interminable wait, the door opened a crack.

"I thought you might enjoy some fresh flowers," she said. "Is everything satisfactory?"

The door was opened a bit wider by a platinum blonde, one of the women who had arrived in the Citröen. She was wearing a wrinkled blue jumpsuit and looked impatient. From somewhere deep inside the house, the old lady heard the tap-tap of a hammer on wood.

"Yes, thank you," said the blonde, opening the door just wide enough to take the flowers. "Everything is in order. We're finding Bellagio restful and attractive. Per our agreement, Signora Tancredi, we shall be departing on the last day of the month." Then she closed the door.

Running upstairs, Rachel watched the old woman in her black dress and brown lisle stockings trudge back to the house next door. Then she rushed into the basement, where the five others were laboring at a series of large tables propped up on sawhorses. The place was strewn with stretcher bars and paintings curled forlornly without their wooden supports. In one corner, Ilana and Luc were wrestling a stiffly rolled canvas into a cardboard tube.

"That was a neighborly call from our landlady," announced Rachel. "Maria, just drop the Carpaccio for a minute and please stick the flowers she brought into a pretty vase. Put it in the upstairs window, where she can see it, so she knows we're nice, respectable people. And tonight, everybody, we're going out for a nice stroll along the lakefront. And stopping for a *gelato*. Just like tourists."

"Damn," said Filippo. "I was looking forward to a few winks before the furniture moving starts again."

Winks? thought Rachel. A few snorts is more like it. The man was a dubious asset, but, unfortunately, indispensable. It was he who had supplied the key to the whole operation and in that typical style of his: carelessly, unwittingly, like a drooling two-year-old trailing a tattered blanket.

True, Rachel had been furious when she learned about the Baron's plans to exhibit -- actually sell! -- the collection. The rank injustice of it still galled her. Damn it, those pictures wouldn't even have existed any more without her work and the work of Maria, Ilana, and Luc. They'd given almost two years of their lives bringing those mildewed hulks back to life -- and complete with the famous painters' autographs.

She walked over to the Carpaccio and studied the tiny painted slip of paper attached to a tree stump in the lower right of the picture. "Victor Carpathivs/finxit M. D. X.," it read, and Rachel resented once again that she had painted the name of that other artist and the date 1510 in that spot. By rights, it was she who in 1950 had planted those iron-shod feet upon the stony path; had limned the gleaming steel and brass rivets of the knight's armor, had recreated the symbol-laden landscape in which he posed: the ermine of the Dukes of Urbino and the oak leaves of the della Roveres representing the knight's forebears; the lilies and irises associated with the Virgin Mary conveying the knight's birthday, March 25, Feast of the Annunciation.

The others had worked on other paintings. This one Rachel had kept for herself, partly because the intricacy of the composition -- landscape, architecture, and the two figures -- challenged her abilities, but mostly because the young knight's sober, reflective gaze and hands resting firmly on a sheathed sword conveyed a stern sense of justice. Such a man, she believed, would not draw his sword rashly, but would ride sternly into battle to slay the enemies of righteousness.

When Helmut Rosenfeld had first mentioned the proposed sale of the pictures, Rachel had exploded in fury.

"That prick! He has no right to sell those things. His grandfather promised they would never be sold privately. I have it in writing. Now the grandson is playing games. He's a lightweight. He doesn't have the capacity to appreciate the things. He can't help that, the poor idiot. But to violate a written agreement, that's wrong, totally wrong."

Helmut was embarrassed by her outburst. "You can't blame the man," he said soothingly. "Look what picture prices are doing. Now that the museums have the cash to bid, the private buyers are ready to spend more than ever. They know that one day they can sell that Canaletto or Bellini to the Cosmopolitan for a mint. And if they want to be really nice about it, they can give it to their neighborhood museum and take a fat tax deduction. That means that other taxpayers are helping the museum to acquire it, but the owner decides when and where it will go."

"No lectures today. Please." Rachel's fingers worked to control her rage. "What the bastard deserves is a major art theft."

Helmut had laughed. So Rachel was stunned when he suddenly appeared at the Chartres studio in that crazy black leather outfit.

"If you're still interested," he coolly announced, "I know how it could be done. And I'll even help you. I have a few scores to settle with Till at the New Museum."

During "an evening," as he delicately put it, with Filippo Cardini, the Italian had told him about a house in Bellagio. It was just one of those ordinary resort villas, a narrow two-story box, its facade flush on the street, an overgrown kitchen garden and cramped garage behind. And it was directly across the street from the Villa Tazzi.

"So?" Rachel tended to get impatient with the reek of Germanic explication in Rosenfeld's discourse. "So, there's a house and it's in that spot. So what?"

Helmut was not to be rushed, however. Methodically (he was, after all, an art historian), he began to relate the history of the Villa Tazzi. It had been constructed just after the turn of the eighteenth century as a summertime retreat for the last of the Gonzagas, who had ruled Mantua since the fourteenth century. The poor feeble scion of this legendary dynasty, Ferdinand Charles, had been able to hang on to the Gonzaga holdings until 1707, when the Hapsburg armies rampaged over northern Italy. Captured upon his return from a summer's dalliance at the lake, he was accused of treasonous contacts with the French and deprived of his duchy.

For almost a century the vacation villa remained empty, gradually decaying into a mournful, evocative ruin. Elsewhere along the lakefront there was plenty of land for new construction, although, as the Hapsburgs tightened their grip on all of northern Italy, few magnates of the old school had the capital or the will to build frivolous retreats. In 1797, with the city of Mantua under siege by Napoleon, the great-grandson of Ferdinand Charles' illegitimate daughter, Francesca, escaped from the city by posing as a mule-driver.

After many vicissitudes (Helmut liked that sort of locution), this last feeble leaf from the great Gonzaga oak, Enrico Galata by name, arrived in Bellagio and took up residence in the ruined villa. While war raged across the fog-shrouded flatlands below, the fact of foreign occupation created new opportunities for those who lived along the lakes at the foot of rugged mountains to the north. As their ancestors had done even in Roman times, they turned to smuggling. Gold, art, even people who were being sought for crimes, were brought to Como for the voyage north.

At Chiavenna, the smugglers transferred their precious cargo to mules and toiled by night over the Passo della Spluga. In the spring and summer, when the water was high enough, they boarded rafts at Splügen for a thrilling ride through the rapids of the Hinterrhein until it joined the Rhine at a ferry-point near Reich. Voyaging on, the travellers or the cargo floated downstream on calmer waters toward Vaduz, to be handed over to a new set of smugglers headquartered in Liechtenstein.

From their strategic perch on a narrow point of land separating the western leg of Lake Como from an eastern leg named Lago di Lecco, the residents of Bellagio would swiftly paddle out to exact a toll from every passing boat. With the proceeds Enrico Galata was able to re-build the villa, eventually creating a fanciful pile of turrets, gables, and gazebos, a vanilla ice-cream confection set in a park of weeping willows and romantically twisted evergreens.

"Helmut, please, get to the point." Rachel restlesssly tapped her foot. "I know they gave you a wonderful education at New York University, but you don't have to cover every little thing you learned."

The dealer smirked insufferably and remained silent for a long time. "I'm getting there," he said at last. "Patience. You'll find it worth the wait." And droned on.

Through most of the nineteenth century, Hapsburg governors came and went in the duchies and principalities of northern Italy, attempting with increasing difficulty to mold these hot-tempered, devious Italians into reliable subjects of the Austro-Hungarian Empire. By the 1830s, Bellagio was among the staging points where Italian patriots sheltered as they tried fruitlessly to foment revolution against foreign rule. After Milan surrendered to Hapsburg forces in August 1848, Giuseppe Garibaldi defiantly led a small band of rebels out of the city and began to harass the Austrians from encampments near the northern lakes.

"So? So the father of modern Italy came to Bellagio," said Rachel in exasperation. "You really are maddening, Helmut. Here we are, trying to get some work done and you're spinning tales of derring-do in days gone by."

"Ah, but now it really gets interesting, I promise," replied Helmut. "Yes, he stayed in Bellagio. At the Villa Tazzi. With the grandson of Enrico Galata. And the Hapsburgs sent a squadron of *Bergjäger*, their best mountain troops, to arrest Garibaldi. They surrounded the villa. Then they broke in and mercilessly searched the place."

"And surprise, surprise," Rachel broke in, "the man escaped."

"Exactly. He made his way to Switzerland and then back to Nice, his birthplace, and, and, and ... I won't bore you with the rest of his story."

"So what else will you bore me with?" She impatiently lit a cigarette.

"Listen and learn. Garibaldi escaped through a tunnel leading to a perfectly innocent house across the street. It was built by Enrico's smuggling pals just in case unexpected visitors came to the villa."

"That's nice," said Rachel. "But that was also a long time ago. I'm begging you, Helmut, what does it all mean today, right this minute? I'm not one of your customers, hanging on every word from the world-famous dealer."

She had often observed Helmut in his New York gallery, as he rambled on about the provenance of a painting on the display easel, attempting to educate a client. Lacking the fund of anecdotes his father poured out to oil a negotiation, Helmut relied, to a maddening degree, on pedantry. Like the clients, Rachel was squirming as the man lectured relentelessly on. And soon, to her surprise, it really did get more interesting.

In 1926, the Villa Tazzi was confiscated from the last remaining descendants of Enrico Galata. Still pursuing the family smuggling business, they had resisted the bureaucratized law and order imposed by Mussolini's Fascist regime. The villa became the summer home of Piero Bardino, a shifty journalist from Milan, who had become wealthy as the publisher of a strident Fascist sheet named *Futurismo*.

"Filippo told me the whole story during our meeting at Garda," said Helmut. "Seems as though Filippo's father was imperiously summoned there for a meeting of the leading local Fascists in northern Italy, I'm guessing in about 1932. And just before the war started, in 1939, Filippo went along with his father to another meeting there. He was looking for some contact to help him stay out of uniform."

"Sounds right in character," said Rachel sourly. "And he spotted the tunnel. Right?"

"Right. Piero Bardino's son showed him how to get some town whore in and out via the tunnel. But I can't resist one interesting digression. You might remember what happened in the last few days before the end of the war."

"I remember a whole lot," Rachel broke in cynically. "I can assure you it had nothing to do with Bellagio."

"The crazy thing is that it's relevant, sort of." Even Helmut sounded a bit apologetic, but pressed on. "Mussolini himself was wandering around that part of the country, trying to elude the partisans roaming everywhere. On April 26, 1945, less than two weeks before the German surrender, he drove up the highway on the west side of Lake Como, with a raggedy entourage of Fascist diehards, hoping to reach the Swiss border. But only a few hours before he got there, the Italian border guards joined the partisans and blocked the route. So he returned to the lake. The story gets very confused and most accounts say he went back to Menaggio, across the lake from Bellagio. But Filippo swears that he really holed up in the Villa Tazzi.

"As it turned out, he and his mistress Clara Petacci spent their last night on earth together in the master bedroom at the villa. The next day, they tried to escape through the tunnel, but by then the partisans were out by the thousands, combing the area for them. But you know the rest. They were captured almost immediately ... by the fifty-second brigade of Garibaldi partisans. The next afternoon at four, they were shot and dumped into a truck. By nightfall, they were hanging by the heels in the Piazzale Loreto in Milan and the mob was throwing garbage at their corpses."

Rachel sighed. "You took the long way around, as usual," she said, "but it was worth it. The one thing about our project that made me hesitate was the prospect of violence. I can't deal with it any more. Now, it looks as though there's a way to avoid it. All we have to do is work like demons to make it happen."

The most difficult part had been the creation of credible substitutes for the pictures which, night after mild May night, the team was removing from the Villa Tazzi. For their success, they had to thank the Baron's grandfather. It was he who had insisted on photographs when the restoration of his paintings was finished, in 1951. The photographer had lugged his bulky eight-by-ten view camera to the castle at Vaduz and had spent many days shooting every single work. The old Baron had collected a set of prints and happily presented a second set to Rachel and her crew. But afterwards, after they had moved into the house in Chartres, bought by the Baron to fulfill his agreement, Rachel went back to Munich, to the photographer's studio. For what seemed like a fortune then, she bought all the negatives. Back then, she didn't know exactly why.

But she knew now. They had used those negatives to make full-size reproductions of the pictures and, in months of concentrated work, had turned them into convincing paintings. Convincing enough anyway to the skeleton staff remaining at the villa during the month of May. Accompanied by his curator and his conservator, The Baron himself was travelling in the United States, touring the museums where his collection would be shown that fall. Wined and dined by museum directors and trustees, the man was having the most fun he would ever get out of the collection, or so Rachel imagined.

Left behind was a housekeeper, whose job was to dust the pictures and vacuum the floors, as well as a night guard, whose most vital task was to monitor the electronic security system. The perimeter of the villa's garden was wired, and so were all the windows and doors. Helmut had a similar system at his New York gallery and was therefore able to get expert advice from his own technician -- all theoretical, of course -- on how the system worked ... and how it could be defeated. Not that it was even necessary, since the tunnel's opening in the villa's basement had been bricked over long before the Baron acquired the building. The opening in the basement of the house across the street, was also bricked over and covered with stucco for good measure.

It took Luc and Ilana all of a day's buzzing with a diamond circular saw to get through the wall at their end. At the Villa Tazzi end, the task was trickier. Working as long as they dared, from midnight until dawn, Luc and Ilana cut through the brick, while the others hauled away and carefully stacked the heavy blocks. The brick would all have to be replaced and repaired when the job was done. In the opening, they carefully fitted a thin plywood panel faced with a layer of textured spackle and perfectly painted to match the adjoining wall. At the beginning of each night's work, while the watchman dozed upstairs next to the serenely blinking red dots of his alarm system, they simply removed the panel. In the morning, they replaced it in its precise position.

Rachel had used Bettman Levin's photos to prepare a scale model of the villa's interior. On its doll's house walls, she had precisely hung a miniature sketch of each painting. Every day, she glued tiny stars to the pictures slated for removal that night. Then the hard work began.

Padding silently in felt slippers and white gloves, the group worked in pairs, sweating in the dank, still air, lifting one heavy painting after another off the wall. At first, only three or four pictures were targeted each night. These they carried back through the tunnel to the makeshift workshop in the basement across the street. There, another team labored to remove frames. For wooden panels, the replacements had been painted on wood and these were relatively simple to jam into the frames and re-hang. Works on canvas presented more of a problem. Each one had to be gingerly pried off its stretchers and the substitute re-stretched before being replaced in its frame. To the maid with her feather duster and to the guard on his morning rounds, the galleries of the Villa Tazzi looked exactly as they had the night before.

After considerable experimenting, Rachel had discovered that she could use wax to fasten a smooth plastic layer over the face of any painting. Any sort of composition could be painted on this surface and easily removed without damage to the underlying pigment. By mid-morning, the entire crew was busy in the basement workshop, creating new works over the old. That was the fun part.

Following the first night's activities, Maria quickly brushed the warm wax onto a meticulously detailed Venetian scene by Canaletto. "Goodbye St. Mark's," she chirped, as Rachel rapidly smoothed the plastic layer into place. "Hello, Mark Rothko," said Ilana, daubing on a mass of crimson lake with a wide painter's brush. Maria added dabs of prussian blue with a narrower brush and then Luc came along to feather in a large patch of zinc white tinted with chrome yellow. It hovered just below the center of the picture, a blinding and mysterious band of light.

"As for the *Doge Francesco Venier*," added Rachel, "let's see what Filippo can do to improve on Titian." She smoothed on the plastic covering and the Italian approached with a bucket of electric blue. He poured a pool of it onto the center of the large canvas and then used a squeegee to distribute the pigment smoothly over the entire surface.

"I can't decide whether to leave it alone and make an Ellsworth Kelly," he giggled, "or add a strip of white tape along one side to make it a Barnett Newman." Filippo had not had so much fun in a long while.

Even Helmut was in a comparatively playful mood. "Pity the poor forgers of the past," he said. "Those guys really had to know something about pigments and painting media. And now? A few tubes of acrylics from the neighborhood paint store and you're in business." He dribbled an elegant pirouette of flat black paint across the plastic covering a satiny oak panel. It was half of an annunciation diptych by Jan Van Eyck. "This one's by a hitherto unknown disciple of Pollock," he intoned. "Notice the energy of the unmediated gesture." He poured on a rough circle from a can of silver radiator paint.

The creations gleamed under strong infra-red flood-lamps to dry. Later that day, Helmut and Filippo loaded the rolled canvases and made their first run across the Swiss border to Lugano, where the dealer had rented a small gallery along the lakefront. After ferrying across Lake Como to Menaggio, Filippo put the Maserati through its paces. They squealed around the hairpin turns as the road climbed sharply above the water. Then they coasted westward into rolling hills, threading through small villages whose stone houses sometimes constricted the road into a single cramped lane. At the Italian customs post, a single *carabiniere* waved them on. Fifty yards further, the Swiss guard asked for their passports and insisted on looking in the trunk.

"Modern art, is it?" He looked dubious.

"Students from Vicenza," said Helmut. "I told them that this sort of work is no longer being done in New York, but they insisted on showing it in Lugano anyhow. They thought maybe we could unload these things on a few tourists. Well, we can try. There's lots more, so we'll be coming back this way quite a few times." He shrugged. "I'm taking it all on consignment, so whatever doesn't sell after a couple of weeks, well, they'll have to take it back." He handed a card for the Lugano gallery to the guard. "Perhaps you know someone who would be interested. We're opening on June 1."

The guard grasped the cardboard as though it were smeared with feces. "Yes, perhaps," he shrugged.

An hour later, Helmut and Filippo passed the same guard on their way back. He waved them on and so did his Italian colleague down the road.

The car droned forward and Helmut scanned Filippo's regular profile. His pale open-necked shirt, the color of chablis, handsomely set off his olive skin and dark hair. But the jowls were becoming apparent and the chin-line showed the first sags of midlife. The softness of the Caravaggio boy's angelic face was beginning to resemble vanilla pudding. The rest of his body also was starting to show the effects of too much pasta and wine, too many late nights, too many chemicals, and too little exercise. Above the belt, the slightest bulge forecast the paunch to come.

"A month of making this same trip," Filippo grumbled. "What a bore. The work is a lot harder than I expected. That Rachel. What a slave driver. Push push. Go, go. All night long."

"She's had a hard life," said Helmut. "I once told you about it, remember?"

Filippo shrugged. "Haven't we all?"

Helmut had first met Rachel almost a decade ago. It must have been her first trip to New York. She had dashed breathlessly into his gallery on a Saturday in June, just before closing time.

"I want to see the Degas you picked up at the Cognacq sale," she ordered curtly.

He suggested that she return the following Tuesday.

"I'll be back in France by then, and who knows when I'll return to New York." She glanced at her watch. "It says 4:33. Your sign says you close at five. That gives me twenty-seven minutes to purchase a $50,000 work … if you insist on leaving on the dot."

She was wearing a severely tailored black wool suit, barely relieved by a white organdy blouse, and low-heeled black patent-leather sling pumps. Her pale hair was pulled up and twisted tightly into a bun. She sat expectantly on the needlepoint directoire chair facing the empty display easel.

Helmut obediently fetched the picture and placed it before her. It was a late pastel, created just after the turn of the century, when the artist's eyesight was failing. These were not the characteristically pretty Degas dancers, pirouetting in fluffy pale tutus. The color cried out stridently, strong ochers and biting blues scintillating against a dark, mottled background. Nor were the faces sensitive or pretty. Instead, they were crudely sketched, and feral, with anxious grimaces.

"I wouldn't expect you to walk out with something like this under your arm," Helmut conciliated. "I usually advise my clients to live with a picture for a while, especially a strong statement like this. It should hang in your home, so you can see how it strikes you in the morning when you're fresh. And then examine it again under the proper lighting in the evening. Try it on, the way you would try on a fur coat."

"I don't put a masterpiece of art in the same category as a fur coat," she said stiffly.

"Of course not." Helmut was annoyed by his apologetic tone. "However, you'd be surprised how many clients view pictures exactly as they would a nice sable or silver fox. Goods. You obviously don't."

Rachel had pulled a magnifier out of her black alligator purse and was scrutinizing the signature on the painting.

"Looks genuine." She sounded surprised. Then she slowly moved the glass, studying, it seemed, the drawing's every pore. "Good, but not the best. It's a late work, done when the poor man's eyesight was failing. By then, he could have painted those dancers in the dark and maybe he did. Are you sure you didn't overpay? Maybe got swept away in the heat of the auction?"

"It was a fair price. The two Renoirs went for more. So did the Manet and the Van Gogh." To his annoyance, Helmut was sounding defensive again.

"I need more light."

Helmut almost ran to bring a floodlamp. When he returned, she had put away her glass and had moved her chair back.

"I don't know where the Cognacqs kept this picture," she said, "but I'm willing to bet that they got afternoon sun through a tall, narrow window."

"Are you a detective by profession?" asked Helmut, hoping that his tone was light enough.

"Not quite. But I do know what causes the white high-lights in a picture to turn yellowish and brittle. When I see that effect in a grid pattern it tells me, 'Too much afternoon sun through a French window.' It happens to paintings, but it's even more noticeable with pastels because, of course, the sun deteriorates the paper."

"If it bothers you, I'm sure that a good restorer ..."

"Oh yes," she interrupted. "A good restorer can do almost anything."

Helmut had ended up spending the evening with Rachel. Over drinks at the Plaza, he heard about the exquisitely appointed conservation studios she and her colleagues had recently opened in the very shadow of the Chartres Cathedral. Over veal parmigiana and chianti at Peter's Backyard in the Village, he heard about the large collection of Old Masters she had finished restoring the previous year.

"The Baritsch collection?" He was stunned. "I just read an article about it in *Burlington Magazine*. Tragic, wasn't it? Just when the old baron gets ready to display his beautifully restored collection to the world, he drops dead."

"Tragedy consists of more than disappointment," said Rachel coolly. "He was old and decrepit. He lived long. Perhaps too long."

"The grandson," Helmut pressed on. "The grandson, I hear, is not exactly an art connoisseur. Do you think he might sell the things?"

"Not a chance," said Rachel.

"But if he did. Dumping that many pictures on the market all at once. It could depress prices quite a bit. Especially just now, when museums all over the world are snapping up any kind of art they can find."

"Not a chance," Rachel repeated.

Over drinks at the Rainbow Room, Helmut heard about Rachel's work on the Prince of Liechtenstein's Leonardo da Vinci.

"*Ginevra di Benci*, what a bitch," Rachel said. "The painting, I mean, not the woman. Although from what I gather, the woman wasn't exactly easy to live with either. Who would be, if they had to paste those tiny little curls into place every morning? It took me weeks to get that hairdo just right. But the most difficult was the *sfumato*."

Helmut felt on solid ground at last. "That's where Leonardo comes through so exquisitely. You know, the other artists of his day marvelled over the delicate smoky shading he achieved. Quite a few of them tried to imitate it. I guess that's what misled Berenson into attributing the *Ginevra* to Verocchio."

"I read somewhere that Leonardo actually tried to use dust for painting," she said. "Of course, I don't have your kind of education."

Helmut, who had always felt a little sorry for himself because his family had fled Berlin so abruptly, listened unhappily to what Rachel told him about herself. Her suffering had been so much greater than his. He had found it painful enough to be thrust into a new school; learning a new language was so traumatic that he could not even remember how it had come about. He had totally repressed German, to the point where he actually had to take a language course in it after entering graduate school. What could have been worse? Now he knew.

They had parted early in the morning, after a long walk through the litter strewn streets of midtown New York back to her hotel near Pennsylvania Station. Helmut had felt exhilarated, especially after she agreed to see him the very next afternoon. Here at last was a woman who interested him. There was something so wild about her, so direct, so determined, so self-assured. It was just a little frightening.

She was waiting in the lobby when he arrived the next afternoon at two, her feet in sandals and her strong legs bare and crossed as she sat in a leather armchair, reading the *New York Times Magazine*. She wore a girlish white cotton dress printed with red cherries. Helmut reached to shake hands European style and she grasped his fingers, pulling herself upright. Then she kissed him.

"I just know we're going to be great friends," she said. "So we might as well act the part." They strolled over to Fifth Avenue and climbed to the open top of the double-decker bus. The wind rippled through her pale blond hair which today she had pulled back into a casual pony-tail, held by a bunch of fake cherries. Helmut gave her a running commentary on the notable places they passed: the Flatiron Building, which had once been New York's tallest building and whose bulk concentrated the wind so powerfully that the 1909 Baedecker warned that passers-by in stormy weather were sometimes whirled off the sidewalk; Union Square, where stray bums in long, shapeless overcoats had replaced all but one or two of the fiery radical speakers; and finally Washington Square, whose stunted arch conveyed the Americans' suspicion of grandiose monuments: it would never challenge the Arc de Triomphe or the Brandenburg Gate.

The park nearby, however, was green and packed with Sunday strollers. A few artists had set up lackluster displays -- clowns, sunsets, seascapes, city views -- and sat nearby, smoking and sunning themselves.

"Everybody says that Greenwich Village is dead," he explained, "but then, they've been saying that for decades. Somehow, the artists in the rest of the country haven't heard that news and when they come to New York, they still head straight for this neighborhood. Only they can't afford to live in the Village itself, so they hole up in all sorts of tenements nearby. Right now, East Tenth Street is getting hot."

He bought them orange popsicles filled with vanilla ice cream and they ambled past red brick row houses dating from colonial days toward University Place, where a few people sat outdoors self-consciously drinking coffee and imagining themselves in Paris. "New York's only sidewalk cafe," he said. "The coffee costs $2."

Rachel had clasped his hand as they walked and Helmut felt somewhat anxious. Much to his parents' disappoint- ment, he had never gotten interested in women. Introduced to this or that daughter of his parents' friends, he had been polite, but had never followed up. At school, both the boys and the girls had considered him a grind. After he had passed his thirtieth birthday he had hoped to slip, unnoticed and with minimum discomfort, into confirmed bachelorhood. Now that his father was gone, his work kept him very busy. And here he was, strolling under the trees on East Ninth Street, with a blonde European female on his arm. What would happen next? How would it all end? The long row of uncertainties left him upset.

Walking and talking, they had covered miles of lower Manhattan and both were glad to sit down when they reached Chinatown. A Sunday's rest never came to those dark narrow lanes jammed with Chinese on mysterious Oriental errands. Ducks lacquered with a brown sauce hung in the windows of busy butcher shops, where cleavers descended with an executioner's finality. At last, they wandered into a basement space totally lacking ambiance. They sank into straight wooden chairs and soon the waiter brought heaping bowls of lobster Cantonese, egg foo young, and fried rice.

"What a magical day," said Rachel, cracking her fortune cookie. "It says, 'A fat purse cannot regain a lost appetite.' That must be the restaurant owner's personal proverb. What's yours?"

Helmut frowned. "Who knows this morning what will happen tonight?" he read.

They walked out into the warm evening and jostled through the crowd toward Chatham Square, where the Bowery's lost souls sat or slept on the sidewalk. A taxi took them back to Rachel's hotel. At the entrance, Helmut stuck out his hand for a formal goodbye and Rachel took it -- but she didn't let go. Without a word, she guided him to the elevator, to her room on the tenth floor, and when the steel door had slammed shut, she embraced him with a passion that left his heart pounding.

"It's too early to say goodbye," she said playfully. "You don't even have to get to work tomorrow. And neither do I.

So..." She kicked off her shoes and removed the fake cherries holding her hair. Then she pulled Helmut's gray cashmere sweater over his head. He should have left immediately, invented another appointment for which he was already late. He should have told her that he was engaged, married, ill, maimed in the war. His face burned as Rachel hiked up her skirt and plunked herself onto his lap. She was unbuttoning his shirt and giggling.

"Bet you thought it would be a great struggle to get me into bed," she said. "Surprise! I've been wanting this ever since I spotted you yesterday, through the window of your gallery. Why do you think I went in?"

Helmut felt overwhelmed by the energy of this grinning, half-naked female. Her scent made him weak and he thought bitterly about the silly message in his fortune cookie. He felt limp as she efficiently unbuckled his belt, unzipped his pants, and then pulled off the dress with the cherries printed on it. Clutching what clothes remained, Helmut stepped primly to the window, which faced a sooty brick wall, and drew the blinds. Then Rachel was upon him, pressing herself against his back and reaching around to loosen his grip on his trousers.

In his early adolescence, Helmut had peeked into relevant pages of medical books in the library, researching what this "it" his contemporaries whispered about really was. This was definitely not the notion of "it" he had acquired there. The heavy breathing was absent and so was the tickling. Neither had the dreams that accompanied his noctural emissions indicated the savageness of sexual encounter. Soberly, he had pictured it more like slipping his foot into a silky sock and had shrugged off the electricity that this act might generate.

No one had described to him the feel of sweating flesh, the odor of bodily secretions, or the eventual loss of control that consumed the isolated self. This last frightened him the most. The woman was so damned unpredictable. Her mouth, her fingers, her hairy places pursued him and challenged him to answer. The response forced him from his habitual observation post high above himself, the parapet from which he serenely monitored the activities of one Helmut Rosenfeld, art expert, picture dealer, individualist.

In the final rush, he felt himself falling, sinking, clawing hopelessly to regain his ledge. Too late. Nerves and muscles he had never been aware of took over, pulsating and exploding in a totally uncontrollable manner. He became aware of Rachel's noises, her grip on the small of his back, and dared not look at a face that sounded contorted and strained.

"So," she said at last. "So we had a virgin to deal with." She laughed. "Scared you, didn't it?"

Somehow, she simply refused to consider his embarrassment, nor did she seem to assign any cataclysmic dimension to what they had just done. All this intimate fiddling and fondling appeared to be no more significant to her than eating a pastrami sandwich. Helmut strenuously analyzed the components of her casualness, but in the end, he never could let go of his innate, protective reserve. Only Filippo, strangely, had eased his anxiety. A weak boy, despite his years; a lump of self-indulgent clay with the slack flesh of a Caravaggio urchin; Filippo posed no threat; flung no challenge.

Helmut considered, once again, the boy-man slumped in the seat behind the Maserati's steering wheel.

"Looks like we can make the 6:30 ferry at Menaggio," Filippo now said. "I need a bath. This road is already a bore. By the time we get through with all these round-trips, I'll be jumping out of my skin."

On the dot of seven, they pulled into the garage of the villa in Bellagio. Helmut wondered what the Swiss border guard had done with his card.

Chapter 9

Portraits

L isette stood beaming at the kitchen door and ceremoni- ously pecked each of the four travellers on both cheeks. Then she briskly clapped her hands.

"No dawdling, *s'il vous plait*. The rice is almost done, the *blanquette de veau* awaits you. And François has brought fresh salad greens from the garden. Wash the hands only and then dinner is served."

Despite Lisette's enveloping love, Rachel felt gritty and exhausted. Even the view of the cathedral's sculptures, illuminated in deep relief by the last sunlight of this June day, failed to give her a lift. The work in Bellagio had been physically gruelling. But even as they sweated and rushed, Rachel had to smooth over a mass of conflicting relation- ships -- including her own. Helmut and Filippo presented a bizarre couple: the dealer trapped in obsession; the collec- tor dissolving in self-pitying dependency. Almost as a reflex, Filippo had tried to seduce Maria. Although unsuccessful, the web of sexual tension had left Rachel feeling strained almost beyond endurance.

The trip back to Chartres had been a nonstop dash. Rachel had slept through the stunning passage over the Simplon Pass -- had not Caesar worked on his accounts while crossing the Alps? -- while Maria took her turn at driving. Stashed in the trunk of the Citröen were the last few of the Baritsch pictures. The rest had gone earlier with Ilana and Luc in a rented van. And now they were all safely tucked into the temperature-controlled sub-cellar, which happened to share a common wall with the Chartres facade.

Rachel smiled as she tried to imagine the scene inside the Villa Tazzi, probably at this very moment. By now, the alarm bells would be ringing in quite a few places around the globe. The Baron was probably on his way home from America. The insurance people might already be there, deciding whether, and when, and how to notify the police. In art thefts, as in kidnappings, there was often consider-able delay, as the owners (or next of kin) awaited a message from the perpetrators.

Well, the message had already been sent. The last pic-ture taken out had not been replaced by a replica in the original frame. Instead, Rachel had thought it amusing to replace the *Toilette of Venus*, a work Rubens had copied almost stroke for stroke from a Titian, with quite a differ-ent picture. Instead of an ample beauty clutching draperies over her nakedness while contemplating her reflection in a mirror held by Cupid, the frame now held a portrait of the Teutonic goddess Freyja.

That would get everybody's attention, especially since the picture was so glaringly new. Frontal, monumental, swathed in draperies, her blond hair streaming like a yellow banner, the figure was more poster than painting. Her sinewed arm pointed stiffly toward a swastika flag, while the rest of the background was daubed in sentimental pinks. Rachel had acquired the picture in Munich from a painter who had risen to prominence under the Nazis for mass producing precisely the sort of work Hitler admired. After the war, the man had turned to picture-postcard landscapes and eventually found a ready market among American soldiers stationed in Germany. He had actually been grateful to barter the portrait of Freyja to Rachel for a jar of Nescafé.

At the time, she had wondered why she had bothered with this exchange at all. Perhaps it was her pleasure in the man's abject thanks. And now, the grotesque Freyja was at last making herself useful. Hands washed, Rachel joined the others at dinner.

※※

Bettman Levin felt the incipient sauna of summer in New York as he turned into the converted warehouse on Lafayette Street in New York's Soho. And this was still June, he reflected, as he entered the battered freight elevator and pushed the button for five. Ascending, he could hear the din of many voices, all coming from the Horus Gallery, where the last opening of the art year was in progress. He stepped into the crush, which had overflowed onto the landing, an assortment of modishly garbed men and women chattering between sips of white wine and studiously turning their backs on the paintings inside.

Pushing through the crowd, Venetia Dimble threw herself around him, and kissed him on the lips before tucking a mimeographed press release into his pocket.

"Bettman darling," she burbled, "I just knew you wouldn't miss the most important show of the year. This is the one people will be talking about all summer. Come and meet the artist."

She clenched his elbow and steered him relentlessly toward a disheveled young man who had not quite outgrown adolescent acne. He was wearing a washed-out black T-shirt above a tie-dyed dhoti and Mexican tire-soled sandals on somewhat grimy feet. In his left nostril beamed a tiny diamond. Introduced by Venetia, Harold Hup ignored Levin's outstretched hand; instead, he bowed gravely and pressed his palms together in an Oriental-style greeting.

"Harold is fascinated by Sanskrit symbolism," said Venetia brightly. "He spent a year in Benares, of all places, immersing himself in it all. Can you imagine? Living in one of those hovels on the banks of the Ganges where the devout Hindus go to die. Bathing in the river. Chanting over the bodies consumed by flames." She shuddered with the thrill of it all.

Without a word, Harold bowed prayerfully and turned away.

"He's on a vow of silence right now," Venetia explained. "He believes that anything he says would dilute the message conveyed by his pictures. It was all I could do to persuade him even to appear at the opening. Such a sensitive soul, he wanted to stay home and meditate."

Above the heads of the crowd, Levin had difficulty viewing Hup's paintings, except to note that the tops of them, at
least, were uniformly painted in a purplish brown monochrome. From the photographs which Venetia had sent to
him in advance, he knew they were oddly shaped: some only
two feet wide and eight feet tall; others horizontal, but of
similar proportions. The color, the advance announcement
reported, symbolized the murk of earthly existence. On
it, in the loose, broad strokes of a billboard- paster's flaccid brush, the artist had painted such symbols as a circle
for the wheel of existence; a triangle for heaven, air, and
earth, and a crude phallus for the god Shiva of creation. The
tall shapes meant to convey humanity's aspirations, while
the wide ones referred to the supine position of mankind's
actual fate.

"Meditating on the human condition?" Zelda looked
up at him from the folds of a gossamer gray cloak, held at
the shoulder by a striking Mexican clasp of onyx and silver.
"Haven't seen you since the last blizzard in February. Why
so withdrawn?"

"Busy," he said vaguely. "Trips hither and yon into
the hinterlands of American culture. Art buffs, you know,
they're everywhere these days, lurking in the cornfields
around Des Moines, blinking in the sunshine in Tucson.
Stick a pin in the map and an art lover will bleed."

Bettman had deliberately avoided contacting her since
that ghastly night when he had fled from her bed. He could
have dealt with his sexual embarrassment; they were, after
all, divorced. But he was not at all certain that he would have
been able to keep from telling her the tale of the *Ginevra di*

Benci. And that tale was far from over. He had not been able to consign the painting to a safe deposit box. Why own it if he could never enjoy looking at it? Never hang it on the wall, where that enigmatic presence could surprise his fantasies? No, it could inspire other fantasies among the housebreaking set. So *Ginevra di Benci* lived in his closet swathed in tissue paper, acid free tissue-paper.

"Heard you had a nice visit with the Baron Baritsch," Zelda said.

"Yes, he was most pleasant. Gave us the complete run of the place for nearly a week. The photos turned out terrific. I've just finished writing the captions. The article will lead off the next issue."

"Well, I hope you have room for a little postscript." Zelda drew closer to his ear. "I can't really talk much about it in the midst of this mob. I really don't know all that much, except that the Baron flew home in tremendous haste last week. Seems that some Nazi painting got smuggled into the Villa Tazzi. A Rubens appears to be missing. The conservators are checking the other pictures now. They all seem to be in place and intact, but something very funny has gone on."

"Well, keep me informed," Levin said lightly. "I must dash. Deadline, you know."

※❀※

For once, the Baron was glad when the sharp sputter of the fishermen's boat awakened him. His clock said 7:23 a.m., but he had no sooner thrown his legs over the side of the bed than his body notified him that it was the middle of the night. Would the doctors ever find a quick cure for jet lag? He had barely brushed the fuzz off his teeth before Franz arrived with the breakfast tray.

"Madame is flying in, arriving in Milan on Lufthansa at ten-fifteen." Franz was was not quite sure how to refer to Rosalinda, but so long as there was no divorce he had decided to act as though she had merely gone to Munich for a weekend.

"Yes. Please leave the tray on the table next to the window. And send the car to meet her."

"I've already taken the liberty of arranging that, Herr Baron."

"Be sure to get the name and number of anyone else who calls. But don't tell them I'm at home. Just say I'll call back when I return. It also might be wise to notify the Bellagio *carabinieri*. Not of anything amiss with the collection, but they might check the streets around the villa for unusual loiterers. All we need is a few *paparazzi* to complicate matters."

Franz withdrew and the Baron turned to his coffee and croissant. The poached egg, clotted in its blue Meissen saucer, looked revolting. Outside the lake shimmered invitingly, the hills and mountains on the opposite shore undulating in the bluish light of early morning. Someone was already out in a tiny sailboat, bouncing in the wake of the departing fishermen. The fragrance of early summer wafted upward from the garden and a bed of Oriental iris just below his window gave new meaning to blue. Even Van Gogh hadn't been able to trap their infinite variations completely.

Showered and dressed in the jeans and red knit shirt he had picked up in America, the Baron walked over to the gallery. He closely studied some of the paintings he had lived with for decades. Everything looked perfectly fine; he was shocked to realize that, except for that disgusting piece of Nazi kitsch, he could have gone for years without perceiving the deception. Of course, a potential buyer would have brought in the experts: X-rays, infra-red photos, spectroscopic studies, chemical analysis, an arsenal of modern science cross-examining the most trivial or innocent expression of an artist's talent.

Awaiting him in the office was his conservator, Martin Strubel, who introduced an insurance investigator, Hendrik Paalen. Strubel, who had flown back with the Baron the previous day, looked wan and kept running his hands through the bushy head of hair he hoped would give him an "artistic" look. Paalen sat with his briefcase centered precisely on knees primly clenched together.

"It's most puzzling," he said. "Thieves usually try to postpone as long as possible any discovery of their foul deeds. Hanging a replica is a favorite device. That's how the robbers of the Budapest National Museum -- you may remember the case a few years ago -- remained undetected for more than a month. Their replicas were crude, but apparently the curators had long ago stopped looking at the original paintings. The fraud was discovered only when one of the pictures was taken away for cleaning. In other instances, the thieves settle for one or two pieces, cut them hurriedly out of the frame and make off. But here we have an altogether more sophisticated scheme."

"I'm truly impressed by the craftsmanship," said the conservator. "The few pieces I've had time to examine could easily pass muster by the naked eye. Except, of course, that atrocity of a Nazi painting. They obviously wanted to announce the foul deed. But why?"

"Certainly there's a message there," said the Baron. "You may recall that my grandfather, who formed this collection, was rather enchanted with Hitler and his Nazis in the early days. He hoped that they would bring order back to Germany. Not that his admiration for their program affected his taste in art. He was appalled by the sort of kitsch they encouraged, although he thought it might be necessary from a propaganda standpoint. Has anyone taken down this so-called Freyja painting?"

In response, the two men rushed out into the gallery and the Baron helped them to detach the large, heavy canvas from its hooks. Neatly taped to the precise center on the back was a plain white envelope. Inside the envelope was a single sheet. The typed message on it read:

The Baritsch collection was formed by an evil man and for an evil reason.

To break the pall of evil that obscures these beautiful works, justice demands that something good be done.

The details will be found in an advertisement to be published once only on June 12 in the classified advertising section of the *Neue Zürcher Zeitung* under "Wanted."

Meanwhile, may the Baron appreciate the aesthetic delights of his art free from financial cares.

P. S. A copy of the Rubens (or, more accurately, our copy of Rubens' copy of the Titian) exists and will be sent after the instructions have been followed.

The paper, a nondescript sheet typed on a machine with dirty keys, rippled in a slight breeze.

"Three days of waiting," said the conservator glumly, "and then who knows what kinds of outrageous demands they'll make."

"The usual procedure in these cases," said the insurance man, "is to notify Interpol immediately. A bulletin then alerts border guards and at least immobilizes the stolen property in one spot. I would recommend that we proceed likewise in this instance."

"But we don't even know when the pictures were stolen." The conservator sounded desperate. "It could have been any time during the month of May. By now, those blasted pictures could be in Timbuktu."

"Blasted?" the Baron's eyebrows lifted mockingly. "Please. The missing items are the grandest expressions of European achievement. Although I must admit that these copies they left behind are quite an achievement too."

"But they're worth zilch," the conservator moaned.

"My, my. This is the first time I can recall that a colloquialism has passed your lips. Goodness coming out of evil? My dear Strubel, we may already be seeing a bit of it emerging. I'm enjoying your straightforward talk, at last. All those stilted circumlocutions can be so tiresome. Carry on. I believe Madame has arrived."

He strode away down the long corridor. Halfway to the great front hall, he opened his arms and actually ran to embrace the blonde figure standing there, in a halo of light from the open doors behind her.

※❖※

The Maserati was eating up the miles, the tunnels and bridges smoothing out the mountains along the autoroute to La Spezia. By late afternoon he would be too far away to change his mind. At some point, Filippo would have to telephone home. He could already hear Carmina's shrill catalog of actual and potential disasters in Vicenza. Well, she would just have to put off the clamor until he could get back.

He had fully intended to drive to Milan for some gallery-hopping. After all the troubles at home, he deserved the kind of deference the dealers there showed him. Already, he could picture Angelo Basani bowing him into the Galleria del Duomo, settling him into a cushy suede chair, sending his boy out for espresso. But at Brescia, he impulsively turned south toward Cremona. At Piacenza, he could still have taken the E2 to Milan, but instead, he continued south and already his depression was lifting as the vague outlines of what to do next emerged. In an hour, he was zipping through the outskirts of La Spezia, where he continued south.

From the twin ribbons of highway clinging to the mountainsides, Filippo could see a thin line of surf far below to the right. The modest resorts along this shore relied heavily on garish blue and orange paint to lure German and Scandinavian campers. He passed the exit for Carrara, where the quarries were still yielding the kind of marble favored by Michelangelo. Maybe he should have bought into sculpture, he thought, instead of betting so heavily on those volatile American painters.

There was nothing intrinsically wrong with the paintings he owned; they just hadn't been properly promoted, he thought. Lots of other artists had been ignored during their lifetimes and then suddenly appreciated beyond all reason. Look at Gauguin. Look at Vermeer, an artist who was practically unknown until about one hundred years ago. Over the centuries, even Rembrandt had his ups and downs on the market. Later generations saw things in those artists' works to which their contemporaries were blind. With the right kind of publicity, Filippo was sure that he could telescope the process.

From Pisa, Filippo called home and endured Carmina's tirade. The car had broken down near Bergamo, he told her; a cracked distributor. A replacement had been ordered from Milan and once it arrived, the mechanic would take more than day to install it. At this news, Carmina's rage subsided, but she certainly didn't sound sympathetic ... yet. Filippo smiled as he contemplated the prospect. Then he placed a call to Naples, person to person.

For the first time in months, Filippo actually felt light-hearted. Usually, long hours of driving caused stabbing agony in his maimed leg, but today it just tingled, not too unpleasantly. Yes, he thought, for too long, he had been passive, waiting for the next blow to fall, reacting to the actions of others. But now the tide was turning; he was taking a strong hand with his own fate and soon lots of people would be scrambling to sort out the cards *he* was dealing. When he reached Civitavecchia, Filippo impulsively wrenched the car off the main highway and drove alongside the shore until the narrow road stopped at an ornate iron gate. Why not surprise Bellanna?

To Filippo's disappointment, there was not much of a party in progress. In the large salon overlooking the water, two couples were dancing desultorily to a tape of some up-and-coming English band; some unkempt combo out of Liverpool, Bellanna explained, called The Beatles. She rolled her brown, liquid eyes and drew Filippo down a hallway into the library. From the intricately inlaid desk, she pulled a drawer exquisitely fitted with drug paraphernalia: a pair of carved miniature meerschaum pipes for smoking hashish; a mirror, razor blade, and tiny spoon for cocaine; an embossed silver syringe for heroin.

"What about it?" she asked, poking his ribs suggestively. "Make yourself at home in the garden of earthly delights."

"Just a little snort for a pick-me-up. It's too early in the day for mainlining."

"A sudden attack of prudence? Perhaps a sign of old age?"

Bellanna had this irritating habit of asking rhetorical questions, but she did pour a generous line of white powder onto the mirror. Frowning, Filippo dipped the tiny spoon into it and adeptly sniffed the contents up one nostril. He did the same with the other.

"Feeling better? Feeling that surge of eternal youth?"

"It's been a long drive," Filippo replied. "I'll be off in the morning. Naples calls."

"Indeed?"

They returned to the salon, where he noticed a cold buffet set on a side table. He selected a plateful of anti-pasto and ate, while the others watched. Somebody had put on a jazz tape. A few more people arrived in a burst of introductions, but conversation languished as those in the room retreated into their own fantasies. Filippo soon went upstairs and let himself into one of the vacant guest bedrooms. He unstrapped his prosthesis and snuggled into the crisp linen sheets. How blissfully one could sleep in someone else's bed.

He awoke soon after sunrise. The villa was silent and before seven he was on the road. By mid-morning he was in Naples, jostling the car through the central city's perpetual traffic stoppage. How could so little movement be accompanied by so much shouting and cursing? It was a relief to tuck the car into a guarded spot near the Piazza Municipio. He walked quickly through the crowded, narrow, nameless alleys of Spaccanapoli, its old pastel buildings spotted, like venerable beasts, with patches of rust and mildew. Above him, housewives were already reeling in dried clothes, brightening the task with shrieked conversations with some neighbor across the way.

In a few minutes, Filippo reached a once-white stucco wall the length of a block and twelve feet high. Glass shards of various colors sparkled along the top. He pressed the unobtrusive bell next to a smooth wooden door painted blue as the mantle of a Renaissance madonna. Apparently, someone had been observing from above, for a buzzer sounded immediately, and when he pushed the door, it opened. He walked across a carefully groomed, symmetrical garden, squinting as the bright sunlight bounced off the pale gravel walk. At the far end, another door was open, like a black hole.

"You're late," said a rat-like little man in a washed-out pink shirt and baggy white cotton trousers. "He's upstairs."

Filippo's eyes adjusted to the gloom as he followed the man up a flight of splintery steps. He was let into a shuttered room, where an immensely fat man reclined in a wicker rocker, reading *L'Osservatore Romano*. He wore a straw hat with a black band.

"You're late," he said, dropping the paper. "Sit." He pointed to a wicker footstool.

Chapter 10

Grissaille

F ranz wondered if the Baron would ever ring for his breakfast. It was almost nine and still not a peep from the master bedroom. Gingerly, Franz allowed a romantic fantasy to swirl briefly inside his stolid Swiss brain. He arranged dewy yellow tea-roses on a gleaming chrome serving cart and smiled. It was good to have Madame home again.

Behind drawn blinds inside the bedroom, a tall hump in the eiderdown marked the spot where Baron Karl T. Baritsch and Rosalinda lay tightly entwined on the king-size bed. Although asleep, they gripped each other's bodies with the blissful relaxation following a passionate night. Karl snuffled softly and immediately fell back into sleep as Rosalinda carefully disentangled herself from his embrace.

The last two days had been an incredible roller coaster. First came Karl's worried call from New York. "Something's gone wrong with the collection." His voice sounded high and tight; she knew that he had telephoned her only after much internal agonizing.

"What do you mean, wrong?" Why did he have to use such flat circumlocutions, even when he was clearly in distress? Rosalinda really did not wish to be drawn back into Karl's staid, repressed, unspeakably boring orbit. Not now, just when she was getting back into the lively Munich scene.

"I don't know exactly what's wrong," Karl said. "I had a call this morning from Carlo Alfieri, you remember him, don't you? The chief guard at Bellagio."

"But of course I remember him," said Rosalinda sharply. "I saw him almost every day for ten years. And I left less than six months ago. Really, Karl, why do you always have to stuff your anxiety into such banal sacks? Clearly, you're very upset about something to do with the collection. So why not convey your worry and fear or whatever to me? Don't hold back. Let go."

Rosalinda was flabbergasted to hear sobs, great racking gales of tears crackling halfway around the world.

"I ... I don't know what passed over me," said Karl in embarrassment when he calmed down. "To be honest, I've been feeling odd ever since you left; detached and disinterested, I guess. And when they told me that something was the matter with the collection ... it was crazy ... I felt glad!"

Rosalinda felt compelled to see for herself what was transpiring in Bellagio. When she spotted Karl sprinting down the hallway toward her the next day, she wondered what had gotten into this taciturn man. And when the rest of the day passed in excited conversation and affectionate gestures, she began to suspect that her stay in Bellagio would stretch on for quite a while.

Hand in hand, they had walked through the galleries, pausing to study each picture. Rosalinda alternately felt grief over loss of the pictures, rage that such a theft was possible, and ... and a creeping feeling of admiration for the replicas.

At the Munich *Alte Pinakothek*, she had often seen fakes side by side with the genuine article. Most fakes were pathetically obvious: the colors too flat or too garish; the brushstrokes nervous or jagged; the textures muddy; the details blurred. Above all, to the eye of a connoisseur a fake lacked the unmistakable aura emanating from a genuine masterpiece. Though its components were hard to explain to the layman, most experts believed in this aura and had experienced it. The great art expert Berenson had described it as a prickling in the back of his neck. Looking at these pictures, Rosalinda sensed neither the golden glow of the masterpiece's aura, nor the leaden footprint of the fake. Instead, the work before her jibed uncannily with the work it replaced. But how could that be?

She felt the Baron's tug on her hand. "Enough of all this sobriety. Have you noticed that it's still a gloriously sunny day out there on the lake?" He led her to the window and pointed to the dock, where a sleek speedboat bobbed lazily against its ropes. "I bet it wouldn't take more than fifteen minutes for Franz to pack a luscious picnic supper into that boat. What about it? Do you think we can jump into our bathing suits and get there faster than he can?"

His lighthearted air carried Rosalinda back to the first day she had met the Baron in the bitter cold of the *Alte Pinakothek* library. She had thought that nothing was left of the spark between them and now, suddenly, it flamed again, fanned by seeming adversity. She had, in fact, overheard Karl ordering the picnic right after lunch.

They reached the boat-landing at the same time as Franz, who solemnly carried, as though it contained the British crown jewels, a gigantic wicker hamper. He tucked it under the back seat. There, Rosalinda glimpsed a towel-wrapped bottle of Piper Heidsieck chilling in an ice-filled silver bucket. Karl pushed the starter and Rosalinda collapsed onto her seat, laughing, as the boat leaped forward.

"I just can't resist buzzing the fishermen's houses," Karl shouted into her ear. "And I do hope we disturb their siestas." He bucked the boat over the wake of the ferry to Menaggio and then turned it south for a flying run toward Grotta Bulgaro. On the shore of this western leg of the lake, the pretty, fragrant resort villages were expanding toward each other and soon would form one tawdry, crowded strip all the way down to Como at the lake's southern tip. Sun-starved Dutch and Germans and Swedes were ruining the very setting they came to savor. Still unspoiled, however, was the tiny village of Grotta Bulgaro. Saved from the motorized mob because the highway engineers had been unable to tunnel through the rocky shale overhang blocking the road to its heart, the village was approachable only by a footpath or over the water. At the town's north end, the lake lapped into a deep and eerie cavern, the *grotta* which gave the place its name.

Rosalinda recalled visiting here only once before, an idyllic afternoon in the first summer they had spent in Bellagio. Karl now guided the boat into the grotto and leaped lightly to the shore to secure the painter. Tucked between willows weeping into the water was a tiny sand beach and here they spread out a blanket and a checked cloth and their portable feast. The champagne cork bobbed away on the lake and they sipped from tulip-shaped goblets and nibbled Dutch cheese crisps.

Rosalinda wiggled on the blanket and then stood up, shedding her bathing suit. The last bit of sunlight formed a halo around her body as she stood above Karl, frankly preening. "Not bad," he said, lazily looking up at her ripe, swelling breasts, her smooth belly, her golden tufts of bush. He reached for her.

"Not so fast." Giggling, she evaded his hand and turned toward the lake with a teasing swagger. He lunged up and just missed grabbing her before she ran lightly into the water. Without a glance around to see if anyone was watching, Karl jumped out of his bathing suit and followed her, with great, frothy splashes. They both slipped on the weeds festooning a hidden rock, collapsing into the water. They went under and reappeared, mimicking the dignified file of ducklings passing offshore. They laughed and grabbed, and went under again.

And then they lay grinning and panting on the blanket. Rosalinda felt deliciously slippery inside and out, open, wanting to show him how vulnerable she really was. He touched her with exquisite lightness, like an egret's feather, caressing elegantly, yet with purpose. She reached out to him. "Please. Now. Now."

The recollection now flooded back into his brain; he stirred languidly in bed as Rosalinda sleepily touched his back. One of this world's great privileges had to be this leisured awakening in the morning; this was the true luxury of the rich, this freedom to hover in the creative limbo between deep sleep and full consciousness. His left hand was groping lazily toward her body for reassurance. A sharp line of sunlight under the blinds hinted at the lateness of the hour and Rosalinda sat stark upright. It was June 12.

She had no sooner pushed the bell than Franz appeared; he must have been lurking outside. He was rolling a cart laden with tempting breakfast possibilities: a crystal bowl of wild strawberries; a pyramid of croissants; a tray of creamy cheeses; a platter of cold cuts. Franz was already pouring coffee from a silver pot when Rosalinda spotted the advertisement, under "Wanted," page thirty-seven, in the *Neue Zürcher Zeitung*.

The letters leaped out at her, a cruel intrusion upon an idyllic scene:

"Confession is good for the soul. The truth shall make you free. Honesty is the best policy. For details, see letter for Freyja, Poste Restante, Bellagio."

"Who gives a hoot anyhow?" Karl was carefully measuring out a sensible dollop of cream over his strawberries. "We can live very nicely without all this art complication. Better than with it."

Rosalinda was inclined to agree. Still, the whole mysterious business was too intriguing to ignore. Besides, if they didn't respond, the thieves might get nasty. They sounded like fanatics. It could even be dangerous.

When Franz re-appeared, he found a couple grinning idiotically at each other among the ruins and scraps remaining of their lavish breakfast. Following a quick run to the post office, he was solemnly bearing a white envelope on a silver tray. He backed out and Karl began to read:

"Sorry for that parade of cliché proverbs, not to mention inflicting the grotesque Freyja upon you. Here's what needs to be done."

It was neatly typed in élite on cheap white notepaper.

"You know damned well that there are no real Baritsch Old Masters. The stolen items are no more genuine than the replacements we left behind and have no more value than Freyja. Therefore, you must cancel the proposed sale and carry on as before."

※❂※

The red telephone on Wesley Till's desk was shrilling. He had tried to dissuade Alex Clarendon from installing this direct line into his office. But the museum president had insisted, saying that it was the only way to maintain secure communication on extremely sensitive matters. Money matters is what he meant, and Till cringed at the crude conversations that were sure to follow after the red phone rang. As though it were a poisonous adder, he picked it up.

"What do you mean cancel the Baritsch sale?" Clarendon often blared into the phone without preliminaries.

"I'm upset about it too, Alex," said Till smoothly. "It seems the Baron's changed his mind. He really didn't explain much; just called to say he's had a change of heart."

"Well, he'll just have to have a change of heart back," said Clarendon curtly. "A lot of people have already decided to bid on those pictures, including me. And the museum absolutely has got to have the funds generated by the commissions, not to mention the exhibition itself. The new building depends on it. You know all that. So why did you even let Baritsch re-open the matter?"

Till was dismayed by Clarendon's disrespectful tone. It was most unseemly coming from this bluff businessman who had amassed a multi-million dollar art collection on the basis of his advice. Clarendon was making him feel like an incompetent errand boy.

"Wes, you're going to Bellagio and you're going to persuade Baritsch to go ahead with the exhibition and ..."

"... and suppose the Baron refuses?"

"Refuses? He's got no damned good reason to refuse. Wes, for years I've watched you persuade people to do things they hadn't dreamed of doing. And now, the entire future of the museum is on the line." He hesitated dramatically. "To be blunt, it's your future too."

The words pounded in Till's ear like a blow.

※❀※

Helmut had arrived in Chartres just in time to partake of one of Lisette's masterpieces. Every year, her brother François made a grand ceremonial when the first *cèpes* of the season burst from the fragrant loam upon the forest floor. This time, he had invited everyone at the Chartres house to his farm near St. Benôit-sur-Loire for the weekend. They had spent most of Sunday in the forest nearby, piling the musky mushrooms into baskets, before returning joyously home with their booty.

Lisette's recipe for mushroom stew was one of those ancient peasant concoctions that never appear in cookbooks. The chunks of meaty mushrooms swimming in a rich brown sauce had probably been a springtime staple already among the forest tribes that harassed Julius Caesar in Gaul. When a friendly chieftain offered him a bowl of this savory stew, the Roman would likely have sopped up the musky juices with bread. Nowadays, boiled potatoes had become *de rigeur*, the waxy texture and parsley aroma being considered the finest complement to the mushrooms' loamy flavor.

"So what are they whispering about in New York?" Rachel thought she knew the answer.

"If you really knew the city," said Helmut, "you'd know they never whisper. They shout. They scream. Or they hint. Either it's huge noises, backed up by professional p.r. people, or it's innuendo ... and sometimes that involves subtle p.r. as well."

"And right now? What's the decibel level?"

"I'm worried because it's nonexistent," replied Helmut. "Till's red telephone rang. Followed by a hasty trip to Bellagio. Followed by his usual summer hibernation in Maine. The museum then signed the Kleist agency to do the p.r. So as best I can tell, the show is on."

"That's nice," said Luc, unenthusiastically.

"Nice?" said Rachel. "What's nice about it? The easiest would have been to persuade the Baron to cancel the show. It seems like we did so, and then Till got him to change his mind."

"If you ask me," said Ilana, "he doesn't much give a damn one way or the other."

"My guess is that the museum is going to do something spectacularly nice for the Baron's collection of modern things," added Maria. "When it comes to making extravagant promises, you know Till is a master."

"No doubt about that," said Rachel. "And he's got so many chips to play with. He could promise the Baron a show of his modern collection. He could sell him some lesser Kandinsky or a Braque out of the warehouse. He could whisper in his ear about the next Chagall some over-greedy speculator wants to put on the market, preferably at a distress price for cash."

Polishing off Lisette's angelic peach tart, they all agreed on the next step.

"So in the morning," said Rachel, "I'll give Bettman Levin his Christmas in July."

❈❈

Ouch. Filippo had leaped out of the car directly onto artifical foot. Damn. He had forgotten how much it hurt to do that after a long stretch of driving. But even the pain couldn't spoil his euphoric mood. The drive from Naples, all fifteen hours of it, had been one long, triumphant fantasy.

Roaring steadily north on the autostrada that ran like a white stripe up the spine of Italy, Filippo allowed his imagination to roll. With only a little outside help -- he had stopped for a joint just once in a rest area near Siena -- he propelled himself through delicious scenarios.

First, there would be the parties. Or would the interviews come first? Then the photographers. They would seek him out in Vicenza. He would immediately have to instruct Carmina and Boldo to clean up the palazzo and order repairs. When the reporters started arriving, those two would learn some respect. Then he would have to spend time in New York. But when would be best? Should he be there when the autumn art season begins in September? No, let them wait. November might be a good time; that's when the New York art parties really got started. On the other hand, Christmas really sparkled in the big city. Yet, the art world practically shut down during the last two weeks of the year.

Filippo sourly abandoned his speculations as Carmina came waddling toward him. Even before he could hear what she said, he saw her arms waving. What now?

✳✪✳

It was a damned nuisance to have Till roosting all summer long in that tumbledown shack of his in Maine. For Zelda Levin, it meant endless trips to the post office to mail off the packets of confidential museum material that just could not be entrusted to the office channels. Trudging through the humid miasma of West 53rd Street, Zelda wished that, for once, the museum director would try spending the summer in the city. Let him experience just a week of the fiendish heat and then maybe he'd agree to close the office for at least the worst summer month.

Unless a miracle came, however, nobody would even get any vacations this summer … except, of course, for Till, who was probably at this very moment paddling his flimsy arms across that arctic pond of his. One dip into its crystalline forty-degree depths had been enough for Zelda. So had the rest of that weekend been more than enough, what with Emily Till drunk the entire time, while her husband studiously ignored her antics. How could he stand being cooped up with that virago of a woman all summer long? It was a question the entire office had inconclusively chewed over many a time.

Today, however, Zelda felt particularly resentful. The Baritsch exhibition was causing an inordinate amount of extra work. For one thing, the trustees were going berserk with devising chic social activities. The night before the opening, Anita Deckman insisted on a sit-down dinner in the museum's galleries, followed by dancing either in the garden or, in case of inclement weather, in the lobby. Then Alex Clarendon added a fund-raising luncheon for building fund donors of $100,000 or more, featuring Baron and Madame Karl Baritsch. But she knew that the chief reason that Clarendon held such an iron grip on the museum presidency was that he knew how to slurp up every last available penny in contributions.

Therefore, the museum would also hold a cocktail reception for donors of $10,000 or more; a wine-and-cheese preview for those who gave at least $5,000, and, finally, a half-hour "private walk-through" for givers of at least $500. All of these events were to take place during the week before the Baritsch collection opened to the public, on September 17. The night before, of course, there would also be the usual mob scene otherwise known as a press preview. Since they had all received voluminous press packets, from which most of them had already written their articles and reviews, the critics had absolutely no further obligation to the exhibition. Free of their duties, they turned into swine.

None of this was new to Zelda. However, this time, an additional, backbreaking task loomed. To make room for the Baritsch exhibition and its attendant hoopla, the New Museum's entire collection would have to spend four months in storage. Even before Till left town, he had scouted various warehouses around the city, winnowing the possibilities down to three, all of which seemed to have equally secure, fireproof, fortress-like facilities. All three were also within a five-mile radius of the museum, less than a fifteen-minute drive away. The security experts all agreed that the only risk -- an infinitesimal risk -- to the museum's collection was concentrated in that tiny segment of time.

The trustees had already authorized the purchase of extra insurance covering that crucial quarter of an hour. There would also be private police to supplement the considerable force supplied by the city to safeguard the move. Till had planned to select from among the three best warehouses, but then had rushed away on his mysterious errand in Italy. Once he was ensconced in Maine, she had badgered him for a decision, all to no avail.

"Can't anything happen down there without my imprimatur?" he had testily scribbled on the margin of a memo asking him about it. "Clarendon has approved all three. So pick the fairest of them all and don't bother me with it again."

Zelda stepped out of the post office into the steambath of the noontime street. She had just ten minutes to get over to the Russian Tea Room, where that charming fellow from the Severini Brothers warehouse had invited her for lunch. Naturally, he was courting a potential customer, but there seemed to be more than a business relationship between them. He was totally different from the cerebral art types she usually met; he was more lighthearted, more amusing and, let's face it, he was certainly more open to new ideas. Zelda had not met an interesting new man in a long time. With luck, she would have five private minutes in the ladies' room to freshen up before he arrived.

※◈※

For weeks, Bettman Levin had been looking forward to this little vacation in the Hamptons. Now that he was in the midst of delicate clothing and accessory decisions, he felt a pang, a worrisome shadow that seemed to have sneaked into his life along with Ginevra di Benci. His first impulse had been to hang the picture; to exult in its sheer magnificence. But suppose the cleaning lady noticed it, what then? It was unlikely that Matilda, the earth mother of the Zion A. M. E. Church, would recognize a Leonardo masterpiece. Yet, she would certainly notice the extra item in her dusting routine. He discarded the idea of a safe deposit box after reading that it was easy for police to get a warrant for searching such places. Not that he was certain that any crime attached to the picture.

So he had kept the picture wrapped in its tissue paper shroud -- he assumed it was acid-free -- tucked behind the luggage which occupied the topmost shelf of his linen closet. Balanced on the stepladder, he dropped a leather valise to the floor and then carefully unwrapped the painting. One more time, he stared into those pitiless eyes and wished that the mouth were softer, the carriage less imperious, and most of all that he had not gotten involved with the lady at all. He replaced her wrappings and wedged her firmly behind another suitcase.

Laid out on his bed was the surprisingly large wardrobe he was packing. The trouble was that one could never anticipate the precise degree of formality in one of these extended summer weekends on the Island. For some stupid reason, asking one's hosts in advance was considered gauche. By contrast, arriving with an overstuffed Pullman case was also considered tacky. The ideal, totally unattainable outside a Bergdorf advertisement, of course, was to bring a small club bag from which one could magically extract tennis and yachting outfits, washed out beachcombing attire, slickers and boots in case of rain, dressy sportswear for luncheon or cocktail parties and (good grief!) formal garb, including a witty printed cummerbund.

Levin was folding his gear into his too-big bag when the phone rang.

"Has the beautiful Ginevra di Benci bent you to her will yet?"

Levin shuddered.

"I don't know what you're talking about," he said stiffly.

"Come off it, Betty. You don't have to play games with your old friend Rachel. You did such a great favor for me. Now I'll do one for you."

"It's OK," said Levin lamely. "I don't want any favors. Just go away."

"But hear me out." She sounded positively manic. "I'm about to give you the art scoop of the century. Free. No strings attached. And it's exclusive for *Art for Tomorrow*."

"You have the greatest talent for barging into my life at the worst moment. Look, I'm leaving for a long weekend in the Hamptons. The limo will be downstairs in just a few minutes. The next issue of *Art for Tomorrow* won't be out until September, so there's plenty of time. Write me a letter with the scoop, okay?"

"Sorry, Betty. I mean, I'm glad your bag is packed. There's a ticket waiting for you at the Pan Am counter. I'll pick you up in Paris tomorrow morning. You are going to be one euphoric journalist when you see what we've got. Ever heard of an art writer winning a Pulitzer? That's how big this story is."

"They all say that," he said wearily. I suppose there's no way I can beg off."

"Not unless you insist on my reporting a certain stolen painting to the N.Y.P.D. I mean, you didn't have to keep the lady if you weren't ready to pay the price."

"Right to the point, as always. *A bientôt.*"

Chapter 11

Sfumato

"The flowers, dammit, where the hell are the flowers?" Anita Deckman was desperately pacing around the museum lobby. Her face was flushed, and the cabbage roses printed on her full skirt churned around as she pirouetted in a frenzied parody of the dance to take place later in the evening. Outside, the temperature hovered around 100 in one of those heat waves that bedevil the northeast in September. The spate of sultry days at that time of year hit hard because no fashion-conscious New Yorker would be caught dead in summer garb after Labor Day. For the tenth time, she flounced through the revolving door and scanned the traffic-choked street outside for any sign of the florist's pink delivery van.

"Freddy promised they'd be here by five," she moaned, darting back inside the air-conditioned lobby.

The last of the visitors to the museum shop were being ushered out by the guards, who impassively endured the public's grumbling about the early closing that had cut short their browsing through worthwhile books and admirably designed goods. The museum galleries had been closed for two days while the entire collection was moved into storage and was replaced by the Baritsch pictures.

A bevy of summer interns from Vassar, Smith, and Bryn Mawr were rushing through the departing crowd, intent on the errands assigned them by Mrs. Deckman. One young woman in a hand-painted silk poncho was arranging engraved programs on a table next to the entry. Another, sweating in a tweed she expected to share with roommates in Poughkeepsie all winter, was gnawing on a pencil while marking up a list of expected guests. A third was nervously pushing her owlish horn-rimmed glasses back up her moist nose while inscribing almost three-hundred name-tags in fine Spencerian script.

The pink truck finally double-parked outside and two burly black men began hauling in great tubs of white chrysanthemums and gilded maple leaves. It took both of them, grunting and straining, to manhandle an eight-foot-tall arrangement of sunflowers through the museum's entry doors. The flowers' association with Van Gogh represented Anita Deckman's most inspired idea for elegant decor, but the short trip in the heat from Madison Avenue and 76th Street had cruelly wilted them.

"Wire them up," she now ordered shrilly, while the florist's driver consulted his clipboard for specific instructions from Freddy. He found nothing there about stiffening the drooping backbones of sunflowers with wire armatures. Anita Deckman ordered him to telephone the florist for instructions.

Upstairs, the scene was equally frantic as Wesley Till directed the hanging of the exhibition. He usually enjoyed the frisson of letting work go until the very last minute, but this one was too close even for his taste. The entire curatorial staff of twelve was now bustling around in mostly useless activity. Till himself sat limply in a wheelchair. Though not crippled, he used it whenever he hung exhibitions as a handy conveyance-cum-throne. He was squinting at his latest arrangement of the wall at the entryway.

Was it really wise to have Hans Memling's *Portrait of a Young Man* facing Titian's *Portrait of Doge Francesco Venier*? The juxtaposition had been one of his last-minute inspirations. It was certainly daring to play the precise brushstrokes, cool palette, and frank-eyed innocence of the German's praying youth against the bravura brushwork, the flaming hues, and the shrewd wisdom in the face of the Italian's mature autocrat. Visible behind the righteous young man was a gentle, orderly landscape; by contrast, the view from the window behind the cunning Venetian ruler included swirling sails and the smoke of naval battle. Paired off, the two paintings enhanced and enriched and explained each other, one and one added up to far more than two. The young man's chaste white linen and praying hands were more pure because of their proximity to the doge's grizzled beard and richly brocaded garments.

But would anyone at all among the opening's festive guests get it? Till pushed back his wheelchair and sighed wearily. So few museum visitors ever bothered to reflect on how and why paintings were hung in a particular order. At an opening, few ever bothered to look at anything at all. It was strange. Having avidly sought an invitation, having paid dearly for it, they were perfectly content to linger in the presence of art masterpieces and guzzle champagne, munch canapés, see and be seen, smile and greet, exchange innocuous, empty remarks. It was not the sort of audience he had envisioned when the creation of a new kind of museum had been his driving ambition.

The past three weeks of frenzied activity had already erased the serenity he had achieved during his summer sojourn in the north woods. He was exhausted; perhaps this contributed to his downbeat mood. But even if the party guests behaved differently, even if they were to crowd around the pictures now occupying the museum's entire exhibition space and exclaim learnedly over this or that painting's sublime qualities, Till knew he would still be dissatisfied. His ideal of art appreciation was a dialogue between the work and the viewer. He enjoyed confronting the artist's creation one on one, *mano a mano*, cross-examining it as to intention and execution before issuing a measured verdict.

Till had felt uncomfortable as he watched the strapping movers lowering the familiar works in the museum's permanent collection from the walls with uncommon tenderness. Till was sad to see the pictures shrouded in gray quilts, and to watch them disappear into the dark cavern of the moving van; so sad that he was glad to be called to his office by a phone call. He had had no children; the consolation for this lack had been his interaction with these inanimate outpourings of the human spirit -- anguished or playful, calm or agitated, a Joseph's coat or monochrome, their meaning blatant or obscure. And then the last of them had been removed from their accustomed place. Late at night, he had stood pensively on the street and watched the parade of vans lumbering away.

The very next morning, another parade of vans began to arrive and another set of movers wearing spotlessly white gloves began carrying the Baritsch pictures across the basement loading dock, into the oversize freight elevators and then into the cavernous, echoing, empty galleries. Till's entire staff had lined up to welcome each of the eighty-three old masters. Using a scale model of the building's interior spaces, he had already made a tentative arrangement for hanging them.

From long experience, however, Till's staff knew that he would continue to arrange and re-arrange obsessively until the very last minute. In fact, he had been known to take pictures down and move them elsewhere all night, long after the guests at the opening had departed. The wheelchair helped to stretch his endurance, while loyalty and awe in the presence of a seeker after perfection kept the staff from fleeing in frustration. Whereas most of the public, including the critics, was blind to them, Till's exhibition hangings were famous among museum professionals for their sensitivity and inventiveness.

The Baritsch pictures had sent Till's staff into aesthetic ecstasies. All the biggest guns of the past were represented, and in the fullness of their mature talent. But one night after everyone had left, Till wandered among them, leaning as they were against the wall, in the places where they were to be hung the next morning. Under spotlights held by a night guard, he had harshly cross-examined them one by one. And he had found them wanting.

Every single picture seemed to be subtly evading his most searching questions. He knew that the provenance was impeccable; each panel had a perfect pedigree: a documented, unbroken chain of ownership stretching from the artist's studio to the present moment. And yet, each picture looked slightly off the mark, vaguely questionable. Finally he had locked up and gone home. And slept poorly, if at all. He awoke at dawn, with a sense of having dreamed chaotically, disquietingly.

The rest of the time had been crowded with activity, decision-making, Anita Deckman's pestering calls about non-alcoholic punch and seating arragements. It was only her two Chagalls, promised but not yet willed to the museum, that had kept Till from exploding in wrath at that terminally silly woman's nervous gyrations. Now she was on the phone again.

"They wired the sunflowers upright," she wailed. "But, Wes, you won't believe it, they sent over the wrong color of wire and now there's a nasty green spiral around the flower stalks. It doesn't match their real color."

Till promised to send a staff restorer to touch up the wire.

"But they'll start arriving in another hour," she groaned, "and what about the caterer and the string quartet. Why aren't they here."

Till promised to investigate these matters immediately.

"Meanwhile," he soothed, "go on home and into a hot bath. Slip into the exquisite dress that I know you've got in the closet. Make yourself beautiful. And get ready to enjoy the party."

He knew that mention of the festivities to come would distract her from further nervous demands. He rolled his chair through the art-decked halls for one last inspection, while the staff followed respectfully behind, picking at imaginary lint and dabbing slices of white bread to erase a few faint fingermarks on the stark white walls. The exhibition was immaculate. And yet the aura, the all-important aura of authenticity exuded by every true masterpiece, this aura seemed faintly, almost imperceptibly, flawed.

Till shook his head. Before the war, he had once tried to see the old Baron's collection, but a sudden opportunity to arrange a Van Gogh exhibition had come up and he was forced to cancel his trip to Munich. That had been most regrettable, especially since the rotting hulks of picture he had examined in Liechtenstein after the war gave no hint of their former glory. Certainly, he had been surprised (stunned is more apt) to learn that someone had been able to resurrect them. In recent years he had included Bellagio on several of his annual trips to Europe. The restorations struck him as a miracle; though he was the son of a devout Methodist, Till did not believe in miracles.

Actually, while admiring the Baron's old masters, Till hoped to interest him in exhibiting his modern works at the New Museum. Who knows? The Baron might even be persuaded to donate something, or to remember the museum in his will. On Till's most recent visit, just before the summer, the Baron had appeared particularly amiable. Till had had no trouble at all persuading him to revoke the abrupt cancellation of the exhibition.

"Then we're on for September," the Baron had said with a puckish smile, as he ushered Till to his waiting car. The museum director was pleased; after more than three decades at his job, he was seldom surprised by the peculiar whims of the rich.

Till's corner office was silent as he wheeled in his chair. He cleared piles of magazines and exhibition catalogs from the stark black leather Mies van der Rohe couch and stretched out. His hands clasped behind his head, resting on the hard cylindrical cushion, he stared at the ceiling. Something was not quite right about the pictures he had just finished hanging, the pictures to be quietly auctioned, the pictures for which bids were already arriving, the pictures whose sales commission would at long last put the museum's finances on a solid basis. To the museum director's peerless eye, the pictures emitted a subtle warning, like a whispered curse.

He had planned a quick nap before it was time to shower and dress in the tuxedo Zelda had picked up from the cleaner's and hung on the chrome clothes tree in the corner. Sleep now was unlikely, but at least he would rest and then adrenalin would carry him through the rest of the evening. But already the adrenalin was pumping.

Till was famous in the art world for his discriminating "eye." In centuries past, the small cadre of dealers and collectors had relied almost completely on their own "eye" to determine what to buy and what to sell and at what price. In the twentieth century, however, the theories and methods of science had spilled over into every scholarly endeavor, even the most subjective and humanistic. Increasingly, art scholars scrutinized archives to piece together a precise chronology of an artist's life and work. They sent bits of paint to laboratories for spectrographic analysis. In many instances, they could date a picture by calculating the atomic half-life of its component pigments. Infra-red photos and X-rays revealed every brushstroke of the artist's earliest intention, from his first tentative sketch to his final alteration.

But Till knew that none of the Baritsch pictures would pass this sort of examination. He had seen for himself how massively all of them had been restored. Though it surely was scientifically possible, no scholar or museum director -- and certainly no dealer -- had dared to draw the cutoff line beyond which the restorer became the painter.

Till had worried about that some years earlier when the one of the New Museum's most valuable paintings, Umberto Boccioni's *The City Rises,* had been charred in a fire. When the weary firemen departed, all that remained of the Futurist masterpiece was a soaked and blackened hulk.

And yet, in twelve months or so it had returned from the restorer's studio, with its restless composition and riotous colors more brilliant than ever. When it was re-hung no one had dared to breathe the word "fake." Amid the champagne toasts during the inevitable festivities marking the picture's return to the museum, Till himself had choked back his qualms. Why stir up trouble?

Rising from the couch, Till stepped into the sleek bath adjoining his office and flipped on the Italian chrome shower.

※⊛※

Riding downtown on the graffiti-smeared Seventh Avenue Express, Bettman Levin closely scanned his fellow-passengers for any sign of hostile intent. He seldom descended into the hellish depths of the New York subway system, but what with the gridlock that a heat wave invariably bred on the city streets, the only reliable way to get to the printer was underground. He tried not to touch any of the banisters, posts, or other fixtures, sticky as they were with black grime and, most likely, colonies of deadly microbes.

At Chambers Street he climbed out of the smelly inferno, crossed to the shelter of a narrow strip of shade and walked north on Hudson Street. The printer occupied all four floors of a cast-iron loft building dating back to the mid-nineteenth century. The facade had not been painted for many decades and its chipped pilasters, arches, and pediments gave off a blistering wave of heat. Inside, a couple of fans stuck in the tops of caked and grimy windows hopelessly stirred the humid atmosphere, trailing fronds of dust. Only Jerry Cooney's office, a cubicle in one corner, set off by a glass partition, boasted a laboring air conditioner.

"Yes, the proofs are ready, and no, you can't change anything." Cooney had greeted Levin with the same formula for at least ten years. The proofs were always ready because Levin always checked by phone before making the trip. The slightest alteration -- there were inevitably a few -- would lead to an overheated shouting match, what passed for a negotiation in this high-strung city.

"How about you bring them in here?" asked Levin. "That way I can read them without leaving sweat-spots."

Cooney looked dubious. He hated to do any special favors for clients. They might think he was a patsy and pretty soon they'd be all over him, maybe even haggling over his prices. Knowing this, Levin tried to look abject.

Certainly, he felt disheveled; the lightweight gray suit he normally enjoyed wearing right after Labor Day encased him like a humid iron maiden. Even if he shed his coat in the airless proof room, the moist wool pants would cling and chafe against his crotch and thighs. He could end up with a tenacious, itchy rash.

"Have a heart, Jerry," he pleaded. "It must be a hundred twenty out there, with all that hot lead in the linotypes."

With the look of St. Peter ushering a supplicant through the pearly gates, Cooney told Levin to clear a bundle of newsprint proofs off a rickety swivel chair. As the printer sauntered out, Levin swept the inky papers to the floor and surreptitiously wiped the seat of the chair with his handkerchief.

"Just don't tell anyone you got special privileges; they could nickel-and-dime me to death." Cooney dropped a stack of slick-paper proofs in Levin's lap. "Here's *Art for Tomorrow* today, ha, ha."

Number three pencil in hand, Levin settled himself at a narrow console table and began to proofread the magazine's October issue. In less than a week, the copies would begin arriving at newsstands. A day or two later, they would appear in subscribers' mailboxes. But even before the magazine came out, the fuse for its explosive content would begin to sputter. The spiciest details were already worked into news releases prepared by Billy Panzer, the magazine's indefatigable publicity agent. The envelopes lay stuffed and stamped in Panzer's office ("poised above the mail slot," is how the man suggestively had put it) waiting for Levin's okay of the proofs. Over the weekend, they would go out and then the media storm would break.

"Who Really Painted the Baritsch Collection?" Levin re-read his own article. It was wonderful how when you had a really good story you didn't have to push it with strong verbs or pump it up with towering adjectives. Simply, directly, it told itself. There were spaces in the proofs for the photographs, keyed to a pile of Xeroxes accompanying the proofs. He gazed at the first one, of the back of a fuzzy figure in white overalls, wielding a tiny brush over a half-painted De Heem flower still life. The scene reminded him of Vermeer's tantalizing *Artist in His Studio*, now often called *Allegory of Fame*. In it, the artist is seated before the easel, with his back to the viewer. He is painting a demure young woman in a blue dress. Her eyes look modestly down, but she stands self-possessed and erect, holding a large yellow book and a brass trumpet. In her neatly plaited blond hair, she wears a laurel wreath. She was the allegory of fame, and the Oriental carpet draped across the picture's upper left, the rich fabrics on a table before her, and the gorgeously detailed map of Holland, with its ships and coats of arms, on the wall behind her signified the wealth and glory of that golden seventeenth century moment in the Netherlands.

The picture was generally considered Vermeer's masterpiece and, of course, the figure of the artist about whose life and personality almost nothing was known, so meticulously painted, baited and provoked the viewer. If only he would turn around; if only he allowed us to meet his gaze. Levin was not the first to harbor that impossible wish. The photograph of the anonymous artist in the first illustration of his article teased him in a similar way as the Vermeer, only he knew who the painter was -- and soon everyone in the whole wide world would know it, too.

Fame? Levin anticipated it with mingled anguish and delight. It was about to burst on him. Would people point him out on the street? Not unless the *National Enquirer* picked up the story. Certainly he would hit the talk shows. But first, the story would sweep through the art world like a tornado. No one would question the truth of what he had written (given the facts and the photos, how could they?), but that wouldn't stop them from slobbering and tearing at him like hyenas.

Typically, the art world lived on rumors and innuendos; many other pictures or whole collections had been questioned in the past, with raised eyebrows, nods, winks, shrugged shoulders, wry smiles. But to publish such a sensational article in a respectable art magazine was another thing entirely. It was against the code and Levin was sure he would pay dearly for transgressing that. On the other hand, the art world had become a stuffy, overheated room and he felt desperate to let in fresh air. As Rachel had emphasized, there had never been a Pulitzer Prize awarded for investigative reporting in art. Maybe this year that barrier would be broken.

❊❊❊

Though they had founded a country without aristocratic titles, Karl thought, the Americans fussed more than anyone else did over calling him Baron Baritsch. That Anita Deckman had actually curtsied in greeting him was really a bit much. He gravely shook her hand and saw her disappointment that he did not kiss it. The cocktail reception in the museum's garden had been brought to an abrupt end by a sudden, spectacular thunderstorm and the rush for shelter in the museum's lobby broke through the stiff formality among the guests, as the rain dissolved some of the elaborate, stiffly lacquered hairstyles of the ladies.

Now the guests swarmed in the lobby and at last the diverse crowd had something in common to talk about -- the storm outside. The caterer's people hastened to bring the bar inside; the disruption certainly did not diminish anyone's thirst. These Americans could stand around for hours, martini glasses in hand, making small talk. They dispensed with titles and called each other by their first names, but everyone seemed nevertheless to know precisely where he or she stood in the class structure.

"You must meet Henry Eckridge. He's one of the genuine self-made tycoons on our board and quite a collector as well." Wesley Till lightly grasped the Baron's elbow and steered him toward the bluff trustee, who was holding forth, for several attentive men on the remarkable staying power of Wall Street's current bull market.

"Ah, the great collector himself." Eckridge greeted Karl with a bone-crushing handshake. "What a pleasure it is to have your marvelous pictures right here in New York City. Frankly, I can hardly wait until we get a glimpse of them later on. I may even sneak away from the dinner table for a little private look-see."

Karl tried to steer the conversation to Eckridge's collection but the man refused to be derailed. It took Rosalinda, in her bouffant pink satin gown, to divert the tycoon from his monologue. At least Eckridge did not struggle with the title and greeted her warmly:

"Madame Baritsch, I presume. You must be sad that your pictures have flown away. Don't worry. We'll take excellent care of them. You never can tell," he giggled archly, "we might even keep some of them permanently."

Karl hoped that the American was not launching into a noisy discussion about the forthcoming auction. That was supposed to be a most private matter, to be talked about, if at all, in glances and whispers. Karl was feeling helpless about the drift of the conversation, when Rosalinda saved the day.

"I understand you've made quite a collection yourself, Mr. Eckridge."

"I'll have to confess," he replied genially. "For most of my life, modern art was all Greek to me. I thought it was a gigantic put-on. I really thought my grand-daughter did better work in her pre-school. But Wesley Till set me right. Invited me to lunch at the Harvard Club and gave a good, fast lecture on the subject. Then, of course, I started reading the headlines about phenomenal prices for your Cézannes and your Toulouse-Lautrecs. I knew that Picasso and Braque couldn't be far behind. Gosh, it was irresistible."

He would have carried on indefinitely, but the lights flashed off and on several times. It was the signal for dinner. The chattering throng began to move toward the escalator, some ascending while still clutching their martini glasses.

"What a relief," Karl whispered to Rosalinda. "I was afraid we would be trapped in that corner all night with that bore."

"Wait till you meet the museum president," she whispered back. "Mr. Alex Clarendon is another one just like that. He's got more money than is good for him and he's discoverd that art is a truly rewarding investment."

They stepped off the escalator into the galleries where the Baritsch Collection was now splendidly displayed. Not that anyone even glanced at the paintings. The partygoers were totally absorbed in finding their names on place-cards at the round tables for eight which filled the floor space. Since the head-table was set up in the corridor outside the galleries, a large black-and-white television screen provided each room with a closed-circuit image of activities there.

On the screen, Karl saw Alex Clarendon giving the two-handed handshake to Wesley Till. Then Henry Eckridge clapped the museum director on the back so hard that Till's slender body seemed to vibrate. Anita Deckman flounced briefly into the picture, her fixed cap-toothed smile contrasting sharply with the tense frown around her eyes. As the Baron and Rosalinda were making their way toward the head table, Karl glanced at the screen once more. A liveried messenger was stiffly handing Till an envelope. The museum director looked puzzled, then thrust it into the pocket of his tuxedo.

As Karl and Rosalinda were getting seated, Clarendon launched into his welcoming address. It sounded boring even to the Baron, who had not attended many such events:

"Wonderful occasion ... excellent turnout ... among the dignitaries present are ... great privilege to be here ... most glittering event of the social season ... unforgettable ... art masterpieces in our midst ..."

Karl's eyes drifted toward Wesley Till, who was fishing the small envelope out of his pocket. Unobtrusively, the museum director ripped it open and extracted a half sheet of white paper with no letterhead. To Karl it looked like there was a typed message of five or six lines. It appeared to be unsigned. Till seemed to blanch as he pushed the papers roughly back into his pocket. Karl saw him whisper a perfunctory apology to Clarendon and then watched Till lurch unsteadily toward the elevator, where he pushed the down button.

Chapter 12

The Black Ship

Helmut was glad he had tolerated the hellish racket of construction, the dirt devils dancing above torn-up streets, the heavy trucks braying under his windows at dawn. Finally, his stoicism was paying off. He had been some sort of urban pioneer back in 1959, leasing this place in the first new apartment house to go up around Lincoln Square since long before the war.

The views from the penthouse on a corner of the 27th floor had been the clincher. To the west, he could make out the open green meadows beyond the industrial badlands of the Jersey shore; in the foreground a green neon sign blinked unforgettably -- "Spry for cooking, Spry for baking." Looking southwest down the river, he could see tiny tugs scudding toward The Narrows.

But on this evening he was looking southeast, beyond the headwall of Central Park South's towers to the illuminated phallus topping the Empire State Building. He leaned on the balustrade of the terrace, savoring a bird's angle on the space two blocks away, where, after three years of non-stop clamor and clanging, the buildings of Lincoln Center were just beginning to emerge. The new Metropolitan Opera House was barely risen from a deep hole in the ground; the New York State Theater no more than a bundle of architects' plans surrounded by the acrimonious hubbub without which no New York endeavor can proceed.

Yet, only an hour ago he had been swept away in Leonard Bernstein's torrential interpretation of Beethoven's *Fifth*. The *Times*' Harold Schonberg might grumble about the acoustics, but the 2,600 who had packed the new concert hall had cheered -- a few boors had whistled -- as the youthful maestro bounced from the wings to the podium for repeated bows.

"More champagne?" Rachel slipped onto the terrace, the Mumm's bottle dripping onto the flagstones.

"Just a drop," said Helmut. "You may have heard about the effect of alcohol on bedroom performance." He stroked her bare shoulder. "Did I ever tell you that the beauty of your clavicle surpasses Botticelli's *Venus*?"

"Is this an art lecture or foreplay?" She clinked his glass. "It's wonderful to live so close to the concert hall. And practical, too. Just a couple of blocks' walk and you're home before the rush of the music wears off."

"Is that a physiology lecture or foreplay?" He drew her close for a long, deep kiss. "Let's go inside for the real thing."

The bed was spread with a woolly Greek flokati rug, onto which the pair now collapsed. Rachel kicked her black satin mules into a corner and then reclined luxuriantly while Helmut slowly lowered the long red zipper down the front of her strapless black satin sheath.

"I can't resist a man in evening dress," she murmured, undoing his black tie. "But goddammit!" Now she was behind him, whispering in his left ear, "Someone's got to do something about those ridiculous studs down the shirt front."

"The top two will do," he said.

"Done."

Helmut was pulling the shirt over his head, while Rachel wriggled out of her panty hose when the phone rang. At the fourth ring, the answering machine picked up. Of all people, it was Wesley Till: "Something awful has happened. Someone seems to have stolen our entire collection. I must see you immediately." Leave it to Wes to speak in complete sentences even in a panic. Helmut picked up the phone. "Where are you?"

"Downstairs."

"Come up. Apartment 27B."

The museum director stood stiff and wan in the doorway a few minutes later. He was still wearing evening dress with his signature red and white polka dot cummerbund and bow tie. "I hate to trouble you at such an hour ... and you've got company, too," he said, nodding to Rachel. "But I don't know whom to consult about this." He almost fell into a leather armchair while Helmut and Rachel, both hastily wrapped in dressing gowns, sat expectantly on the facing sofa.

Till drew from his tuxedo pocket a small white envelope, the kind that usually holds a greeting card. The outside was utterly blank. From inside, Till's long fingers -- some had called them sensitive -- drew a white paper and a Polaroid photo. The museum director's face looked mottled and gray; his eyes glittered with tears as he handed Helmut both items.

The typed message said: "Your 'children' are in a safe place … for now. Their environment is temperature and humidity controlled and they enjoy extremely competent nannies. Don't do anything rash. We'll be in touch."

The Polaroid showed a double-tiered rack with canvases neatly filed into vertical slots. Leaning against one corner was Humberto Boccioni's *The City Rises*. Even this tiny, grainy image conveyed the power of this Futurist fantasy. In shock, Helmut saw the great swirls of red, blue, white, and flaming oranges of the original as it had hung in the museum's central gallery. The artist had cunningly compressed the anxieties of a world in chaos, a riotous confusion of figures swirling tragically amid smoke and fire against a backdrop of scaffolded buildings. Helmut had always been intrigued by the ambiguity of the picture's title. Was it the energy of a city raising monumental constructions? Or did it depict a city's furious inhabitants rising against an oppressive modern society?

He recalled another panicked consultation with Till several years ago. The director had summoned him in the dark of night. During construction of a new gallery, a welding torch had ignited a pile of rags. Till himself had wielded a fire extinguisher on that ghastly afternoon, while his staff hauled pictures and sculptures out into the museum's walled garden. Almost everything was saved, but when the flames were quelled, this painting lay in a pool of oily water on the gallery floor, a black, ruined mass.

"It's gone, Wes; forget it," Helmut had coldly told Till, whose face was still smeared with black soot. "Take the insurance money. Buy something else."

But Till refused. "It's the central image in our Futurist collection. People come from all over the world to see this picture. It sums up the whole Futurist manifesto: destroy the old; build the new. And besides, it's too gorgeous... *was* too gorgeous. And it will be again."

Early the next morning, two curators wrapped the charred remains in a quilted shroud, not easy with a painting more than six feet tall and almost ten feet wide. They lifted it tenderly into a plywood box, nailed it shut and manhandled the awkward package to the back loading dock. There, five burly workmen loaded the crate into an unmarked truck.

A year later, Helmut was stunned to see *The City Rises* hanging again in its customary spot. It was the closest he would ever come to witnessing a resurrection: The canvas was perfect, the color fresh and vibrant, the scene of those churning bodies as beautiful and disquieting as ever. But was it a Boccioni? Till had shrugged off that question with an enigmatic smile.

Not a trace of a smile flickered on Till's face now. A slight tic was agitating his left cheek, and his fingers fussed nervously over the empty white envelope. "I've got to get back to the party," he said somberly. "They'll suspect a problem. They all hate problems, especially in the midst of a party."

"Not without a little bracer." Rachel handed him a snifter of cognac.

"Alcohol is not the answer," said Till primly. But he dutifully drank, grimacing as though it were a draft of bitter medicine.

"We'll keep the note and the photo," said Helmut. "In the morning, we'll start making discreet inquiries. Let's meet again as soon as we know something new."

Till was already moving toward the door.

"Don't worry," said Rachel. She couldn't resist a tiny jab. "You'll get the goods back ... or a reasonable facsimile, like the Boccioni."

※※

Chattering with the guests at her table, Zelda Levin had barely noticed Wesley Till's hurried departure from the head table. Diarrhea, she concluded; the poor man's guts often rebelled during these sociable occasions. He completely lacked small talk. His wife was even worse; she often zinged out barbed comments: Anita Decker still winced over, "Green is an unfortunate color for you." And Zelda had also been flicked by this lady's sharp tongue. As Till stood helplessly by, his wife had once trilled at his executive secretary: "You can quit ogling him; he's just not viable in that department."

Zelda, by contrast with the directorial pair, loved the dizzy *melange* of famous names, trendy places, and expensive objects that spiked the conversation around her. Her fellow diners fondly recalled summer idylls in Capri, St. Tropez, Hilton Head, Corfu, Portofino and a new, close-by sensation: the Hamptons. When no more posturing seemed possible, Zelda turned to her dining companion, a gall bladder specialist at New York Hospital.

"I visited Cross Wreckner's studio last week," she murmured. As she had expected, the table talk instantly ceased. Zelda scanned their curious faces, forked up a morsel of *tournedos Rossini*, and daintily chewed. Swallowing, she sipped at her 1952 Mouton-Cadet, "A fine year," she said, "fleeting overtones of cherries and raspberries, but not overbearing." Her audience was rapt.

"Cross? Well, yes," she continued. "He's off the bottle these days and is on to a new style. It's not so confrontational. It's softer, more tender, almost sentimental. The black and white stripes are history." She watched a couple across the table smile; for the past three years, the vibration of those oversized stripes flanking the mantle had driven dozens of their dinner guests to an early departure.

At his one man show during the previous winter, Zelda recalled, Cross Wreckner had made a memorable impression. He had arrived drunk, his blue and white striped overalls and black steel-toed boots spattered with paint. Even his raddled beard, his bushy eyebrows, and the dark sunglasses he affected at all times were speckled. A Pollock that walks and talks, someone had whispered, but when that boozy figure opened its mouth, most listeners recoiled from the gigantic belch that issued.

Lurching over to Wesley Till, the artist grabbed the signature polka-dot bow tie, burbling, "Love that shade of red. Gimme a sample for my next picture." As the museum director froze, Wreckner pulled the tie off and stuffed it into his gaping fly, where a loose end remained hanging outside, like a spent and speckled penis.

"Spots and stripes forever," the artist hooted as two beefy rent-a-cops in gray flannels and blue blazers approached. "Aw shucks, boys, I'm just having a little fun," Wreckner bleated. "Sure, Cross," said one cop firmly grasping the artist's right elbow. "We want to help you get home," said the other gently, clenching the left arm. As the trio moved smoothly toward the door, Zelda had noticed that Cross Wreckner's boots were not touching the floor.

Several people at the table had witnessed that episode, and savored the thrill of encountering genuine artistic temperament. The gall bladder doctor had in fact been consulted by the artist, diagnosing the man's abdominal distress as Stage II cirrhosis of the liver. Nevertheless, everyone listened raptly as Zelda gave further details about Wreckner's new paintings.

"They're big and bold," she said, "but the colors remind you of ripe Brie and pink champagne. The new paintings bubble with life. They're optimistic. And unfortunately so are his new prices, $10,000 for the little ones and twice as much for the giant economy size. If Warhol can get that much for a Brillo box, his dealer, Casatti, is determined to go one better. He's already promised us one for the museum, a gift."

Waiters had meanwhile cleared the main course, and Zelda was contemplating the miniature Vesuvio of *profiterolles* before her, its lava flow of bittersweet chocolate sauce drizzling temptingly down onto the fluted ivory china plate. The demi-tasse cups were being passed when Zelda noticed that Wesley Till had resumed his place at the head table. His pale face looked almost transparent; his left eye twitched in a momentary tic. She saw his knuckles white as he pushed himself erect. A spoon clinked against the rim of a glass to quiet the crowd.

"This is a landmark occasion for our museum," Till said. "Tomorrow morning at ten, the public will begin viewing the greatest exhibition of Old Masters this city -- no, this country -- has ever enjoyed. We who savor modern art know that all the wonderful work being done today has its roots in the past, and so, for the next four months, we can study the details of that glorious past inside these walls."

Zelda saw his tight, monkish smile before he continued. "The public is already extremely excited about this show. Tickets for every time slot during the first month are practically sold out. I see no reason to regret storing our permanent collection in order to do this worthy educational and aesthetic work. And now, please enjoy the party."

Always the missionary, Zelda thought, as applause pattered around the room. The band struck up a smart bossa nova. She knew that the Tills would not stay on to dance the night away, but she was surprised to see them dodging out so hastily, without the usual circuit of the room to shake hands and attempt -- hopelessly, to be sure -- light conversation. Then Bettman Levin appeared, and whisked her onto the dance floor.

"What's going on with Till," he asked her as soon as they were rhythmically swaying.

"Beats me. I think he's hitting the Pepto again. His gut always rebels at these make nice occasions."

"But he looks ghastly; more cadaverous than even during his worst attacks of the runs."

Levin was not about to share the revelations in his article in *Art for Tomorrow,* which would appear soon enough. Let them all gnash their teeth. During the social hour he had strolled through the exhibition, silently interrogating each picture close up -- Dürer's Orientalesque monogram, Memling's ravishing renditions of furs and satins, Gentile da Fabriano's lavish applications of gold leaf. The he had stepped back, his connoisseur's antennae quivering to discern the aura great art exudes. Every brushstroke appeared to be in place, but aura? No. He had felt no tightening in his crotch, and was faintly disgusted that the well-known "eye" of the connoisseur appeared to be located, not in the refined intellect, but somewhere between his testicles and the end of his prick. He fingered the crisp Nile-green taffeta stretched over Zelda's rather bony ribs. And he couldn't resist asking: "So what do you make of the Baritsch collection?"

"Great, but not good," she replied, frowning slightly. "The names are all there. The provenance is impeccable, but ..." she broke off, frowning. "Something's not right. I don't feel the passion."

"Neither do I," he admitted. "Have any bids come in?"

"You bet. That's why I can't understand Till's disappearing act. There was no reason for him to be anxious. The tickets are selling faster than we dreamed. Attendance should set a record. And this crowd," she rolled her eyes at the elegant couples swaying on the dance floor, "this crowd is drooling over a chance to shlepp home a world-famous masterpiece. Bet we sell out before the show closes."

Bettman Levin said nothing as the music ended and he escorted Zelda back to her table. He was bursting to tell her about the article, so much so that he quickly excused himself and strode away. Zelda had hoped he would ask to take her home, just so she could beg off -- "It's been a tough, long week." Why did she enjoy teasing this earnest man who clearly was still in love with her? Grasping the tiny beaded pouch containing lipstick, house keys, and a $20 bill, she made her way to the exit.

It *had* been a gruelling week ... more like a gruelling month, she thought as the taxi dashed downtown. First, the immense labor of packing up the entire permanent collection; then the sheer drudgery of hanging the Baritsch pictures. Till could loll back in his wheelchair, squinting at each possible arrangement and dithering obsessively over height, spacing, combinations, lighting. At those times, Zelda took over as virtual director, answering phone calls and presenting a pile of letters for his signature at the end of each day. In all but name, damn it, she was a wife.

"Give me back $2," she told the driver as they reached her building. "And please stay here until I get through the front door." In the last six months, eight women had been mugged by bandits darting from the shrubbery between the street and the front door. Only last week, there had also been a rape. Zelda was relieved to enter the lobby and hear the door click shut behind her. Under harsh fluorescents, the elevator waited. At the 21st floor, Zelda scurried toward her apartment, key in hand. Inside, she set three different locks, perhaps an illusory defense against the perils of the street.

She kicked off her pumps, Nile-green taffeta dyed to match the dress, which followed the pumps to the floor. At midnight, the air was still warm, considering that October was almost upon the city. Carrying a small snifter of Calvados, Zelda sank into the redwood chaise that almost filled her tiny terrace. The strings of lights winking from the Brooklyn and Manhattan Bridges to the south resembled fairy pincers grasping a dark and mysterious land -- Brooklyn. She hardly knew the place, despite having grown up on the top floor of whitestone walkup near Borough Hall.

In that apartment of her youth, everyone faced west, toward Manhattan. For them, the F train did not run eastward and then south toward Prospect Park, Ebbetts Field, or the teeming flesh sprawled on the beach at Coney Island; it moved only westward, its stuffy carriages rattling and swaying into the daylight over the East River toward West 4th Street, then north to Rockefeller Center. In the dark expanse of Brooklyn, her parents were at this very moment sleeping in that same apartment, their genteel snores now muffled by the roar of a new window air conditioner.

Last May, Zelda had delivered that bulky machine in a taxi, a Mother's Day gift offered to atone for her infrequent visits home. Week would pile upon busy week until her mother would telephone, usually at a hectic moment at the museum. Her whining voice was shrill, and Zelda would interrupt with a whisper: "The director needs me. I'll call you from home." That evening she would forget to call, and the next, too. When guilt finally forced her to the phone, Zelda heard herself mouthing apologies, and then was trapped for an hour, listening to detailed descriptions of her aging parents' bodily processes. She would promise to visit soon. The call over, she would pour herself a brandy.

Her parents were increasingly needy strangers, lapel-clutching intruders in the life she had constructed for herself. She felt vaguely at fault for the blows the Depression had inflicted on their lives. Her father, a stockbroker ruined in the market crash, had become a hollow man trudging hopelessly to the subway each morning to his job as a bookkeeper for a small time millinery supply house on West 38th Street. Her mother, a lady who had loved to spend lazy afternoons shopping at Altman's, had ended her working life as a seamstress in the alterations department of that very store. They had been forced to move from a smart Beekman Place flat with a view of the East River to that cramped three-room place in Brooklyn.

Zelda recalled the stifling summers in that apartment under the roof. She would shower just before bedtime and then creep, still dripping wet, under a sheet on a fold-out couch in the living room. At suppers of macaroni and cheese, boiled carrots and Wonder bread, her parents would trade resentful accounts of the day's humiliations at work. "So that fat Jew comes marching in just before lunch -- would you believe? -- and he pounds on the desk and says the factor needs last month's p. & l. by five." Her father was almost sobbing, sweating in his limp undershirt in that airless kitchen. "We should pay attention to that Hitler in Germany," he would add. "He has some good ideas."

"They're taking over the whole city," her mother chimed in. "Today I heard they're promoting Hilda Horowitz to head seamstress. She was hired after me, but I didn't have a chance, not at Altman's lousy Jewish department store."

Listening, Zelda wondered about what evil secrets these Jews used to attain success. Lots of them at school were let out early to attend Hebrew School; maybe that's where they learned how to shove people like her parents aside. She had a church too. Sunday mornings, her family would ride the bus to St. Edmund's on Montague Street in Brooklyn Heights, her father squeezed into an outdated gray flannel suit, her mother in a flowered chemise topped by a navy blue pillbox, with a veil. While Father Farnsworth postured and prayed, Zelda's eyes roamed the cool, pillared sanctuary.

Most absorbing to her were the windows, their late nineteenth century panes not so much stained in brilliant colors as painted in dusky grisaille. She studied Saint Sebastian: why was he smiling with all those arrows stuck in his body? But then, there was Saint Francis, feeding birds, and a Tree of Jesse based on the famous window at Chartres.

Zelda seldom reviewed her Sunday mornings at St. Edmund's without recalling how much those childhood fugues from boredom affected her further education: admission to the elite girls' high school attached to Hunter College, an art major at Brooklyn College, a fellowship that allowed her to pursue an art history doctorate at New York University.

While researching her dissertation on the atmospheric lighting favored by the Impressionists of Southern California she had met Bettman Levin. An art history graduate student at Columbia, he had fastened upon a San Diego sculptor for his thesis: "Graven Images: Southwest Indian Motifs in the Work of Donal Hord." They were both spending the summer in California, ostensibly immured in the library of the San Diego Museum of Art. Actually, as July melded into August, the beach increasingly lured them away from books and archives.

In her recollection, the magic of those endless stretches of sand and water seemed to her as alluring as what she had heard about trips triggered by LSD. One day, they picnicked at Mission Beach, where an antique wooden rollercoaster was rattling into decrepitude; another day, they lingered at Coronado, from which open sand stretched for miles down beyond the border with Mexico. They drove to the rugged rocks rimming The Cove in La Jolla, up to the dunes at Torrey Pines, and even further north to Leucadia and Cardiff-by-the-Sea, where only a sprinkling of surfers roosted like prehistoric amphibians among the waves, waiting for The Big One.

They kissed playfully at Silver Strand; passionately, deeply, and protractedly at Wind and Sea; and were on the way to coitus at Tourmaline Beach when a passing lifeguard interrupted. They finally connected under a rickety pier jutting into the sea at the Scripps Institution of Oceanography. They had camped nearby at sunset. Sprawled on a souvenir serape from Tijuana, they lazily munched a bag supper from Fidel's Hacienda while industriously scanning the horizon for the legendary green flash said to appear just as the sun settled in the waters to the west.

"It's gone. We missed it," Zelda said at last, when the sea lost its sparkle and the first star appeared.

"Maybe it's just some myth put out by the Chamber of Commerce," he said.

Far out, a formation of pelicans was making a last, skimming pass over the breaking surf. A velvety night fell quickly. They had just furled the serape around their shoulders. In the stillness of low tide, they reached for each other like desperate swimmers. And then they were grappling desperately, lasciviously, rolling into the damp sand. There was nothing elegant about their lovemaking. Their passion drove them, just like the elemental drive that periodically propels tiny, silvery fish called grunion to spawn in the shoreline here. The pair hastened toward climax without pause or finesse, and then lay, limp as kelp, upon the roiled sand.

"Now I saw the green flash," she murmured, smiling.

In October, they were married at New York's City Hall. The event, witnessed by two colleagues, was but a brief diversion from her all-night cramming for orals and his preparation for defending his thesis. Her parents had bitterly refused to attend the wedding; his parents grudgingly fed them supper, their silence eloquently deploring a *schicksa* in the family.

Now, rising from the chaise on her terrace, Zelda gazed once more upon Brooklyn. High up on Manhattan Bridge, a brightly lit subway train was carrying its sparse and weary nighttime cargo toward the twenty-two stations ending at Surf Avenue in Coney Island. On the river below the bridge, gliding through the oily waters toward New York Bay, she saw a black ship.

Chapter 13

Perspective

By 7 a.m. two days later, Till was already on the phone, rousing Helmut and Rachel from deep slumber. Forty minutes later, the museum director was at their door, gaunt, hollow-eyed, with a bloody nick on his chin where the razor had slipped. To Rachel he proffered a white paper bag. It felt warm.

"Fresh bagels," he said. "I assumed you'd not eaten breakfast."

Rachel smiled. That's New York, she thought, nothing moves in this town without a *nosh*. When they're nervous, they eat; when the roof caves in, they're snacking. She'd even heard of muggers with a gun in one hand and a pretzel in the other. "So tell us exactly what transpired on the loading dock when they came to pick up the collection."

"According to the curator in charge, everything was normal," said Till. "That's the troubling part of it. Every van was clearly marked Severini Brothers; we've dealt with them for years. To be truthful, I didn't stick around to watch the whole operation. I was called to the phone. But, the papers were in order. The pictures were securely crated. They trav-elled under armed guard, and of course we assumed they reached the warehouse. But they didn't. So where are they?"

The man looked so thoroughly miserable that Rachel impulsively hugged him. Her father would have been about this man's age, she thought, had he survived Buchenwald. Rachel and Till both heard the rustle of paper in his coat pocket at the same time. Till extracted a small envelope of greeting card size. With fingers totally unnerved by this dis-covery, he ripped it open and withdrew a typed note:

> As said, your 'children' are safe...under heav-ily armed guard. They will be returned in time to resume their customary places in your museum after the Baritsch show ends on January 5. But only if:
>
> 1. You maintain total silence about this happen-ing. No police. No reporters. No whispers to anybody in that gossipy art crowd, especially your trustees.
>
> 2. You place all proceeds from sale of the Baritsch pictures into a Swiss bank account. You will receive the number shortly before the payment is due.
>
> 3. You make no effort to trace their whereabouts.

Till was shaking his head in disbelieving rage when Helmut appeared from the kitchen with a tray. "On an empty stom-ach, none of us can think clearly," he said. "Let's just sit down calmly, Wes. Let's have some bagels and coffee, and figure out what to do."

Till sat, but was still extremely agitated. "That note was not in my pocket when I left the house," he said. "This coat was fresh from the cleaners'. I stabbed my finger trying to pry off that blasted little stapled tag before I put it on. The doorman called me a cab. I made the driver wait while I picked up the bagels." Then he slapped his palm against his forehead. "Of course! When I came out of the bakery, a man collided with me on the street; a business type with a brief-case. He quickly apologized and dashed on down Broadway. I didn't even get a look at him."

"Doesn't matter," said Helmut soberly. "Lots of people are involved in a job this big. What does matter is that they're following you. By now, they'll know you came to see us. For $10, that fat concierge downstairs would turn in his own grandmother."

"So now they know that you've consulted us," said Rachel. "But the consultation could be about many matters related to the museum, an acquisition from Helmut, a resto-ration from me. We'll have to convince them that your visit this morning was about something like that."

During her years in the concentration camp, another day of life had often hinged on deviousness and guile. She had, of course, spun her own sophisticated deception around the Baritsch collection. Their authenticity had been drastically compromised by her own massive restorations following their wartime stay in Liechtenstein. For almost fifteen years, Rachel had remained silent when the Baron's Dürers had travelled all over the world for exhibitions. Let the catalogs call them authentic, and spin yarns about their "perfect preservation."

But the copies recently left behind in the Villa Tazzi were obvious fakes, not that the Baron had ever murmured a word about their existence. She had wanted to punish the Baron for violating his grandfather's agreement never to sell these pictures. Bettman Levin's article about the fraud (though not about the perpetrators) would soon appear; it would be a blockbuster all right, not a blockbuster exhibition, but a powerful bomb. Now, the theft of the museum's collection had put a new spin on the whole complicated scheme.

She replenished Till's coffee mug, calmly saying: "I have a confession." Rapidly, she described the fakes smuggled into the Villa Tazzi in Bellagio. These were the pictures now drawing the crowds of eager visitors to the museum; the pictures at this moment attracting sealed bids from the museum's trustees and other art insiders; the pictures soon to be exposed by Bettman Levin's article.

Where are the originals?" Till demanded.

Rachel shrugged. "There are none."

"What?! What?!" He was shouting. Till appeared unable to absorb yet another shock.

"You shouldn't be surprised," said Rachel. "You yourself saw the pitiful condition of old Baritsch's collection right after the war. Did you see a single brushstroke of Memling or Dürer remaining on that pathetic pile of mold and cobwebs? My crew and I reconstituted those pictures from photos. Yes, they were beautifully done; not a hair was out of place; every ripple of satin gleamed; and the skin tones glowed with life. But, you must agree that those original artists no longer had anything to do with the stuff in the world-renowned Baritsch collection."

Her voice dripped with sarcasm. "Ours were the signatures that should have appeared on those works. But never mind. We modestly stayed in the background so long as the Baron lived up to the promises his grandfather made when we resurrected his dead collection. But when we learned that Baritsch was going to scrap the deal; that you, of all people, were about to market these goods; we had to act."

Till's bony shoulders sagged. He realized at once that his grand plan for curing the museum's finances had collapsed.

"Act?" he asked forlornly. "How act?"

Rachel's voice was harsh. "Simple; at least it's simple to describe, not to carry out, I can assure you. We made a second set of copies, which copies the Baron blithely shipped to you without notice. Oh yes, I gather that he did try to cancel the show, but you rushed over there to convince him to go forward. Those are the masterpieces now hanging in your hallowed halls."

"But what about the originals?" asked Till.

"As said, the originals were reduced to smelly piles of mold by years of neglect in that Liechtenstein cellar. The copies we created then, your so-called originals, are safely in storage under our control ..." she couldn't resist a slight jab" ... unlike a certain museum's permanent collection."

Now Till was furious. "I don't care what happens to me," he shouted. "I've been losing my taste for manipulating those rich bastards for some time. They don't care about art, only money and their precious status. But I very much care about the permanent collection. Sure, I cut a few moral corners to create it, but it represents my whole life's work." He threw up his hands in despair.

Helmut touched Till's shoulder. "Look, we're just a devastated as you about this horrible theft. We had nothing to do with that. Whoever did it can't possibly escape. They can't possibly market such famous images. Why not get down to your office? Carry on with your usual routine. Meanwhile, we'll make discreet inquiries."

Till shambled disconsolately to the door and departed, lamely saying, "Keep in touch."

He was no sooner gone than Helmut strode to the phone and dialed an interminable string of numbers. "I must speak with Count Cardini," he said. "Not there? But where is he?"

Off the phone, Helmut turned to Rachel. "They said he's in New York. What a mess! Who knows where he could be roosting in this huge city?"

"It's got to be in Manhattan," Rachel said drily. "A character like that would never take his miserable ass to the outer boroughs. That cuts the possibilities down from ridiculous to merely impossible."

"I think I can do better," said Helmut thoughtfully, picking up the phone. He dialled the Horus Gallery, where Filippo had been a steady customer.

Rachel wandered toward the bedroom to shower and dress. So much had happened since Till's early morning phone call, and it was still only 11:15 a.m. She felt sorry for the museum director, and even sorrier for Helmut, whose entire career could be destroyed if the art world learned of his connection with the faked pictures. She had not intended that the hoax would hurt anyone except in their overstuffed pocketbooks. But, with the museum's permanent collection in the hands of unknown criminals, her relatively harmless deception could spin out of control.

Too late now to kick herself over involving that wretched Count Filippo Cardini in this caper. She basked in the shower's robust spray. It was not like the anemic dribble most Europeans tolerated, nor did the sparse stream issue from a hand-held contraption insecurely dangling -- if you were lucky -- from a hook fastened at some implausible location on the wall. No, this was a veritable Niagara, a valuable, yet unsung, amenity peculiar to New York City. Fortunately, too, Helmut had not succumbed to Americans' habitual stinginess with towels. Stepping out of the shower, Rachel wrapped her body in a luxuriantly proportioned bath sheet, pale blue in color.

In the bedroom, she found Helmut fastidiously picking up the garments tossed in various corners during the previous night's passionate embrace. She wished she could turn the clock back to the early morning, before Till's phone call; to her anticipation of a lazy morning's sexual dalliance. Helmut was just beginning to take the initiative in bed, and Rachel burned to learn where that would lead. But not now.

"You're pretty calm and collected," she said, examining the possibilities in the closet.

He smiled. "Filippo's been sighted at his usual haunts, several of those sleazy dealers he likes to tease about buying something. Harry Zick saw him yesterday morning, late. In the afternoon, he paid a call on Casatti. But I hit the jackpot at the Horus Gallery. There, Filippo seemed interested in a modest-size creation by Jeffrey Boos, so much so that he asked to 'live with it' for a day or two in his room. They delivered it to him late yesterday afternoon at the Chelsea Hotel."

Alice Goldfarb Marquis

"Leave it to him to find the shabbiest digs in town," grumbled Rachel. Was she just a bit jealous of Helmut's flings with Filippo? "That place was rushing downhill back in the Thirties when Thomas Wolfe was there, scribbling his endless novel," she snapped.

"How do we know that?" asked Helmut calmly.

"Everybody knows that," said Rachel. She appreciated his judicious calm, his tendency to assess all sides of any issue, to tolerate ambiguity, and to reserve judgment. Rachel usually leaped in with both feet; none of this on-the-one-hand-on-the other-hand dithering. She avoided suspense. Decisiveness had, after all, saved her life: snatch that extra slab of gray bread, eat; pull a torn, dirty jacket off a corpse, keep warm. Run, hide, smile, grab -- but whatever you do, do it now. Use feral cunning to buy yourself another hour, another day, another chance.

Helmut was something else. At first, she had been repelled by his detached ways, his distance, his cool assessment of every situation. She had chafed at his slow, prudent mulling of all the possibilities. Now, she found that he often balanced her hasty rush to action. She was beginning to appreciate his thoughtful deliberations. Moreover, for the first time in her life, she glimpsed herself as part of a pair. Their time together was slowly changing from the rush of passionate embrace into something less torrid, but more sustainable. The raging flame was mutating into a warming hearth. She was by no means certain that she wanted Helmut permanently in her life, but, dammit, she felt sad thinking of life without him.

At least she could be decisive about Filippo.

"Look, we know where he is," she said, tucking a brick-red T-shirt into scuffed blue jeans. "Let's just go down there and get him. I don't care what it takes. The guy is a wimp. He's probably loaded on something. If he doesn't tell us everything, I wouldn't mind getting rough. He deserves a good beating."

Helmut was stepping into gray flannels. He seemed oblivious to Rachel's heated remarks. Silently, he unfurled a fresh pale blue shirt and slipped his arms into the sleeves. Rachel watched, seething, as he pulled a navy blue blazer out of the closet.

"Help me with the necktie," he said softly. "The red knit? Or do you like the tiny print Italian silk?"

"I can't even hear the word Italian," Rachel snapped. "The very sound of it feels like a dagger at my throat." She was about to explode, but stepped to his side and obediently studied the tie rack. He must have something in mind, she thought, but, good grief! does he have to keep me in suspense? She kept silent, and suddenly realized that she trusted him. Yes, he could be insufferably pedantic, but, while she lunged impetuously up and down, he steadily plodded forward.

She pulled a sober burgundy and navy stripe out of the rack.

"Good lord, it's almost lunch time," he said.

"Just about when that good-for-nothing is stirring in the fleabag sheets," she said.

"I feel like something light," he said. "Maybe a plate of that mushroom and barley soup we shlepped home from Ratner's the other night."

"Let's cut out the small talk. Do you think I can sit here passively eating soup while that slimy dope fiend is plotting who knows what further mischief?"

Without reply, Helmut led her by the arm into the kitchen. "No, we won't passively eat soup," he said. "We will quite actively, quite aggressively plan how best to deal with Count Cardini. But first ... a brief history."

"Brief? When it comes to history, Helmut, I have never known you to be brief." She was shocked to realize that this was the first time she had called him by name. She shrugged, knowing that no amount of urging could abbreviate his lecture. On the other hand, something worth knowing usually emerged at the end. She sat back in the chrome and plastic chair at that minute Formica rectangle that passed for a table in that dusky cubicle that passed for a kitchen.

He stirred the soup as it heated on the stove. "My father didn't jump on the first train out of Berlin when the Nazis came," he began. "No, he carefully studied the options. First he took some his best pictures off their stretchers ... my mother's favorite Renoir, a juicy nude ... a Blue Period Picasso saltimbanque ... a Cézanne ... a Gustav Klimt, stuff like that." Helmut ladled soup into two bowls. "My father carried those pictures in a shopping bag to his friend, Oskar Schirmer, who was still quietly running his umbrella factory out in Potsdam. The pictures left Germany rolled up inside a shipment of umbrellas to Brussels. Poor Schirmer, he couldn't bring himself to give up the factory; insisted the Nazi madness would pass; died in Dachau, and quickly, a blessing.

"My father's best picture was one that made me swear off meat, a bloody beef carcass that only Rembrandt could have chosen for a subject. He traded that to a jeweler in Munich for a small bag of diamonds. The man had a son who was a regular ski bum; every Sunday in winter he was on the train to the mountains. That particular Sunday, he takes the train as usual to Garmisch. He rides the cog railroad to the top of the Zugspitze. But, instead of descending into Germany, he skis down on the other side to Austria. There, he takes the train to a little town in Switzerland and stays in a ski hut overnight. When the little country bank opens in the morning, he's there. The little bag goes into a safe deposit box. It travelled in a hollowed-out niche under the ski binding."

As Helmut brought spoons, napkins, and a box of Ritz crackers to the table, Rachel squirmed. "Stories," she said wearily. "Everybody in the camp had some god-forsaken story. And what was the good of it? Not many happy endings there."

"Happy?" said Helmut. "I don't recall much talk about happy when we finally left. At the last stop in Germany before the Dutch border, the guards pulled us off the train. Our papers were not in order. I watched my father carrying his briefcase into the customs shed. My mother grabbed onto my hand as we waited on the platform. And, by God, just as the train was beginning to move, my father rushed out and we all jumped aboard. It was a long time before he talked: 'It seems they still like Dürer,' he said. 'It pays to plan ahead carefully.'

"I was taking a graduate seminar in German Renaissance art when my father told me how three little Dürer etchings saved our lives. 'It pays to plan ahead carefully.' He was not a terrific father; it cost plenty for a shrink to help me come to terms with that stiff old man. But I can't help agreeing with that litle motto: 'It pays to plan ahead carefully.'"

Rachel was surprised to find herself spooning up Ratner's rich mushroom and barley broth. She was becoming a New Yorker: when the going gets tough, have a nosh. "So what have you so carefully planned ahead?"

"It's evening in Chartres," he said. "They're probably sitting around the dinner table scarfing up one of Lisette's great creations."

"What do they have to do with this?"

"Not they; just Maria. Remember, Filippo spent a lot of time peeking down the front of her smock when we were busy in Bellagio. I watched him ogle her sweet little rump many a time when she bent over to wipe some spilled paint from the floor. He just didn't dare to press further because he was afraid of you ... and because of me. We might still be good for something, he was maybe thinking. But on her own, Maria could probably get the Count to sing as sweetly as that sensational new young tenor, Pavarotti...."

Before Helmut could continue, Rachel was at the phone, dialling Chartres. And then she was arguing with Lisette: "Yes, I know about your asparagus soufflé. I wish I were there to eat it myself before it falls. Only an emergency would cause me to interrupt your meal, *ma chérie*, but I must speak to Maria."

Helmut was loading the dishes into the Kitchen Aid when he felt Rachel's arms around his waist. "You look so cute," she said. "Where's your apron?" He blushed. "Maria's catching the first morning flight from Paris. She'll call us with arrival time just before she boards. Luc is driving to Vicenza to check out the Count's so-called palazzo. And Ilana will take a quick jaunt down to Bellagio; see if there's any activity at the Villa Tazzi. And we?" She raised the dishwasher's door and kissed Helmut's ear. "This funny guy once told me, 'It pays to plan ahead carefully,'" she whispered, nudging him gently toward the bedroom.

"Some planning ahead," Helmut grumbled. "I just made the bed." But Rachel was already pulling off the spread.

"Can't be helped," she said. "Or do you have a better way to deal with the tension of waiting?"

He cradled her face with two hands and brought it close to his. He looked into her eyes. "Am I in love with you?"

She placed a finger on his lips. "Sure," she said glibly, "whatever turns you on."

Rachel immediately regretted the remark. Why so flip in reply to his earnest question? She reached eagerly for his belt.

The sun was sinking in pink and purple glory toward the pig farms of Secaucus when Helmut and Rachel strolled out onto the terrace. Wrapped in plush white terry robes, they sat down at a glass-topped table. From a frosted silver shaker, he poured martinis, while she nibbled from a bowl of salted almonds.

"I don't think I know what love is," she said pensively. "I've never had time to experience it."

"Don't worry about that now," he said, lightly brushing her fingers. "There'll be plenty of time after this is over."

The setting sun was turning the river into liquid silver. Beating upstream toward a wharf on the Weehawken shore, far to the south, they noticed a black ship.

Chapter 14

Vernissage

A klaxon sounded shrilly across the lake, stopped, then shrilled again.

"Is it time already?" Rachel lazily trailed her finger in the water. Though not yet warm enough for swimming, the lake undulated invitingly in the noonday sun on this Thursday in the middle of May. "I hate to go back."

But Helmut, always dutiful, was already paddling the boat toward the dock. "How can you resist the fabulous lunches the Baron's kitchen conjures up?"

"I guess I don't want any of this to end," she said. "After all we've been through, I can't get enough peace and quiet and predictability. I can't deal with a single further surprise."

"Not even a special antipasto on the buffet?" Helmut stopped paddling momentarily, and grasped her moist fingers. "I'm famished."

The lapping water pushed the boat toward the dock, where Ilana and Luc waited to capture it with boathooks.

"Haven't you two gotten tired of making goo-goo eyes at each other?" Ilana held out a hand to pull Rachel onto the dock.

"Seems to me a certain couple has been giving free lessons in that technique," said Helmut, as they headed toward the house. The gravel path wound in gentle curves through a garden on the cusp of its springtime glory. Behind banks of blooming yellow jonquils and deep blue iris, the tender shoots on hundreds of rose bushes were poised for a spectacular summertime display. On a gentle rise beyond the garden, the Villa Tazzi fairly flaunted its complex architecture, the pale yellow stucco and white trim pristine; it was freshly painted.

As they entered, they saw a boy in white linen striding through the hallways, enthusiastically sounding the luncheon gong.

"Can we dress in five minutes?" Rachel seized Helmut's arm and pulled him toward their room.

"I thought the Baron said it was casual," said Helmut, "just a few loose ends and a final accounting. Maybe he'll even tell us something about future plans. On the other hand ..."

"Forget about the other hand," Rachel interrupted. "We're on vacation."

Holding hands, they slipped into their bedroom. "I'm glad we don't face the lake," said Helmut. "I rather like the view of the town. Do you think Signora Tancredi is peeking at us from her upstairs window?"

"I do wonder how she feels now about her famous tenants," said Rachel, stepping out of her shorts and into a lavender voile skirt, printed with tiny blue forget-me-nots. "We must pay her a visit. Is this too summery?"

Helmut was zipping the fly on a crisp pair of khaki chinos. "I doubt that she's aware of all the details. But no doubt the news involving Villa Tazzi has persuaded all the townspeople that they can raise their summer rental fees."

"She's probably doubled the rent on her house already."

They headed for the dining room, where the kitchen staff had outdone itself with the buffet. A huge poached perch reposed on a bed of fresh spring greens, surrounded by carved radishes, carrot roses, and tiny, glistening black olives. Fat shrimp were heaped on a round platter around a crystal bowl of creamy green mayonnaise. On a scrubbed pine board, pale cheeses reposed, all specialties from local farms. A gleaming silver tray offered succulent raw beef, thinly sliced and sprinkled with chopped basil and capers.

The Baron's guests drifted into the dining room: Luc and Ilana, whispering over some private joke; Maria, with Bettman Levin on her arm, carrying a basket of wild strawberries; Zelda Levin holding the arm of Wesley Till, who was still limping a bit; Karl Baritsch, rubbing his hands expectantly, followed by Rosalinda.

The Baron cleared his throat. "Ladies and gentlemen, we have a few final details to settle. Please enjoy your lunch, then we shall assemble in the library."

"Why so formal?" Rosalinda broke in. "You're addressing a bunch of seasoned veterans, who are all famished. Let's eat."

They carried loaded plates to a dining table that overlooked the lake. Sparkling silver and glassware set off the pink damask tablecloth and napkins. In the center, a shallow white china bowl floated the spring's first pink camellias. Behind each place, Franz stepped soundlessly to pour a straw-colored local soave.

No one at the table seemed be interested in discussing anything serious. But, given their realms of expertise, not a person there failed to notice the magnificent still life hanging above the buffet. It celebrated the plenitude of a rich table: grapes, peaches, cherries, plums, and a bursting fig spilling out of a rush basket, with a butterfly hovering above; a vermilion lobster on a pewter plate, and beside it, a half-peeled lemon, a crusty loaf, and sprigs of currants. The whole composition of Jan Davidsz. de Heem's *Still Life with Lobster* spoke of genteel taste masking robust appetites and playful desire. It would have been gauche for anyone at the table to subject this canvas to professional scrutiny. But Rachel could not help a discreet glance toward the lower left corner of the painting, where another name was faintly discernible beneath de Heem's signature. The others attended studiously to consuming the real food before them.

"I read about some doctor who found a relationship between cholesterol from fatty foods and heart disease," Bettman Levin said, dipping a shrimp into the green mayonnaise on his plate.

"Ach, these doctors," groaned the Baron. "Why don't they research the dangers of eating too much spinach. We're here to enjoy life, aren't we?" He rose to help himself to a few more of the suspect shrimp and mayonnaise.

Wesley Till wondered briefly whether the sliced raw beef would upset his delicate stomach. He tentatively tasted a morsel. "*Carpaccio*, if I'm not mistaken, like the Venetian painter. I tried it decades ago, when I spent a couple of weeks in the Ticino." He took another bite. "It's a wonderful area ... all the vivaciousness of Italy, but with Swiss prim and proper order. "You went there to recover, as I recall," said Zelda, "after one of those grueling sessions with Picasso. I saw your letter in the files, where you described how you wangled that first exhibition of his work at the museum."

"How come we never got that story for the magazine?" asked Bettman Levin. "That's just the kind of little tidbit our readers love."

Till glanced at the critic. "Seems to me you've had quite a few 'little tidbits' in the magazine this past year. More than you would ever have gotten from me."

"That why we journalists cultivate a lot of different sources," replied Levin, with a smug smile.

Seeing everyone leaning back replete, the Baron rose. "Shall we take petit fours and coffee in the library? It's time to review the press reports of our recent adventures."

They rose and followed him into a spacious corner room with two exposures on the lake. Tucked amid the books lining the remaining walls hung a rather macabre painting about nine inches tall and only 14 inches wide. In it, a human skull rested on an ancient book; in the foreground, an overturned inkwell and a quill pen. The somber colors of this Pieter Claesz composition reflected its sobering title: *Vanitas*.

They settled into flowered chintz and cosy velour around a spacious Tunisian copper table. On it lay several scrapbooks bound in red leather and a stack of video reels.

"May I suggest," said the Baron, "that we follow a strict chronological order." He looked meaningfully at Bettman Levin. "So we begin with the article in *Art for Tomorrow*. Ah yes, here it is." He held up the topmost scrapbook, open to the first page.

THE BARITSCH COLLECTION: GREAT OLD MASTERS OR FABULOUS FAKES?

Visitors thronging the world-famous Baritsch Collection opening this week at New York's New Museum will be shocked to learn that they are not in the presence of genuine, blue-chip Old Masters. *Art for Tomorrow* has obtained startling evidence that the works in this exhibition, which is expected to be on view through the end of the year, are re-creations of precious masterpieces which no longer exist.

The originals were unfortunately destroyed while stored in a damp Liechtenstein dungeon during the Second World War. The pictures now on view were re-created by a team of expert restorers, all survivors of Nazi concentration camps, led by Rachel Haberman.

"When I first saw these pitiful wrecks," Miss Haberman told *Art for Tomorrow* in an exclusive interview, "virtually nothing but mold and mildew remained. The old Baron was heartbroken, and begged me to do whatever was possible to restore them. Restore? There was nothing to restore. However, the old Baron was able to provide us with excellent photographs of these works before their destruction."

Haberman and her three colleagues labored for two years to re-create the Baron's beloved paintings. The old man, ill and dying, cried with joy, she said, when his treasures were returned. As payment, he provided the group with a magnificent studio and living quarters in the shadow of the cathedral at Chartres.

"We would have been perfectly happy to carry on there forever," said Haberman, "if the rest of our agreement had been followed."

She described a contract which provided that the pictures would be available to the public on a permanent basis, and would never be sold. When she learned of the New Museum's plan to exhibit the most precious works in the Baritsch Collection, Haberman said, she felt a pang of anxiety. But when word reached her that the museum was accepting secret bids for the pictures, she said, 'I could not let that happen. I had to act.'"

Rachel caught Bettman Levin's eye. "I don't believe that my language was quite so ladylike," she said. "You made it sound as though we chatted over tea at the Plaza. Can't you share the real story with your friends in this room?"

Levin blushed. "I was hoping to save it for my memoirs. Maybe to whisper it to my children." He shyly grasped Maria's hand. "Maybe I could substitute another exclusive... we're expecting an heir, due somewhere around the end of September."

"Very nice," said Rachel. "Congratulations. I'm so glad you fell in love with the lady Maria. But please tell us about that other lady, the one that bewitched you in the beginning.

Without her, you know, there would have been no article at all."

"*Ginevra di Benci*?" Levin smile. "My dear Rachel. I sus-pected she was a fake right from the beginning. But I wasn't sure until I sent her to the Chicago Art Institute for X-rays. Interesting ... the panel was old, but the paint? Strictly 20th century, they said ... no sketch, no underpainting ... chemical dyes ... and they even found a few hairs from a brush. Those were identified as American beaver."

Till stirred on the sofa. "So it was a copy," he said. "That's most intriguing. The National Gallery's been courting *Ginevra* for years. Whenever I see John Walker, the director, he groans about wasting a good part of every European trip on fruitless visits to Liechtenstein. He must have her. It's become an obsession. But every time he raises the ante, it's the same story. There they sit in the prince's drawing room, sipping cognac and smoking cigars. And from her perch above the mantelpiece, that divine woman gazes down upon these two miserable mortals with the faintest of smiles."

"That was the hardest part," said Ilana. "We all took a crack at it. We tried enlarging the photo, painting over it, and then reducing the result to the original size. We tried projecting a transparency onto the panel. Luc, remember how you got so frustrated that you painted a moustache on her, just like Duchamp did with the *Mona Lisa*? I guess the final result was pretty successful; it fooled the director of the National Gallery."

"That's when I decided we should make a second copy," said Rachel. "It might come in handy in the future, we thought ... some kind of insurance."

"Speaking of insurance," the Baron broke in, "let's move on in our scrapbooks." He leafed to another page. "Remember this?"

It was clipping from *Time* magazine. He began to read:

LLOYD'S LOSES FACE— AND MUCH MORE

Baffled and furious.

That's how executives at Lloyd's of London reacted to the news that the Baritsch Collection, now showing at New York's New Museum, is nothing but a farrago of fakes. Angrily gesturing, the chairman of the venerable insurance house, Lord Ironsides, spluttered over the revelations published this week in a little-known art periodical.

"Little-known, indeed," growled Bettman Levin. "That was then. They sure know about us now."

Maria patted his hand. "Easy. We're not here to fight a magazine war. Let's hear the rest of it."

'Such a fraud would never have succeeded in England,' the peer told worried Lloyd's investors. 'Unfortunately, our American cousins are not so sophisticated when it comes to artistic heritage.'

Embarrassed over issuance of a massive policy -- the precise amount remains unclear -- for the Baritsch "masterpieces," Lloyd's could suffer a mortal blow from other claims.

In his teak-panelled Wall Street office, tycoon Henry Eckridge, longtime museum trustee and sometime investor in Lloyd's, was glum. He confessed that the museum expected to achieve permanent financial stability through "discreet sales" of the Baritsch masters.

Wringing his hands, New Museum director Wesley Calvin Till nervously paced to and fro in his stark, white inner sanctum...

Till sprang to his feet, and winced as pain shot through his leg. "Pacing, yes," he cried, "but hand-wringing? Never. That *Time* researcher never set foot in my office. We just talked on the phone. Who wrote that drivel? We'll never know; they don't have by-lines."

Zelda pulled him back onto the loveseat they shared. "Now Wes, it's just a figure of speech. Remember your ulcer. Karl, please continue."

"Where was I? Oh yes, the stark, white inner sanctum."

Problem was not the Baritsch picture hoax, but a mega-theft: the museum's entire collection apparently had gone astray on the way to storage in the Severini Brothers' forbidding, windowless warehouse.

The disappearance of the Western world's most comprehensive collection of modern art sent Lloyd's managers rushing for their tranquilizers. Reason? They faced a bankrupting payment of $1 billion if the collection were lost.

Meeting late into the night at the syndicate's historic headquarters on London's Leadenhall Street, executives mournfully mulled over their options. Dustmen making their rounds noticed a haggard Lord Ironsides emerge just before dawn. A chauffeured Bentley delivered the portly Lloyd's chairman to Broadcasting House, the Art Deco BBC headquarters at Portland Place and Langham Street. Thirty minutes later, Britons were absorbing the stunning news with their tea and biscuits: Lloyd's would pay a $10 million reward for safe return of the New Museum's collection.

"So much for *Time* magazine's report. I suggest a brief recess for refreshments," said Baron Baritsch, "while we prepare for showing the video tapes. We were able to borrow a viewing machine from a television station in Milan. I haven't the faintest idea of how to run that gadget, but my dear wife, Rosalinda, had a few sessions with the technicians there.

"I suppose you've heard," he continued, "that she's doing an educational series on Italian art for the American public broadcasting network. The people in Milan are in charge of the actual taping. It's quite convenient. She can scoot down there easily from here. Frankly, I'm looking forward to getting a real education in art when we start location filming."

All except the Baron's wife made for a side table, where an assortment of petit fours was surrounded by petite

Rosenthal china bowls of Jordan almonds, chocolate coated espresso beans, and morsels of candied ginger.

"I'm surprised the *New York Times* wasn't on top of the story," said Helmut. "What a scoop."

Levin nodded. "I couldn't figure that out either. I finally got the story a couple of weeks ago, right after the Pulitzer Prizes were announced. It seems they couldn't decide which departments should cover the story -- the art critics wrangled with the crime reporters, and then the financial page weighed in. I happened to visit that bar on 43rd Street where they all hang out and heard all about it. There was still a lot of bitterness."

Maria squeezed Levin's arm. "I know the Pulitzer is a great honor," she said, "but I was a little disappointed that it was just a piece of paper. Somehow, I thought a gold medal was in order."

"Save the medals for the real heroes of this little adventure," he replied.

Rosalinda briskly clapped her hands. "Places please. We're ready for the TV show."

The group clustered around the television screen, which came to life with a burp-like sound. Walter Cronkite's fatherly face appeared, saying, "The big story tonight is a daring raid by New Jersey State Police and FBI agents on an abandoned warehouse on the Weehawken waterfront. Dan Rather is on the scene."

The picture shifted to a windowless concrete hulk of a building, from which wisps of smoke were rising.

"They're still cleaning up after the terrific battle that took place here just a few hours ago, Walter. With me is

Captain Bill Ringwald, New Jersey State Police. What brought you to this isolated spot?"

"We were acting on an anonymous telephone call informing us that a valuable art collection was inside the building."

"Did you have any idea of how valuable it was?"

"Not until our helicopter reported activity there. A number of armed men were loitering on the dock and at the entrances to the building. That's when we called in the FBI."

"Please tell our viewers what happened then."

"We first scouted the warehouse from the river. Then we acted quickly. A diversion was created behind the building."

"I understand you set off several smoke bombs on the landward side," said Rather.

"That I am not authorized to reveal."

"I understand that under cover of this diversion, your main force landed from several pleasure yachts on the river."

"I'm sorry. The FBI has not authorized anyone to describe actual details."

"But we do know that a number of shots were fired," Rather persisted. "Can you tell us if anyone was injured."

"Only a civilian. As the main force was entering the building, this man pushed past our sentries. At the time, we had no idea who he was. The man seemed to have the kind of superhuman strength that you sometimes see with people who are high on drugs or insane. He rushed straight into the shootout."

"Do you now know who that person is?"

"I have now been informed by the paramedics that he is a museum director named Wesley Calvin Till."

"Thank you Captain Ringwald. The sun is now setting on what could have been the most tragic loss of art in American history. Back to you, Walter."

"We have a report now from Lesley Stahl, at New York Hospital."

"The ambulance carrying Wesley Till, the director of New York's Museum of the New arrived here late this afternoon. He is still in the operating room. With me is Dr. Morris Gross, the emergency room physician who first saw Mr. Till. Can you tell us about his condition, doctor?"

"He was very weak from loss of blood, but conscious."

"Did he say anything about what happened?"

"Only about his children. He kept repeating that he had to save his children."

"Can you tell us about his injuries?"

"A serious bullet wound in the abdomen and several lesser injuries. Remember, the man was caught in the middle of a shootout."

"When can we expect further word?"

"I doubt we'll have any information before morning. He's still in surgery."

"Thank you Dr. Gross. We're standing by and will bring you further word as soon as it's available. Back to you, Walter."

"Thank you, Lesley Stahl. Police are holding five men in connection with this daring robbery, and more arrests are expected. In other news tonight ..."

Rosalinda switched the tape machine off. "Whatever made you dash into the middle of a shootout, Wes?"

The museum director shrugged. "I felt I had nothing to lose. The works in that building *were* my children; they always will be, no matter who runs the museum. I blamed myself for losing them to begin with. I should never have sent them into storage. I was too eager to please the trustees. I lost sight of my basic values."

Zelda grasped his fingers. "Aren't you being awfully hard on yourself?" she said.

"Hard to decide," said Till, "but ultimately irrelevant. I should never have allowed the trustees to talk me into showing the Baritsch pictures. Showing those Old Masters, even if they were genuine, had nothing to do with the museum's mission ... and everything to do with money. Basically, we were showing goods for sale ... as it turned out, questionable goods."

"I'm somewhat to blame as well," said Karl. "I knew about the fakery last spring, of course, when that horrible Nazi painting confronted me. I wanted to cancel the show. I was sick and tired of dealing with these pictures, even if they were genuine. Then Wes rushed over and urged me to go forward as planned. As always, he was extremely persuasive. The museum needed the money ... the trustees were determined ... the public was snapping up tickets ... bids for the pictures were already on hand ... the social events were planned. I just didn't have the heart to tell Wes that he was getting a museum full of fakes. That was wrong."

"You didn't have to," replied Till. "They didn't look right when I was hanging them; too slick, and not a crack or wrinkle in the lot. By then, it was too late to send the poor things out for X-rays. In a way, I have all of you to thank for the happy outcome."

"Which is?" asked Zelda. "Why not share the good news with these colleagues."

"I've had my last conversation on that blasted red telephone," said Till. "For a while last fall, it seemed to ring every couple of minutes. And what perturbed our dear museum president, Alex Clarendon, so deeply? The possible destruction of our permanent collection? Oh no, just the loss of ticket revenue when the fake show closed after three weeks instead of four months. Clarendon told me that, of course, I was fired. But the announcement would have to wait several months, since the museum couldn't survive two serious blows to its prestige in close succession."

"That's when Zelda handed me the second great scoop of the year," said Bettman Levin. "You were in the hospital, Wes. She arrives at my apartment with a Brillo Box. No, not a Warhol, alas, but valuable in other ways. She'd made copies of all the letters in Till's files documenting how the museum trustees bought pictures at special prices from museum shows, how they got Till to buy pictures for them, how they speculated on artists slated for shows at the museum."

"Remember how furious you were, Betty," said Zelda, "when I said you couldn't use them ... yet?"

Maria broke in: "Betty? How charming." She giggled. "My one qualm about our future life together was forever having to call you 'Bettman.' At least now I know what to call the baby."

"So you threatened the trustees with exposure," said Rachel.

"What else could I do?" said Zelda.

"And that's when Clarendon showed up at the hospital," said Till. "Brought me those gorgeous purple gladiolas, a giant bouquet, and offered to pay me more in retirement than I'd ever gotten while working my tail off at the museum. As soon as we finish here, Zelda and I are off to Paris. We're working on the definitive book about Boccioni."

Helmut smiled. "Maybe in it you'll tell us about the ultimate meaning of *The City Rises*."

"Maybe we will," replied Till. "Anything we can read in the museum's wonderful re-creation, with his name on it."

"Ladies and gentlemen," the Baron broke in. "As you can see, there's a great deal more in these scrapbooks before us. I have just one more to share this afternoon. The rest you can read at your leisure."

He opened the second volume and displayed a clipping from the *National Enquirer*.

ART SCANDAL ENDS IN MURDER

Police in New York City this week were piecing together a bizarre blackmail plot ended by a grisly death.

When the body first washed ashore near a tiny abandoned lighthouse under the George Washington Bridge, police knew that the victim was no suicide. The man's hands were tied behind his back and his legs were bound. In a bizarre detail, one foot was missing. A gang murder, they concluded -- until they searched his pockets.

There was no wallet, no identification, but only the address of an art gallery in Soho. At the morgue, art dealer Leon Casatti identified the body. He told police that when he last saw the victim, about two weeks ago, the man talked about blackmailing the Museum of the New.

The museum's director, Wesley C. Till, was still hospitalized with injuries received in a spectacular shootout on the Weehawken waterfront. His assistant, Zelda Levin, revealed details of the blackmail attempt.

"A note came in the mail about a week before Mr. Till was injured," she said. "It was scribbled in block letters on cheap paper in pencil. 'If you ever want to see your collection again,' it said, 'these artists must have a show at your museum.' He listed ten or twelve contemporary painters, all second, if not third-rate."

"Mr. Till was too worried about the loss of his collection (see story on page 2) to pay much attention to this crude threat," Miss Levin added, "but he did make a few inquiries."

The murdered man was identified as an Italian art collector, who was disappointed that his art collection had not appreciated in value as so many others have. He hoped to force the museum to endorse the works he owned by exhibiting them.

Sources told *The Enquirer* that the victim had squandered his inheritance on speculations in contemporary art. He looted the palazzo that had been in his noble family for almost 400 years, selling off priceless antiques and paintings. With the proceeds, he bought huge canvases painted in white and purple stripes, multi-colored dribbles, and solid blue.

"The Count wagered and lost," said respected New York art dealer Helmut Rosenfeld. "He had not informed himself enough about art. Rather than developing his own taste, he followed the fashion of the moment. That's dangerous."

"That's not exactly what I said," Helmut broke in. "These reporters...they'll misquote you every time."

"Not so fast," broke in Bettman Levin. "That's a pretty broad brush. I haven't heard you complain about my article revealing Baron Baritsch's ingenious plans for his collection."

Now the Baron broke in. "Ingenious? I see it as a way of educating the public. There's altogether too much froufrou surrounding art. Now, the public will be able to see for itself the true genius of restorers, especially the four in this room." He pointed at Maria, Luc, Ilana, and Rachel.

Rosalinda touched his arm. "You haven't mentioned our plans for the opening of the Museum of Restoration. There's not going to be a single posh dinner or fund-raising party. What a relief! No, we're inviting the entire population of the villages around the lake for a gigantic picnic. It'll be at the end of August, after the tourists go home. Of course, you're all invited, too."

"But before the public arrives," said Rachel, "Helmut and I hope you'll attend another celebration." She blushed, and Helmut squeezed her hand. Her voice faltered. "I never thought this would happen to me ... we're getting married. But before you hear the details, I have a confession."

The room was dead silent, the festive atmosphere swallowed by Rachel's sobriety. Luc, Ilana, and Maria exchanged glances, shrugged, then sat back in resignation. "Are you sure you want to ...," Ilana's tentative question trailed off as Rachel surveyed all those present: "Yes, I want to, in fact, I have to. It's time to put the past behind us, to trust the good friends you have all become."

The sun outside disappeared behind a dark cloud as Rachel softly continued. "In all these years of intimacy with great art, I had always felt separated from it by a curtain -- my own history, terror and despair, the sense of endless evil in the world. All that time we were bringing those exquisite paintings back to life, I was obsessed with their intimations of decay and death. My work was driven by the need to wipe it away, to make these broken wrecks whole again."

Helmut shifted restlessly. "Good heavens! You've always accused me of long windedness. Aren't you being a bit grim?"

"Yes, but also truthful. Sure, we did excellent work, but paintings were as much objects to me as they are to your museum trustees, Wes, just valuable objects. That's why I had no trouble with hatching this fantasy of stealing your permanent collection. I persuaded my partners to go along with the plot, to hold the whole collection for ransom and force the museum to give up its hare-brained -- illegal, I might add -- scheme for selling the Baritsch pictures. But Filippo, poor fish, intervened with his own foolish intrigue."

"Foolish? Hardly," said Helmut drily. "It was suicidal. I see his whole life now as a downhill rush to extinction. Sure, I was seduced by his resemblance to Caravaggio's pampered youths. Now, I'm struck by how much Filippo's life also resembled Caravaggio's."

"Get ready for a long lecture," she said to the room at large, "but worth it."

"Not so long, I promise," said Helmut, "and maybe worth it. It puts us back in touch with flesh and blood. Here was a painter, Caravaggio, whose career exploded like a rocket around the turn of the seventeenth century: sales to the nobility, patronage by a cardinal, commissions from the Vatican. At age 33, he killed an opponent in a duel over a tennis game and fled to Naples. The next year, he escaped to Sicily from a Maltese prison. Back in Naples, enemies beat him so severely that he was crippled for almost a year. At the age of 38, having influenced every leading painter of his time, he died of a fever."

"So Filippo had a model," said Rachel. "Only Filippo had no talent, just dreams, and sordid ones at that. Not so much different from my own grandiose dreams of revenge. Maybe the kindest thing he ever did was to save me from turning those dreams into reality."

"Enough postmortems," said the Baron briskly. "Those of you who feel energetic still have time for a brisk walk along the lakefront before cocktail hour. The rest have time for a nap."

Brushstroke!

He rose, taking Rosalinda's hand, and the others soberly followed them from the room.

THE END.

About the Author

ALICE GOLDFARB MARQUIS (1930-2009) was a German refugee art historian, biographer and critic, an art collector with a Ph.D. in History from the University of California, San Diego who published critically acclaimed biographies of Marcel Duchamp, Clement Greenberg, and Alfred H. Barr, Jr., as well as *The Art Biz: The Covert World of Collectors, Dealers, Auction Houses, Museums and Critics.*

Brushstroke! is her only novel.

www.ingramcontent.com/pod-product-compliance
Lightning Source LLC
Chambersburg PA
CBHW030128180626
46812CB00002B/598